Courtin' Christina ~ *Wee* Macgreegor *Enlists*

by

J. J. BELL

With an introduction
by

BRIAN D. OSBORNE

The Publisher would like to dedicate this volume to David Blaikie and Allan Boyd – companions in the spirit of the Hebrides, the spirit of literature and the spirit of whisky – for all their help and support.

17 Roseneath Street, Edinburgh

Typeset in Monotype Plantin by
ROM-Data, Falmouth, Cornwall
and printed and bound by
Cox and Wyman Ltd, Reading

A CIP record for this book is available
from the British Library

ISBN 1 874744 10 6

Contents

Introduction

The World of Wee Macgreegor

"Can I get oarin', Paw?"

The insistent cry of Macgregor Robinson to his ever-tolerant father, John, echoes from a rowing boat in Rothesay Bay in the first years of the twentieth century. It carries with it memories of traditional Glaswegian holidays "doon the watter". Like so much else in the stories of Wee Macgreegor the custom of family holidays at the coast has largely disappeared, as has its essential preliminary – the voyage down-river on a Clyde paddle-steamer. Those glorious, but now vanished, vessels were appreciated for their utility, their happy associations and for the excitement their wakes gave to holiday-making hirers of rowing boats who, like John Robinson, could take their families out "...to get a wee shoogy-shoo wi' thon steamboat's waves". An experience which naturally delights Macgreegor, "I like when the boat's whummlin' aboot" and equally naturally appals Lizzie, his mother, "We'll get sookit into the paiddles, as shair's death!"

More than just the transport arrangements and popular recreations have changed since 1901 when Wee Macgreegor first made his way into the hearts of readers of the *Glasgow Evening Times*. Many of the customs and attitudes described in the stories have been quite transformed. It might even be difficult to find an exact modern equivalent of Aunt Purdie. This dire exemplification of the dangers of upward social mobility is married to Lizzie's brother Robert, a well-doing Glasgow grocer. Like the Robinsons they live in that archetypal Glasgow dwelling – the tenement. Naturally the Purdies, as befits their status, live in a superior example of the species. The Purdies indeed were typical of the numerous, fairly modest, Glasgow households that could afford to keep a maidservant. No fewer than 25,947 domestic servants were recorded in the Glasgow Census of 1901. Aunt Purdie is always addressed as "Mrs Purdie" by her somewhat overawed sister-in-law, who warns her husband that Mrs Purdie is a "rale genteel wumman, an' awfu' easy offendit". So set is Mrs Purdie on aping "gentry ways" that she invites the Robinsons to Christmas Dinner, instead of having a party at New Year like ordinary folk. Christmas Day was then, and for decades afterwards, a normal working day for the vast majority of the Scottish population. Robert Purdie, thankfully, is a more approachable character, "a herty man". Even so John is warned by Lizzie against making him "lauch abin his breath" – laugh out loud – a clear sign of un-genteel behaviour likely to raise Aunt Purdie's eyebrows.

Wee Macgreegor and his immediate family are firmly of the Glasgow working-class. When our hero grows up he first of all goes to work as a painter before joining his uncle Robert in the grocery business. The Robinsons are depicted as forming part of the sober, decent, comfortable element of the urban working class. John Robinson is promoted to be foreman at an engineering works and the family's income is always sufficient for them to be able to find a penny to buy Macgreegor some toffee or take him to the Zoo for a treat. Like his better-known contemporary, Neil Munro's, stories about Erchie Macpherson, the Glasgow waiter and church beadle published as "Erchie, My Droll Friend", these little tales did much to establish the idea that the life and manners of the Glasgow working class was an appropriate subject for literature. A later, and perhaps better-known, school of working class Glasgow fiction concentrated on the violence and poverty of the slum dwellers. Until the coming of the 1914–18 War the world of "Wee Macgreegor" and his family is safe and ordered and the worst that can happen is being barred from the Sunday School soirée or breaking a tea-cup at one of Aunt Purdie's tea-parties.

Despite her unremitting attempts to bring up Macgregor properly: "...ye're no' to be askin' fur jelly till ye've ett twa bits o' breid an' butter... An' ye're no' to dicht yer mooth wi' yer cuff..." Lizzie and John Robinson are fond and tender parents. Our stereotyped view of the repressed and strictly brought up Victorian and Edwardian child being "seen and not heard" certainly gains no support from these tales. John Robinson is an indulgent father while Lizzie tries, with varied success, to keep both husband and son in some sort of control. Despite her distaste for her sister-in-law Purdie's affectations and social pretensions Lizzie, in her own way, tries her best to raise her family in the social order. She drags the family off to the photographer to "get likenesses tooken" with John uncomfortable in a stand-up collar; she prudently ensures that Macgregor's birthday half-crown from his grandfather ends up in the Savings Bank. Lizzie even takes the sadly mistaken decision to buy Macgregor an alpine hat with a feather in it, for Sunday best, instead of another Glengarry bonnet. This aspirational purchase exposes Macgregor to the mockery of strangers and friends alike and leads to his throwing the new hat on the floor and crying "I winna be gentry!" – an act of nascent class consciousness and outright defiance of authority only equalled by his sympathetic father's kicking the hat out of the kitchen window into the street below – where a conveniently passing dog obliges by tearing it to bits.

A more conventional, more mature, though still sensitive, Macgregor spends a couple of years "Courtin' Christina" – the formidable, intelligent and attractive Miss Baldwin. Christina, a shop assistant, is socially perhaps a little above the Robinsons – Lizzie, for one, feels somewhat shy of her. In part this is due to her "proper" way of speaking. In fact Christina displays the remarkably common Scottish talent of utilising two quite separate linguistic registers and tends to break into Scots under the stress of emotion. Her linguistic variety should not be confused with the comic malapropisms perpetrated by Aunt Purdie in her aping of the middle classes and their ways. The latter lady, in discussing the Doctor's wife observes: "Mrs McCluny is very highly connected, quite autocratic, in fact" or in describing a traffic accident which befell her husband's shop assistant remarks that "Robert's young man got conclusion of the brain".

On his nineteenth birthday, Macgregor, like many another young man in 1914 and 1915 answered the call and enlisted – in Macgregor's case in the 9th Battalion Highland Light Infantry (The Glasgow Highlanders). Emboldened by the prospect of a kilt and with his mind focussed by impending mortal danger he plucks up the courage to propose to Christina and in "Wee Macgreegor Enlists" we have the story of their engagement and estrangement and his early days as a soldier. By the end of the book Macgregor has been wounded in action in Flanders and shipped back to hospital in England where he is visited by and reconciled with his Christina.

Bell, unlike some writers of the period, took a realistic and unromantic approach to the war. The opening of the chapter dealing with Macgregor's front line service: "Like a trodden, forgotten thing Private Macgregor Robinson lay in the Flanders mud, under the murk and rain": is far from being a jingoistic glorification of war. The horrors, excitement and fears that men experience in combat are quite sensitively handled in the context of what is, after all, a piece of light, comic, prose.

The wounded Macgregor is rescued by his childhood friend, Willie Thomson, a weak and inadequate personality who finds strength and purpose in his army service. Indeed, a significant feature of Bell's writing is the diversity of character he manages to draw in these stories. He brings a fairly wide range of observation within the bounds of a typically sentimental example of a genre that the historian of the Glasgow novel, Moira Burgess, has described as the "urban kailyard" school. Bell pictures for us the decencies of John and Lizzie Robinson; the weaknesses of Willie Thomson and the unattractive nature of his unloving aunt; the warmth and kindliness of Granpaw Purdie; the shallowness, vanity and pretensions of Aunt Purdie; the curious party-throwing habits of the sociable Mrs M'Ostrich, who to host such events has to borrow a good tea-pot from her neighbours; the stubborn determination of Macgregor himself and the pride and spirit of Christina (who reflected ruefully after one of her regular quarrels with Macgregor that "He had actually departed without being dismissed; worse still he had had the last word").

Whether these stories are to be seen as a social document, or as a classic of Scottish humour, their considerable popularity at the time of writing and later is testimony both to Bell's skill as a literary craftsman and his ability to depict with sympathetic charm, particularly in the earlier stories, the minor daily joys and sorrows of Glasgow tenement life. Their author went on to write many other books but in his long list of novels and topographical works it is unlikely that he won as many hearts as he did with the creation of the enduring, endearing personality of Macgregor Robinson.

Brian D. Osborne

Glossary

A', all
ABIN, above
ABLOW, below
AULD, old
AVA' at all
AWA', away

BA', ball
BASS, a door mat
BAIKIE, rubbish receptacle
BAUN', band
BAWBEE, halfpenny
BAWR, jest, "lark"
BEGOOD, began
BEW, blue
BLATE, backward, ashamed
BLETHER (TO), to talk nonsense
BRAW, fine, handsome
BREID. bread
BREITH, breath
BUITS, boots

CA' (TO), to call
CA' (TO), to drive, to force
CAIRRIT, carried
CANNY, careful
CARVIES, sugared caraways
CALLER, fresh
CHEUCH, tough
CHEUCH JEAN, a toffy sweet
CHIEF, friendly, "chummy"
COME BEN, come in
COORIE DOON (TO), to crouch in sitting position
CLAES, clothes
COUP (TO), to upset, to fall
CRACK, conversation

DAFT, silly stupid
DAIDLEY, pinafore
DAUNER, stroll
DOO, dove
DOUR, stubborn
DROOKIT, drenched

EEN, eyes
ERNED, ironed

FASH (TO), to worry
FA' (TO), to fall
FECHT, fight
FILE (TO), to soil
FIN (TO), to feel
FIT, foot
FLY, sly, sharp
FRAE, from
FREEN', friend
FRICHT, fright
FRIT, fruit
FURBYE, also
FURRIT, forward

GAB, mouth

GAR (TO), to induce, compel
GAUN, going, go on!
GEY, rather ("pretty")
GLAUR, mud
GREET (TO), to weep
GRUMPHY, pig
GUID-SISTER, sister-in-law

HAP (TO), to cover cosily
HASSOCK, stuffed foot-stool
HAUD (TO), to hold
HAVERS, nonsense
HOAST, cough
HOGMANAY, New-Year's Eve
HUNNER, hundred
HULLABALOO, noise, disturbance
HURL, ride (in a vehicle)

INGIN, onion
INTIL, into

JAWBOX, sink in kitchen
JOOG, jug, mug

KEEK (TO), to peep
KIST, chest
KEP (TO), to catch
KIST, cheat
KITLY, tickly
KIZZEN, cousin

LET BUG (TO), to show, to inform
LEEVIN', living
LOUSE (TO), to loosen, to unlace
LUG, ear
LUM, chimney
LYIN' BADLY, lying sick

MAIRRIT, married
MAUN, must
MUCKLE, great, big

NAB (TO), to seize
NEB, nose
NE'ERDAY, New-Year's Day
NICK, policeman
NICK (TO GET THE), to be "run in"
NICKIT, caught, captured
NOCK, clock

OARIN', rowing
'OOR, hour
OOSE, OOSIE, wool, woolly
OOTBYE, out of doors
OWER, over, excessively
OXTER, arm

PARTINS, crabs
PECHIN', panting
PEELY-WALLY, sickly, feeble-looking
PEERY-HEIDIT (TO BECOME), to "lose one's head"
PICKLE (A), a few
PLUNK (TO), to play truant
POOSHUN, poison
POKE, a (paper) bag
POTTY, putty
PREEN, pin
PUIR, poor

QUATE, quiet

RID, red
RIPE (TO), to pick (one's pocket)

SAIR, sore

SARK, shirt
SCALE (TO), to spill
SCART (TO), to scratch
SCLATES, slates, scales
SCLIM (TO), to climb
SHAIR, sure
SHIN, soon
SCOOT (TO), to squirt
SCUD, to smack, to whip
SHOOGLY, shaky, insecure
SKELP (TO), to whip
SIC, such
SILLER, (silver) money
SOJER, soldier
SOOM (TO), to swim
SOOPLE, supple
SLITHERY, slippery, slimy
SNASHTERS, dainties (cakes)
SPEIR (TO), to enquire
SPELDRON, a small dried fish
STAUN' (TO), to stand
STAIR-HEID, stair landing
STEERIN', restless, energetic
STRACHT, straight
STRAVAYGIN', wandering
STRIPPIT, striped
STROOP, spout
SUMPH, a lout
SURREE, soiree
SYNE, ago
SYNE (TO), to wash out
SWEIRT, unwilling

TAE, toe
TATE, a small portion
TAURRY-BILER, tar-boiler
TAWPY, a "softy"
TAWTIE, potato
TEWKY, a chicken
THOLE (TO), to bear, to endure
THAE, these
THUR, those
THON, THONDER, yon, yonder
THRANG, busy, occupied
TIL, to, unto
TIM (TO), to empty
TOORIE, ornament on bonnet
TOOSIE, untidy
TOSH UP (TO), to tidy up
TWAL, twelve

UNCO, very, extremely

WANNERT, wandered
WAUR, worse
WARL', world
WEAN, child
WHEEN, some
WHAUR, where
WHUMLIN' tumbling, rolling
WULKET (TO TUM'LE THE), to throw a somersault
WICE, wise
WINDA-SOLE, window-sill
WULK, whelk
WUR, our

YIN, YINST, one, once

Courtin' Christina

I

MRS. ROBINSON conveyed sundry dishes from the oven, also the teapot from the hob, to the table.

"Come awa'," she said briskly, seating herself. "We'll no' wait for Macgreegor."

"Gi'e him five minutes, Lizzie," said Mr. Robinson.

"I'm in nae hurry," remarked Gran'paw Purdie, who had come up from the coast that afternoon.

"I'm awfu' hungry, Maw," piped a young voice.

"Whisht, Jimsie," whispered daughter Jeannie.

Said Mrs. Robinson, a little impatiently: "Come awa', come awa', afore everything gets spiled. Macgreegor has nae business to be that late." She glanced at the clock. "He's been the same a' week. Haste ye, John."

John opened his mouth, but catching his wife's eye, closed it again without speech.

Excepting Jimsie, they came to the table rather reluctantly.

"Ask a blessin', fayther," murmured Lizzie.

"Shut yer eyes," muttered Jeannie to her little brother, while she restrained his eager paw from reaching a cookie.

Mr. Purdie's white head shook slightly as he said grace; he had passed his five and seventieth birthday, albeit his spirit was cheerful as of yore; in his case old age seemed to content itself with an occasional mild reminder.

John distributed portions of stewed finnan haddie, Lizzie poured out the tea, while Jeannie methodically prepared a small feast for the impatient Jimsie. Gran'paw Purdie beamed on the four, but referred surreptitiously at brief intervals to his fat silver watch.

It is eight years since last we saw the Robinson family. Naturally we find the greatest changes in the younger members. Jimsie from an infant has become a schoolboy; he is taller, more scholarly, less disposed to mischief, more subdued of nature than was Macgregor at the same age; yet he is the frank, animated young query that his brother was, though, to be sure, he has a sister as well as parents to puzzle with his questions. At thirteen Jeannie is a comely, fair-haired little maid, serious for her years, devoted to Jimsie, very proud of Macgregor, and a blessing to her parents who, strangely enough, rarely praise her; her chief end seems to be to serve those she loves without making any fuss about it.

As for John, he has grown stouter, and to his wife's dismay a bald spot has appeared on his crown; his laughter comes as readily as ever, and he is just as prone to spoil his children. But by this time Lizzie has become assured that her man's light-hearted, careless ways do not extend to his work, that his employers have confidence in their foreman, and that while he is not likely to rise higher in his trade, he is still less likely to slip back. She is proud of the three-roomed modern flat in which she and hers dwell, and her sense for orderliness and cleanliness has not lost its keenness. In person she is but little altered: perhaps her features have grown a shade softer.

"Ye see, Maister Purdie," John was explaining, "Macgreegor's busy the noo at a job in the west-end, an' that's the reason he's late for his tea."

" 'Deed, ay. It's a lang road for him to come hame," said the old man. "An' is he still likin' the pentin' trade?"

"Ay, ay. An' he's gettin' on splendid – jist splendid!"

"It's time enough to be sayin' that," Lizzie interposed. "He's no' ony furder on nor a lad o' his age ought to be. I'm no' sayin' he's daein' badly, fayther; but there's nae sense in boastin' aboot what's jist or'nar'? – Na, Jimsie! it's no' time for jeelly yet. Tak' what Jeannie gi'es ye, laddie. – Ay, the least said – "

"But his employer's pleased wi' him; he tell't me as much, wife," said John. "An' if ye compare Macgreegor wi' that young scamp, Wullie Thomson – "

"Oh, if ye compare a man wi' a monkey, I daresay it's no' sae bad for the man. But, really, John – "

"Maw, where was the man wi' the monkey?" enquired Jimsie through bread and butter.

"I'll tell ye after," whispered Jeannie, and forthwith set her mind to improvise a story involving a human being and his ancestor.

"It's easy seen," said Gran'paw, once more consulting his watch, "that Macgreegor's workin' for his wages. Surely he'll be gettin' overtime the nicht. I hope his employer's a kind man."

"I've nae doot aboot that," Lizzie returned. "He gi'es Macgreegor money for the car when he's workin' in the west-end."

"That's a proper maister!" cried Mr. Purdie, while John smiled as much as to say, "Ay! he kens Macgreegor's value!"

"An' I'm thinkin'," Lizzie continued, "that Macgreegor walks hame an' keeps the pennies to buy ceegarettes."

"What?" exclaimed the old man; "has the laddie commenced the smokin' a'ready?"

"Oh, naething to speak aboot," said John, a trifle apologetically. "They commence earlier than they did in your day, I suppose, Maister Purdie. No' that I wud smoke a ceegarette if I was paid for 't."

"He's far ower young for the smokin'," observed Lizzie.

"*I* can smoke," declared Jimsie indiscreetly. Jeannie pressed his arm.

John guffawed, Gran'paw looked amused until Lizzie demanded: "What's that ye're sayin', Jimsie?"

"But I'm no' a reg'lar smoker," mumbled Jimsie, crestfallen.

"Ay," said John, with a jocular wink at his father-in-law, "ye're feart ye singe yer whiskers, ma mannie."

"John," said Lizzie, "it's naething to joke aboot ... Jimsie, if ever I catch ye at the smokin', I'll stop yer Seturday penny, an gi'e ye castor ile instead. D'ye hear?"

"Hoots!" cried Gran'paw, "that's a terrible severe-like punishment, Lizzie!"

"I wud rayther tak' ile twicet an' get ma penny," quoth Jimsie.

"Hear, hear!" from John.

Lizzie was about to speak when the bell rang.

Jeannie slipped from her chair. "I'll gang, Maw," she said, and went out.

"It's Macgreegor," remarked John. "Ha'e ye kep' his haddie hot for him, Lizzie?"

"What for wud I dae that?" retorted Mrs. Robinson in a tone of irony, going over to the oven and extracting a covered dish.

"Haw!" laughed John. "I kent ye had something there!"

"What for did ye ask then?"

She came back to the table as her son entered, a very perceptible odour of his trade about him – an odour which she still secretly disliked though nearly three years had gone since her first whiff of it. "What kep' ye?" she enquired, pleasantly enough.

It is possible that Macgregor's dutiful greeting to his grandfather prevented his answering the question. He appeared honestly glad to see the old man; yet compared with his own the latter's greeting was boisterous. He returned his father's smile, glanced at his mother who was engaged in filling his cup, winked at his young brother, and took his place at the table, between the two men.

"Ye'll be wearied," remarked John.

"No' extra," he replied, stretching his tired legs under cover of the table.

"Did ye walk?" his mother asked, passing him his tea.

"Ay."

"It'll be three mile," said John.

Jeannie came from the fire and put a fresh slice of toast on his plate. He nodded his thanks, and she went to her place satisfied and assisted Jimsie who had got into difficulties with a jam sandwich that oozed all round.

"What way did ye no' tak' the car, laddie?" enquired Lizzie.

"I'd as sune walk," he replied, shortly.

"It's fine to save the siller – eh, Macgreegor?" said Mr. Purdie.

Macgregor reddened.

"It's something new for Macgreegor to dae that," Lizzie quietly observed.

"Tits, wumman!" muttered John.

"Wi' their cheap cars," put in Mr. Purdie, "Glesga folk are like to loss the use o' their legs. It's terrible to see the number o' young folk that winna walk if they've a bawbee in their pooch. I'm gled to see Macgreegor's no' yin o' them." He patted Macgregor's shoulder as he might have done ten years ago, and the youth moved impatiently.

"I'm no' complainin' o' Macgreegor walkin' when he micht tak' the car," said Lizzie, "but I wud like to see him puttin' his savin's to some guid purpose."

At these words Macgregor went a dull red, and set down his cup with a clatter.

"Ha'e ye burnt yer mooth?" asked John, with quick sympathy.

"Naw," was the ungracious reply. "It's naebody's business whether I tak' the car or tramp it. See's the butter, Jeannie."

There was a short silence. An outbreak of temper on Macgregor's part was not of frequent occurrence. Then John turned the conversation to a big fire that had taken place in Glasgow the previous night, and the son finished his meal in silence.

At the earliest possible moment Macgregor left the kitchen. For some reason or other the desire to get away from his elders was paramount. A few minutes later he was in the little room which belonged to him and Jimsie. On the inside of the door was a bolt, screwed there by himself some months ago. He shot it now. With a towel that hung on the door he rubbed his wet face savagely. He had washed his hands in turpentine ere leaving the scene of his work.

He donned a clean collar. As he was fixing his Sunday tie a summons came to the door. He went and opened it, looking cross.

"Weel, what are ye wantin', Jimsie?"

"Did ye bring ma putty, Macgreegor?"

"Och, I clean forgot."

Jimsie's face fell. "Ye promised," he complained.

Macgregor patted the youngster's head. "I'll bring it the morn's nicht, as sure as death," he said. "I'm sorry, Jimsie," he added apologetically.

"See an' no' forget again," said Jimsie, and retired.

Macgregor closed the door and attended to his tie. Then he looked closely at his face in the mirror hanging near the window. He was not a particularly good-looking lad, yet his countenance suggested nothing coarse or mean. His features as features, however, did not concern him now. From his vest pocket he brought a knife, with a blade thinned by stone and polished by leather. He tried its keen edge on his thumb, shook his head, and applied the steel to his boot. Presently he began to scrape his upper lip. It pained him, and he desisted. Not for the first time he wished he had a real razor.

Having put the knife away, he looked at his watch – his grandfather's prize for "good conduct" of eight years ago – and proceeded hastily to brush his hair. His hair, as his mother had often remarked during his childhood, was "awfu' ill to lie." For a moment or two he regarded his garments. He would have changed them had he had time – or was it courage?

Finally he took from his pockets a key and two pennies. He opened a drawer in the old chest, and placed the pennies in a disused tobacco tin, which already contained a few coins. He knew very well the total sum therein, but he reckoned it up once more. One shilling and sevenpence.

Every Saturday he handed his wages to his mother, who returned him sixpence. His present hoard was the result of two weeks' abstinence from cigarettes and walking instead of taking the car. He knew the job in the west-end would take at least another week, which meant another sixpence, and the coming Saturday would bring a second sixpence. Total in the near future:- two shillings and sevenpence. He smiled uncertainly, and locked up the treasure.

A minute later he slipped quietly into the passage and took his cap from its peg.

The kitchen door opened. "Whaur are ye gaun, Macgreegor?" his mother asked.

"Oot," he replied briefly, and went. Going down the stairs he felt sorry somehow. Sons often feel sorry somehow, but mothers may never know it.

When Lizzie, hiding her hurt, had shut the kitchen door, Mr. Purdie said softly: "That question an' that answer, ma dear, are as auld as human natur'."

As Macgregor turned out of the tenement close he encountered his one-time chum, Willie Thomson. Macgregor might not have admitted it to his parents, but during the last few weeks he had been finding Willie's company less and less desirable.

Willie now put precisely the same question that Mrs. Robinson had put a minute earlier.

"I'll maybe see ye later," was Macgregor's evasive response, delivered awkwardly. He passed on.

"Ha'e ye a ceegarette on ye?" cried Willie, taking a step after him.

"Na."

"Ye're in a queer hurry."

"I'll maybe see ye later," said Macgregor again, increasing his speed in a curious guilty fashion.

Willie made no attempt to overtake him. He, too, had been finding a certain staleness in the old friendship – especially since Macgregor had stopped his purchases of cigarettes. Willie was as often out of employment as in it, but he did not realise that he was in danger of becoming a mere loafer and sponge. Yet he was fond of Macgregor.

Macgregor passed from the quiet street wherein he lived into one of Glasgow's highways, aglow with electric light, alive with noise out of all proportion to its traffic. He continued to walk swiftly, his alert eyes betraying his eagerness, for the distance of a couple of blocks. Then into another quiet street he turned, and therein his pace became slower and slower, until it failed altogether. Beneath a gas lamp he questioned his watch, his expression betokening considerable anxiety.

It was a fine October night, but chilly – not that he gave any sign of feeling cold. For a space he remained motionless, gazing up the street. Possibly he would have liked a cigarette just then.

As though rousing himself, he moved abruptly and proceeded slowly to the next lamp post, turned about and came back to his first halting-place, where he turned about again. For a long half-hour he continued to stroll between the two posts. Few persons passed him, and he did not appear to notice them. Indeed, it may as well be frankly admitted that he shamefully avoided their glances. When at last he did stop, it was with a sort of jerk.

From one of the closes a girl emerged and came towards him.

II

MACGREGOR'S acquaintance with Jessie Mary was almost as old as himself; yet only within the last three months had he recognised her existence as having aught of importance to do with his own. This recognition had followed swift on the somewhat sudden discovery that Jessie Mary was pretty.

The discovery was made at a picnic, organised by a section of the great drapery store wherein Jessie Mary found employment, Macgregor's presence at the outing being accounted for by the fact that in a weak moment he had squandered a money gift from his grandparents on the purchase of two tickets for Katie, his first love (so far as we know), and himself. The picnic was a thorough success, but neither Macgregor nor Katie enjoyed it. It was not so much that anything came between them, as that something that had been between them departed – evaporated. There was no quarrel; merely a dulness, a tendency to silence, increasing in dreariness as the bright day wore on. And, at last, in the railway compartment, on the way home, they sat, crushed together by the crowd, Katie dumb with dismay, Macgregor steeped in gloom.

Opposite them sat Jessie Mary and her escort, a young man with sleek hair, a pointed nose, several good teeth, and a small but exquisite black moustache. These two were gay along with the majority of the occupants of the carriage. Perhaps in her simple sixteen-year-old heart Katie began to realise that she was deserted indeed; perhaps Macgregor experienced prickings of shame, not that he had ever given or asked promises. Still, it is to be hoped that he did not remember then any of Katie's innocent little advances of the past.

Affection 'twixt youth and youth is such a delicate, sensitive thing, full of promise as the pretty egg of a bonny bird, and as easily broken.

Macgregor was caught by the vivacious dark eyes of Jessie Mary, snared by her impudent red mouth, held by the charm of her face, which the country sun had tinted with an unwonted bloom. Alas for the little brown mouse at his side! At briefer and briefer intervals he allowed his gloomy glance to rest on the girl opposite, while he became more and more convinced that the young man with the exquisite moustache was a "bletherin' idiot." Gradually he shifted his position to the very edge of the seat, so as to lessen his contact with Katie. And when Jessie Mary, without warning, presented to his attention her foot in its cheap, stylish shoe, saying: "I wish ye wud tie ma lace, Macgreegor," a strange wild thrill of pride ran through his being, though, to be sure, he went scarlet to the ears and his fingers could scarce perform their office. There were friends of Jessie Mary who declared that Macgregor never would have noticed her at all that day had she not been wearing a white frock with a scarlet belt; but that was grossly unfair to Jessie Mary. The animation and fresh coquetry of eighteen were also hers.

Nigh three months had gone, autumn had come, and here in a dingy side-street the captivated youth had lingered on the bare chance of a glimpse of the same maiden in her every-day attire, his mind tormented by his doubts as to his reception, should she happen to appear.

And now she was approaching him. For the life of him he could neither advance nor retire. Still, such of his wits as had remained faithful informed him that it was "stupid-like" to do nothing at all. Whereupon he drew out his watch and appeared to be profoundly interested in the time. At the supreme moment of encounter his surprise was, it must be confessed, extremely badly managed, and he touched his cap with the utmost diffidence and without a word.

"Hullo!" Jessie Mary remarked carelessly. "Fancy meetin' you, as the man said to the sassige roll!"

It had been a mutton-pie at their last meeting, Macgregor remembered, trying to laugh. Some comfort might have been his had he known that this flippancy, or its variant, was her form of greeting to all the young men then enjoying her acquaintance. Jessie Mary usually kept a joke going for about three months, and quite successfully, too.

"Did ye no' expec' to meet me?" He stumbled over the words.

Jessie Mary laughed lightly, mockingly. "I wasna aware yer best girl lived in this street."

"It – it's no' the first time ye've seen me here," he managed to say.

She laughed again. "Weel, that's true. I wonder wha the girl is." He would have told her if he could, poor boy. "But I must hurry," she went on, "or the shops'll be shut."

"Can I no' gang wi' ye?" he asked, with a great effort.

"Oh, ye can come as far as Macrorie's," she answered graciously, mentioning a provision shop.

Young love is ever grateful for microscopic mercies, and Macgregor's spirit took courage as he fell into step with her. Jessie Mary was a handsomely built young woman; her shoulder was quite on a level with his. There were times when he would fain have been taller; times, also, when he would fain have been older, for Jessie Mary's years exceeded his own by two. Nevertheless, he was now thinking of her age without reference to his own. He was, in fact, about to speak of it, when Jessie Mary said:

"I'm to get to the United Ironmongers' dance on Friday week, after a'. When faythe was at his tea the nicht, he said I could gang."

She might as well have poured a jug of ice water over him. "Aw, did he?" he murmured feebly.

"Ye should come, Macgreegor," she continued "Only three-an'-six for a ticket admittin' lady an' gent."

"Och, I'm no' heedin' aboot dancin'." said Macgregor, knowing full well that his going was out of the question.

"It'll be a splendid dance. They'll keep it up till three," she informed him.

With his heart in his mouth he enquired who was taking her to the dance.

"Oh, I ha'ena decided yet." She gave her head a becoming

little toss. "I've several offers. I'll let them quarrel in the meantime."

Perhaps it was some consolation to know that she had not decided on any particular escort, and that the rivals were at war with one another. While there is strife there is hope.

"Ay; ye'll ha'e plenty offers," he managed to say steadily, and felt rather pleased with himself.

"I'm seriously thinking o' wearin' pink," she told him as they turned into the main street. "It's maybe a wee thing common, but I've been told it suits me."

Macgregor wondered who had told her, and stifling his jealousy, observed that pink was a bonny colour ... "But – but ye wud look fine in ony auld thing." Truly he was beginning to get on.

So, at least, Jessie Mary seemed to think. "Nane o' yer flattery!" she said with a coquettish laugh.

"I wud like fine to see ye at the dance," he said with a sigh.

"Come – an' I'll gi'e ye a couple o' dances – three, if I can spare them." Hitherto Jessie Mary had regarded Macgregor as a mere boy, and sometimes as a bit of a nuisance, but she was the sort of young woman who cannot have too many strings to her bow. "I can get ye a ticket," she added encouragingly.

For an instant it occurred to Macgregor to ask her to let him take her to the dance – he would find the money somehow – but the idea died in its birth. He could not both go to the dance and do that which he had already promised himself to do. Besides, she might laugh at him and refuse.

"It's nae use speakin' aboot the dance," he said regretfully. Then abruptly: "Yer birthday's on Tuesday week, is't no'?"

Jessie Mary looked at him. His eyes were on the pavement. "Wha tell't ye that?"

"I heard ye speakin' aboot yer birthday to somebody at the picnic."

"My! ye've a memory!"

"But it's on Tuesday week – the twinty-third? I was wantin' to be sure."

"Weel, it's the twinty-third, sure enough." She heaved an affected sigh. "Nineteen! I'm gettin' auld, Macgreegor. Time I was gettin' a lad! Eh?" She laughed at his confusion of face. "But what for d'ye want to ken aboot ma birthday?" she innocently enquired, becoming graver.

The ingenuousness of the question helped him.

"Aw, I jist wanted to ken, Jessie Mary. Never heed aboot it. I hope ye'll enjoy the dance – when it comes." This was quite a long speech for Macgregor to make, but it might have been even longer had they not just then arrived at the provision shop.

"Here we are," said she cheerfully. She had the decency to ignore the smile of the young man behind the counter – the young man with the sharp nose and exquisite black moustache; nor did she appear to notice another young man on the opposite pavement who was also gazing quite openly at her. "Here we are, an' here we part – to meet again, I hope," she added, with a softer glance.

"I'll wait till ye've got yer messages," said Macgregor, holding his ground.

She gave him her sweetest smile but one. "Na, Macgreegor; it'll tak' me a while to get the messages, an' I've ither places to gang afterwards. Maybe I'll see ye floatin' aroun' anither nicht."

"But I'm no' in a hurry. I – I wish ye wud let me wait."

Her very sweetest smile was reserved for the most stubborn cases, and she gave it him now. But her voice though gentle was quite firm. "If ye want to please me, Macgreegor, ye'll no' wait the nicht."

He was conquered. She nodded kindly and entered the doorway.

"Guidbye, Jessie Mary," he murmured, and turned away.

There were no other customers in the shop. Jessie Mary took a seat at the counter. The young man, stroking his moustache, gave her a good-evening tenderly.

"I'm to get to the dance," she said, solemnly.

The young man's hand fell to his side. "Wi' me?" he cried, very eagerly.

"I ha'ena made up ma mind yet, Peter. I want a pair o' kippers – the biggest ye've got."

III

THE outside of the shop had been painted but recently. Above door and window were blazoned in large gilt letters the words:

STATIONERY AND FANCY GOODS.

Just over the doorway was very modestly printed in white the name of the proprietor:

M. TOD.

What the M stood for nobody knew (or cared) unless, perhaps, the person so designated; and it is almost conceivable that she had forgotten, considering that for five and thirty years she had never heard herself addressed save as Miss Tod.

For five and thirty years M. Tod had kept her shop without assistance. For five and thirty years she had lived in the shop and its back room, rarely going out of doors except to church on Sunday mornings. The grocer along the way had a standing order: practically all the necessaries of life, as M. Tod understood them, could be supplied from a grocer's shop. A time had been when M. Tod saved money; but the last ten years had witnessed a steady shrinking of custom, a dwindling in hopes for a peaceful, comfortable old age, a shrinking an dwindling in M. Tod herself. A day came when a friendly customer and gossip was startled to behold M. Tod suddenly flop to the floor behind the counter.

A doctor, hastily summoned, brought her back to a consciousness of her drab existence and dingy shop. She was soon ready to go on with both as though nothing had happened. The doctor, however, warned her quite frankly that if she did not take proper nourishment, moderate exercise and abundance of fresh air, she would speedily find herself beyond need of these things.

M. Tod did not want to die, and since she never laughed at anything she could not laugh at the doctor. To some of us life is like a cup of bitter physic with a lump of sugar at the bottom, but no spoon to stir it up with; life, therefore, must be sweet – sooner or later.

On the other hand, obedience to the doctor would involve considerable personal expenditure, not to mention the engaging of an assistant. When M. Tod had reckoned up the remnants of her savings and estimated her financial position generally, she incontinently groaned. Nevertheless, she presently proceeded to prepare a two-line advertisement for the *Evening Express*. She was still in the throes of composition – endeavouring to say in twenty words what she thought in two hundred – when Mr. Baldwin, traveller for a firm of fancy-goods merchants, entered the shop. Acquainted with his kindly manner in the past, she ventured to confide to him her present difficulties.

Mr. Baldwin was not only sympathetic but helpful.

"Why," said he, "my niece Christina might suit you – in fact, I'm sure she would. She is nearly sixteen, and only yesterday finished a full course of book-keeping. More than that, Miss Tod, she has had experience in the trade. Her aunt before her marriage to – er – myself – had a little business like your own, at the coast. I had thought of getting Christina a situation in the wholesale, but I believe it would be better for her to be here, for a time at least. I know she is keen on a place where she can have her own way – I mean to say, have room to carry out her own ideas." Mr. Baldwin halted in some confusion, but speedily recovered. "Anyway," he went on, "give her a trial. Let me send her along to see you this evening."

M. Tod assented, possibly because she feared to hurt the traveller's feelings. "Nearly sixteen" and "keen on a place where she can have her own way" did not sound precisely reassuring to the old woman who had no experience of young folk, and who had been her own mistress for so long.

That evening Christina came, saw and, after a little hesitation, conquered her doubts as to the suitability of the situation. "I'll manage her easy," she said to herself while attending with the utmost demureness to M. Tod's recital of the duties required of her assistant – "I'll manage her easy."

Within six months she had made good her unuttered words.

It was Saturday afternoon. M. Tod was about to leave the shop for an airing. Time takes back no wrinkles, yet M. Tod seemed younger than a year ago. She had lost the withered, yellowed complexion of those who worship continually in the Temple of Tannin; her movements were freer; her voice no longer fell at the end of every sentence on a note of hopelessness. Though she had grown some months older, she had become years less aged. She glanced round her shop with an air of pride.

From behind the counter Christina, with a kindly, faintly amused smile, watched her.

"Ay," remarked M. Tod, "everything looks vera nice – vera nice, indeed, dearie. I can see ye've done yer best to follow ma instructions."

It had become a habit with M. Tod to express observations of this sort prior to going out, a habit, also, to accept all Christina's innovations and improvements as originally inspired by herself. Even the painting of the shop, which, when first mooted by the girl, had seemed about as desirable as an earthquake, had gradually become her very own bright idea. Happily Christina had no difficulty in tolerating such gentle injustices; as a matter of fact, she preferred that her mistress should be managed unawares.

"Tak' a squint at the window when ye gang oot," she said, pleasantly. "Ye ha'ena seen it since it was dressed. There's a heap o' cheap trash in it, but it's trash that draws the public noo-a-days."

"Oh, I wudna say that, dearie," said the old woman. "I've aye tried to gi'e folk guid value."

"Ay! Ma aunt was like that – near ruined hersel' tryin' to gi'e the public what it didna want. What the public wants is gorgeousness – an' it wants it cheap. Abyssinian Gold an' papermashy leather an' so on. See thon photo-frames!" –

Christina pointed – "the best sellin' photo-frames ever we had! In a week or so, they get wearit sittin' on the mantel-piece, an' doon they fa' wi' a broken leg; in a fortnight they look as if they had been made in the year ten B.C.! Behold thon purses! Safer to carry yer cash in a paper poke, but the public canna resist the real, *genuine* silver mounts. Observe thon – "

"Weel, weel," Miss Tod mildly interrupted, "it's maybe as ye say, an' I canna deny that custom's improvin'. But it's a sad pity that folk winna buy the best – "

"Oh, let the folk pity theirsel's – when they get sense – an' that'll no' be this year. Gi'e them what they want, an' never heed what they need. That's the motto for a shop-keeper. Come ower here for a minute till I sort yer bonnet, or ye'll be lossin' twa o' yer grapes. I hear figs an' onions is to be the favourite trimmin' next Spring. Ye could dae wi' a new bonnet, Miss Tod."

"So I could," the old woman wistfully admitted as she submitted her headgear to her assistant's deft fingers. "I couldna say when I got this yin."

"Oh, I'm no' keen on dates. But" – encouragingly – "we'll tak' stock next week, an' when we've struck the half-year's balance I'll no' be surprised it ye tak' the plunge an' burst a pound-note at the milliners." Christina administered a final pat to the ancient bonnet. "Noo ye're ready for the road. See an' no' catch cold. I'll ha'e the kettle at the bile against yer return at five."

"I'll no' be late," replied M. Tod who, to tell the truth, was already wishing it were tea-time, and moved to the door.

"I suppose," said Christina, "ye wudna care to call at the Reverend Mr. McTavish's an' politely ask for payment o' his account – consistin' chiefly o' sermon-paper. He's a whale for sermon-paper!"

"Oh, dearie, dearie, I couldna dae that," faltered M. Tod, and made her escape.

"If that account isna paid sune," Christina murmured, "I'll ha'e to gang masel' an put the fear o' death into the man. Business is business – even when it's releegious."

She looked round the shop to discover if aught required her attention; then being satisfied that nought could be improved, she seated herself on the stool and prepared to do a little book-keeping.

As she dipped her pen, however, the door of the shop was slowly opened, the bell above it banged, and a young man – so she reckoned him – came in. In her quick way, though she had never seen him before, she put him down in her mind as a purchaser of a half-penny football paper. But having recovered from the alarm of the bell and carefully shut the door, he hesitated, surveying his surroundings.

Christina flung back her thick plait of fair hair, slipped from the stool, and came to attention.

"Nice day," she remarked in her best manner. She contrived to get away from the vernacular in her business dealings.

"Ay," The young man smiled absently.

"Nice teeth," thought Christina. (That Macgregor's teeth were good was entirely due to his mother's firmness in the matter of brushing them during his younger days. He was inclined to be proud of them now.)

"Just take a look round," she said aloud.

Macgregor acknowledged the invitation with a nod.

"Was it anything special you wanted to see?" she enquired.

Macgregor regarded her for a moment. "I had a look at yer window," he said, his eyes wandering once more, "but I seen naething dearer nor a shillin'."

"Oh!" exclaimed Christina. Then recovering her dignity – "The window is merely a popular display. We have plenty of more expensive goods within." She felt pleased at having said "within" instead of "inside."

At the word "expensive" Macgregor shrank. "Aboot half-a-croon?" he said diffidently, taking a step towards the door.

"Half-a-crown *and* upwards," said Christina very distinctly. As a matter of fact, the shop contained few articles priced as high as two shillings, the neighbourhood not being noted for its affluence; but one of Christina's mottoes was "First catch your customer and then rook him." "Oh, yes," she added pleasantly, "our goods at half-a-crown are abundant."

For a moment Macgregor doubted she was laughing at him, but a veiled glance at her earnest face reassured him – nay, encouraged him. He had never bought a present for a lady before, and felt his position keenly. Indeed, he had left his home district to make the purchase in order that he might do so unrecognised.

So with a shy, appealing smile he said:

"It's for a present."

"A present. Certaintly!" she replied, lapsing a trifle in the excitement of the moment. "Male or female?"

Macgregor gave her an honest stare.

"Is it for a lady or gent?" she enquired, less abashed by the stare than annoyed with herself for having used the wrong phrase.

"Lady," said Macgregor, with an attempt at boldness, and felt himself getting hot.

"Will you kindly step this way?" came the polite invitation.

Macgregor proceeded to the counter and bumped his knee against the chair that stood there.

"Useful or ornamental?"

"I – I dinna ken," he answered between his teeth.

"I'll break that chair's neck for it some day!" cried Christina, her natural sympathy for suffering getting the better of her commercial instincts. Then she coughed in her best style. "Do you think the young lady would like something to wear?"

"I dinna ken, I'm sure." Macgregor pushed back his cap and scratched his head. "Let's see what ye've got for wearin' an' – an' no' for wearin'."

Christina, too, nearly scratched her head. She was striving to think where she could lay hands on articles for which she could reasonably charge half-a-crown.

Without very noticeable delay she turned to a drawer, and

presently displayed a small green oblong box. She opened it.

"This is a nice fountain-pen," she explained. "It's price has been reduced – "

"Aw, I'm no' heedin' aboot reduced things, thank ye a' the same."

"I'll make it two shillings to you," Christina said persuasively. "That's a very drastic reduction." Which was perfectly true. On the other hand, the pen was an old model which she had long despaired of selling. "Nothing could be more suitable for a young lady," she added, exhibiting the nib. "Real gold."

But Macgregor shook his head.

With apparent cheerfulness she laid the pen aside. "It's for a *young* lady, I think you said?"

"Ay, it's for a young lady, but she's no' that young either. Aboot ma ain age, maybe."

Christina nearly said "about twelve, I suppose," but refrained. She was learning to subdue her tendency to chaff. "I perceive," she said gravely. "Is she fond of needlework?"

"I couldna say. She's gettin' a pink dress, but I think her mither's sewin' it for her."

"A pink dress!" muttered Christina, forgetting herself. "Oh, Christopher Columbus!" She turned away sharply.

"Eh?"

"She'll be a brunette?" said Christina calmly, though her cheeks were flushed.

"I couldna say," said Macgregor again.

Christina brought forward a tray of glittering things. "These combs are much worn at present," she informed him. "Observe the jewels."

"They'll no' be real," said Macgregor doubtfully.

"Well – a – no. Not exactly *real.* But everybody weers – wears imitation jewellery nowadays. The west-end's full of it – chock-a-block, in fact." She held up a pair of combs of almost blinding beauty. "Chaste – ninepence each."

"Ay," sighed Macgregor, " but I'm no' sure – "

"Silver belt – quite the rage – one shilling."

Macgregor remembered the scarlet belt at the picnic. He had a vague vision of a gift of his in its place. He held out his hand for the glittering object.

"You don't happen to know the size of the lady's waist?" said Christina in a most discreet tone of voice.

"I couldna say." He laid down the belt, but kept looking at it.

"Excuse me," she said softly, lifting the belt and fastening it round her waist. She was wearing a navy skirt and a scarlet flannel shirt, with a white collar and black tie. "My waist is just about medium." She proceeded to put the combs in her hair. "Of course they would look better on a brunette." She permitted herself the faintest of smiles. "But you can see how they look when they're being worn."

Was there a hint of mockery in the bright grey-blue eyes? Macgregor did not observe it; nor was he shocked by the crudity and gaudiness of the ornaments in broad daylight. But perhaps the general effect was not so shocking. Christina, having previously experimented with the ornaments, had a pretty good idea of how they appeared upon her. It would be difficult to describe precisely what Macgregor thought just then, but it is to be feared that he made the sudden and unexpected discovery that Jessie Mary was not the only pretty girl in the world.

"I'll tak' them," he said uneasily, and put his hand in his pocket.

"Thank you," said Christina. "Will that be all to-day?"

"Ay; that'll be a'." He had purposed spending the odd penny of his fund on a birthday card, but for some undefinable reason let the coin fall back into his pocket.

Christina proceeded to make a neat parcel. "You're a stranger here," she remarked pleasantly.

"Ay. But I dinna live far awa'." Now that the ordeal was over, he was feeling more at ease. "Ye've a nice shop miss."

"Do you think so? I'm very glad you got something to suit you in it. Thank you! Half-a-crown – two-and-six exactly. *Good* afternoon!"

It may be that Macgregor would have stopped to make a

remark or two on his own account, but just then an elderly woman entered the shop.

"Guidbye, Miss," he murmured, touching his cap, and departed with his purchase.

Christina dropped the silver into the till. To herself she said: " I doobt he's no' as green as he's cabbage-lookin'." Aloud: "Nice day, Mrs. Dunn. Is your little grandson quite well again?"

IV

FOR some weeks Macgregor had nourished an idea of making the birthday presentation with his own hands. In fancy he had beheld his own gallant proffering of the gifts, and Jessie Mary's shy acceptance of the same. Why he should have foreseen himself bold and Jessie Mary bashful is a question that may be left to those who have the profound insight necessary to diagnose the delicate workings of a youthful and lovelorn imagination. At the same time he had harboured many hopeful fears and fearful hopes, but to divulge these in detail would be sacrilege.

On the day following the purchase of the gifts, however, his original plan, so simple and straight-forward, would seem to have lost something of its attractiveness. Perhaps he was suddenly assailed by the cowardice of modesty; possibly he argued, in effect, that the offering would gain in importance by impersonal delivery. At all events, he endeavoured, on the way to church, to borrow from Willie Thomson the sum of threepence – the charge for delivery demanded by a heartless post-office. Unfortunately Willie's finances just then were in a most miserable state, so much so that on this very morning he had been compelled to threaten his aunt, with whom and on whom he lived, with the awful vow never to enter a church again unless she supplied him with twopence on the spot. (This, of course, in addition to the customary penny for "the plate.")

He jingled the coins in his pocket while he confided to Macgregor his tale of a hard world, and continued to do so while he waited for the sympathy which past experience of his friend led him to expect.

It was therefore something of a shock to Willie when Macgregor, privately fondling the penny which he had not spent on a birthday card, replied: "I could manage wi' the tuppence, Wullie. An' I'll pay ye back on Seturday, sure."

"Eh?" Willie stopped jingling and clutched his coins tightly.

Macgregor repeated his words hopefully.

"Aw, but I canna len' ye the tuppence," said Willie, almost resentfully; adding, "But I'll gi'e ye a ceegarette or twa when I buy some."

"I'm no' wantin' yer ceegarettes," Macgregor returned, his eyes on the pavement.

Willie shot at him a curious glance. "What for d'ye want the tuppence? Ha'e ye been bettin' on horses?"

For a moment Macgregor was tempted to plead guilty of that or any other crime on the chance of gaining the other's sympathies and pence. Instead, however, he answered with caution: "I'll maybe tell ye, if ye'll len' me the tuppence."

Willie laughed. "I'm no' sae green. Ye best get yer faycher to gi'e ye the money."

"Clay up!" snapped Macgregor, and remained silent for the rest of the journey.

Had the money been required for any other object in the world, Macgregor would probably have gone straightway to his father and frankly asked for it. But the limits of confidence between son and parent are reached when the subject is a girl. Nevertheless, it was to the boy's credit that he never dreamed of attempting to obtain his father's help under false pretences.

That night he came to the dismal decision to deliver the package himself at Jessie Mary's door, at an hour when Jessie Mary would be certain to be out. There was nothing else for it, as far as he could see just then.

The following morning's light found him at his work – no longer, alas! in the far west-end with its windfall of pennies for the car, but in the heart of the city. The man under whom he worked found him so slow and stupid that he threatened to report him to his employer. Altogether it was a dreary day, and Macgregor, who usually paid enough attention to his duties to escape the burden of time, was more than glad when the last working hour had dragged to its close.

He went home by an unaccustomed though not entirely unfamiliar route. It led him past the shop wherein he had made the birthday purchases on Saturday afternoon. The window was more brightly illuminated than the majority of its neighbours; the garish contents were even more attractive than in daylight. Macgregor found himself regarding them with a half-hearted interest. Presently he noticed that one of the sliding glass panels at the back of the window was open a few inches. This aperture permitted him to see the following: A hand writing a letter on a sloping desk, a long plait of fair hair over a scarlet shoulder, and a youthful profile with an expression very much in earnest yet cheerful withal.

Macgregor could not help watching the writer, and he continued to do so for several minutes with increasingly lively interest. He was even wondering to whom the letter might be written, when the writer, having dipped her pen too deeply, made a horrid, big blot. She frowned and for an instant put out her tongue. Then, having regarded the blot for a space with a thoughtful gaze, she seized the pen and with a few deft touches transformed the blot into the semblance of a black beetle. Whereupon she smiled with such transparent delight that Macgregor smiled also.

"What are ye grinnin' at?" said a voice at his elbow.

He turned to discover Willie Thomson. At no time in the whole course of their friendship had he felt a keener desire to hit Willie on his impudent nose. "Naething," he muttered shortly. "Are ye gaun hame?"

"Ay," said Willie, noting the other's discomposure, but not referring to it directly. "This isna yer usual road hame."

"Depends whaur I'm comin' frae," returned Macgregor, quickening his pace. "Ha'e ye got a job yet, Wullie?" he enquired more graciously.

"I tried yin the day, but it's no' gaun to suit me. But I've earned ninepence. I can len' ye thon thruppence, if ye like."

"Aw, I'm no' needin' it noo."

"Weel, ha'e a ceegarette." Willie produced a yellow packet.

"Na, I'm no' smokin', Wullie."

"What's wrang wi' ye?"

"Naething ... What sort of job was ye tryin'?"

Willie told him, and thereafter proceeded to recount as many grievances as there had been hours in his working day. Macgregor encouraged him to enter into all sorts of detail, so that home was reached without reference to the shop window which had caused him amusement.

"So long," said Willie, lighting a fresh cigarette. "Maybe see ye later."

"Ah, it's likely," Macgregor replied, and turned into the close, glad to escape.

"Haud on!" cried Willie.

"What?" Macgregor halted with reluctance.

Willie sniggered. "I seen ye we' Jessie Mary the ither nicht."

"Did ye?" retorted Macgregor feebly.

"Ay; an' if I was you, I wud let girls alane. They're nae fun, an' they're awfu' expensive."

With which sage advice Willie walked off.

Macgregor made up his mind not to leave the house that evening, yet eight o'clock found him at the foot of the street wherein Jessie Mary lived. But he did not go up the street, and at the end of five minutes he strolled the way he had taken two hours earlier. As he approached a certain shop the light in its window went out. He marched home quickly, looking neither right nor left.

On the following evening he hired a small boy for the sum of one halfpenny to deliver the package to Jessie Mary at her abode, and straightway returned to the parental fireside, where he blushed at the welcome accorded him.

That night, however, fate willed it that John Robinson should run out of tobacco. Macgregor, who had been extremely restless, expressed himself ready to step down to the tobacco shop in the main street.

Here it must be mentioned that the gifts had reached Jessie Mary at precisely the right moment. They had raised her spirits from the depths of despair to at least the lower heights of hope. Only an hour before their arrival she had learned how the young man with the exquisite moustache had treacherously invited another young lady to accompany him to the Ironmongers' dance; and although to the ordinary mind this may appear to have been the simple result of a lack of superhuman patience on the young man's part, Jessie Mary could perceive in it nothing but the uttermost perfidy. So that until the arrival of Macgregor's present – "to J. M. from M. with best wishes" (an "l" had been scraped out where the second "w" now stood) – she had felt like tearing the pink frock to tatters and preparing for the tomb.

They met near the tobacconist's – on Macgregor's home side, by the way – and he could not have looked more guilty had he sent her an infernal machine.

"It was awful kind o' ye," she said sweetly; "jist *awful* kind."

"Aw, it was naething," he stammered.

"They're jist lovely, an' that fashionable," she went on, and gradually led the conversation to the subject of the United Ironmongers' dance.

"Ye should come," she said, "an' see hoo nice I look wi' them on. The belt'll be lovely wi' ma pink frock. An' the combs was surely made for black hair like mines. Of course I tried them on the minute I got them."

"Did ye?" murmured Macgregor. Where was all the feverish joy, the soft rapture anticipated three nights ago? "Did ye?" – that was all he said.

She made allowance for his youth and the bashfulness she had so often experienced. "Macgreegor," she whispered, slipping her hand through his arm, in the darkness of the street leading to her home, "Macgreegor, I believe I wud suner dance wi' you than onybody else."

Macgregor seemed to have nothing to say. The touch of her hand was pleasant, and yet he was uneasy.

"Macgreegor," she said presently, a little breathlessly, "I'm no' heedin' aboot ony o' the chaps that wants to tak' me to the dance. If ye had a ticket – " She paused. They had halted in the close-mouth, as it is locally termed. "I'm sayin', Macgreegor, if ye had a ticket – " She paused again.

The boy felt foolish and wretched. "But I canna gang to the dance, Jessie Mary," he managed to say.

She leaned closer to him. "It'll be a splendid dance – at least" – she looked at him boldly – "it wud be splendid if you and me was gaun thegether."

In his wildest of wild dreams he may have thought of kissing this girl. He might have done it now – quite easily.

But he didn't – he couldn't.

"Na; I canna gang," he said. "An' – an' ma fayther'll be waitin' for his tobacco. Guidnicht." He glanced at her with a miserable smile, and departed – bolted.

Poor Jessie Mary with her little natural vanities!

Poor Macgregor! He went home hot and ashamed – he could not have told why. He did not grudge the gifts, yet vaguely wished he had not given them.

And he dreamed that night of, among other queer things, a shop window, a plait of fair hair on a scarlet shoulder, and a black beetle.

V

"MERCY, laddie!" exclaimed Mrs. Robinson, as her son entered the kitchen, a little late for tea. "What ha'e ye been daein' to yer face?"

The colour induced by the question seemed almost to extinguish the hectic spot at Macgregor's left cheek-bone.

"Washin' it," he answered shortly, taking his accustomed chair.

"But it's cut."

"Tits, Lizzie!" muttered Mr. Robinson. "Are ye for toast, Macgreegor?"

"He's been shavin' his whiskers," said Jimsie. "Did ye no' ken Macgreegor's gettin' whiskers, Maw?" he went on in spite of a warning pressure from sister Jeannie. "Paw, what way dae folk get whiskers?"

"Dear knows," returned his father briefly. "Lizzie can ye no' gi'e Macgreegor a cup o' tea?"

Lizzie lifted the cosy from the brown teapot. "Where did ye get the razor, Macgreegor?"

"He hasna got a razor, Maw," said Jimsie. "He does it wi' a wee knife."

"Shurrup!" Macgregor growled, whereupon Jimsie choked and his eyes filled with tears.

"Macgreegor," said his mother, "that's no' the way to speak to yer wee brither."

"Macgreegor," said his sister, "I'll mak' ye a bit o' hot toast, if ye like."

"Ay, Jeannie," said John quickly, "mak' him a bit o' hot toast, an' I'll look after Jimsie." He turned the conversation to the subject of a great vessel that had been launched into the Clyde that morning.

Sullenly Macgregor took the cup from his mother's hand and forthwith devoted his attention to his meal. Seldom had resentment taken such possession of his soul. Another word from his mother or Jimsie, and he would have retorted violently and flung out of the room. The mild intervention of his sister and father had saved a scene. Though his face cooled, his heart remained hot; though hungry, he ate little, including the freshly made toast, which he accepted with a gracelessness that probably shamed him even more than it hurt Jeannie. Poor sensitive, sulky youth! – a hedgehog with its skin turned outside-in could not suffer more.

For the first time in the course of his married life John Robinson really doubted Lizzie's discretion. It was with much diffidence, however, that he referred to the matter after Macgregor had gone out, and while Jeannie was superintending Jimsie's going to bed.

"Lizzie," he began, eyeing his cold pipe, "did ye happen to notice that Macgreegor was a wee thing offended the nicht?"

Mrs. Robinson did not halt in her business of polishing a bread plate. "Macgreegor's gettin' ower easy offended," she said, carelessly enough.

John struck a match and held it without application to his pipe until the flame scorched his hardened fingers. "Speakin' frae experience," he said slowly, "there's twa things that a young man tak's vera serious-like. The first – "

"Wha's the young man?"

"Macgreegor… . Aw, Lizzie!"

"Macgreegor's a laddie."

"He's a young man – an' fine ye ken it, wife!"

Lizzie put down the plate and took up another. "An' what does he tak' serious-like?" she enquired, coolly.

"Firstly," said John, with a great effort, and stuck.

"Ye'll be preachin' a sermon directly," said she. "Can ye no' licht yer pipe an' speak nateral?"

"Hoo can I speak nateral when I ken ye're makin' a mock o' me?"

"Havers, man!" she said, becoming good-humoured lest he should lose his temper; "licht yer pipe. I'm listenin'."

John lit his pipe in exceedingly methodical fashion. "Weel, Lizzie," he began at last, "I jist wanted to say that when a young man's gettin' hair on his face, ye – ye shouldna notice it."

"I didna notice it."

"Weel, ye shouldna refer to it."

"It was the cut I referred to."

John sucked at his pipe and scratched his head. "That's true," he admitted. "Still, if yer sister had a wudden leg, ye wudna refer to the noise on the stair. It wasna like ye, Lizzie, to hurt Macgreegor's feelin's."

Mrs. Robinson put down the plate with an unusual clatter. Hurt Macgreegor's feelings! – She? – The idea! "Are ye feenished?" she snapped.

John nerved himself. "There's anither thing that it's best no' to refer to – anither thing that a young man tak's vera serious-like. When a young man begins to tak' an interest in the lassies – "

"Oh, man, can ye no stop haverin'?" she cried. "Ha'e ye forgot the laddie's age?"

"It's the shavin' age, an' that means – "

"Ma brither Rubbert was nineteen afore he put a razor to his face."

"Yer brither Rubbert was never what I wud ca' a female fancier. Of course that wasna his fau't; he was jist as the Lord made him, and he's turned oot a vera successful man, an' for a' we ken his wife Sarah's maybe better nor she's bonny. But yer son Macgreegor – "

"Macgreegor wud never look at the lassies. He's ower shy."

"Whiles it's the kind that doesna look that leaps the furdest. But there's waur things in the world nor razors and lassies," said John, with a feeble laugh, "an' I jist wanted to warn ye no' to ask questions, even though ye should see Macgreegor weerin' his Sunday tie every nicht in the week! I hope ye're no' offended, Lizzie."

But it is to be feared that Lizzie was offended just then. She had not been the better half for eighteen years without knowing it; she had grown to expect her easy-going husband's cheerful acquiescence in practically all she did, and to regard her acceptance of his most mild remonstrances as a sort of favour. And now he was actually giving her advice concerning her treatment of her firstborn! It was too much for her pride.

She set her mouth in a hard line, threw up her head, and proceeded with her polishing.

John waited for a couple of minutes, then sighed and took up his evening paper.

Meanwhile Macgregor was having his troubles. He contrived to dodge Willie Thomson, who nowadays seemed always to be where he was not wanted, but the operation involved a *detour* of nearly a quarter of a mile, in the course of which he was held up by another youth of his acquaintance. Ten minutes were wasted in listening with ill-concealed impatience to fatuous observations on the recent play of certain professional footballers, and then he continued his journey only to fall, metaphorically speaking, into the arms of Jessie Mary emerging from a shop.

"Hullo, Mac! I thought ye was deid!" was her blithe greeting, the 'sausage roll' phrase having at long last served its day. "Ye're in a hurry," she added, "but so am I, so ye can walk back to the corner wi' me."

Macgregor mumbled something to the effect that he was in no special hurry, and, possibly in order to give a touch of truth to his falsehood, turned and accompanied her.

"Ye've no' been gi'ein' the girls a treat lately," she remarked. "I ha'ena noticed ye floatin' aroun'. Ha'e ye been keepin' the hoose at nicht?"

"Whiles," he replied, and enquired with some haste, "Hoo did ye enjoy the dance last week, Jessie?"

"Oh, dinna mention it!" she cried, with a toss of her head. "I didna gang to it."

"Ye didna gang to the dance!"

"If I had went, it wud ha'e meant bloodshed," she impressively informed him. "Ye see, there was twa chaps implorin' me to gang wi' them, an' they got that fierce aboot it that I seen it wudna ha'e been safe to gang wi' either. A riot in a ballroom is no' a nice thing. An' if I had went wi' a third party, it wud ha'e been as much as *his* life was worth. So I jist bided at hame."

Macgregor began, but was not allowed to complete, a sympathetic remark.

"Oh, I was glad I didna gang. The dance turned oot to be a second-rate affair entirely – no' half-a-dizzen shirt fronts in the comp'ny. An' I believe there wasna three o' the men could dance for nuts, an' the refreshments was rotten."

They had now reached the appointed corner.

"Jist as weel ye didna gang, then," absently said Macgregor, halting.

"Come up to the close," said Jessie Mary. "I've something to show ye. Ay; it was jist as weel, as ye say. But there's a champion dance comin' off on the nineteenth o' November – the young men o' the hosiery department are gettin' it up – naething second-rate aboot *it.* Ye should come to it, Macgreegor." She touched his arm – unintentionally perhaps. "Plenty o' pretty girls – though I wudna guarantee their dancin'. I've no' decided yet wha I'll gang wi'." She paused. Macgregor did not speak. "Ye see, I'm parteec'lar wha I dance wi'." she went on softly, "an' I expec' you're the same. Some girls are like bags o' flour an' ithers are like telegraph poles, but there'll be few o' that sort at the hosiery dance. An' onyway" – she laughed – "ye could aye fa' back on *this* girl – eh?"

"I dinna think ye wud be that hard up for a partner," said Macgregor, suddenly stimulated by a flash of her eyes in the lamplight. "But I'm no' awfu' keen on the dancin'."

"Ye danced fine when ye was a wee laddie. I mind when ye danced the Highland Fling in the kitchen, on Hogmanay. That was the nicht I had to kiss ye to get ye oot o' the ring. Ye was ower shy to kiss me. An' you an' Wullie Thomson started the fightin', because he laughed. D'ye mind?"

"That's an auld story," he said, with embarrassment.

"I suppose it is," she admitted reluctantly. Then cheerfully: "Weel, here we are! But wait till I let ye see something." She halted at the mouth of the close and began to unbutton her jacket.

"Ye've never seen the belt since ye gi'ed it to me, Macgreegor. I weer it whiles in the evenin'. There ye are! It looks fine, does it no'? Maybe a wee thing wide. I could dae wi' it an inch or twa tighter. Feel."

She took his hand and slid his fingers between the metal and the white cotton blouse. Jessie Mary had at least one quite admirable characteristic: she doted on white garments and took pride in their spotlessness. A very elemental sense for the beautiful, yet who dare despise it? In these grimy days purity of any kind is great gain.

This girl's hunger for the homage and admiration of the other sex was not so much abnormal as unrestrained. Her apparent lack of modesty was in reality a superabundance of simplicity – witness her shallow artifices and transparent little dishonesties which deceived few save herself and the callowest of youths. Men "took their fun off her." And even Macgregor was not to be entrapped now. There is nothing so dead as the fallen fancy of a boy. Moreover, Macgregor was still at the stage when a girl's face is her whole fortune, when the trimmest waist and the prettiest curves are no assets whatsoever.

For a moment or two he fingered the belt, awkwardly, to be sure, but with as much emotion as though it were a dog's collar.

"Ay," he said, "ye're ower jimp for it." And put his hand in his pocket.

Then, indeed, it was forced on Jessie Mary that somehow her charms had failed to hold her youngest admirer. The knowledge rankled. Yet she carried it off fairly well.

"Ye're no' the first to tell me I've an extra sma' waist," she said, with a toss of her head. Then, as if struck by a remembrance of some duty or engagement: "But I've nae mair time to stan' gassin' wi' you. So long!" She ran briskly up the stone stair, humming a popular tune.

"So long," returned Macgregor, and resumed his interrupted journey, rather pleased than otherwise with himself. He realised, though not in so many words, that he had conducted himself in more manly fashion than ever before.

It did not for a moment occur to him that he had left a big "Why?" behind him, not only in the mind of Jessie Mary, but in Willie Thomson's also.

His pilgrimage ended at the illuminated window of M. Tod's stationery and fancy goods shop. Jingling the few coppers in his pocket, he appeared to be deliberating a weighty problem of extensive purchases, while, as a matter of fact, he inwardly debated the most profitable ways of wasting a penny. While he would now gladly have given all he possessed – to wit, ninepence – to win a smile from the girl with the scarlet blouse and the ripe-corn-yellow pigtail, he was not prepared to squander more than he could help for the benefit of her employer. The opaque panels at the back of the window were closed, the door of the shop was composed chiefly of ground glass; wherefore he had no inkling as to which person he was likely to encounter at the receipt of custom. He was hoping and waiting for a customer to enter the shop, so that he might gain a glimpse of the interior with the opening of the door, when suddenly the lights in the window were lowered. Evidently it was near to closing time.

Hastily deciding to "burst" the sum of one penny on the purchase of a pencil – an article for which he had more respect than use – he entered the doorway and turned the handle. He had forgotten the spring bell. When he pushed the door inwards, it "struck one" – right from the shoulder, so to speak. Who will assert that the ordinary healthy youth has no nerves? 'Tis a hoggishly healthy youth who does not bristle with them. The sturdy Macgregor wavered on the threshold; and as he wavered he heard behind him a badly stifled guffaw.

Next moment a hearty push in the small of the back propelled him into the shop. With a hot countenance he pulled up, guessing who had pushed him, and strove to look as if this were his usual mode of entering a place of business. In his confusion he missed the quick glance of the girl seated at the desk on the window-end of the counter. Her head was bent low over her writing. He noticed, however, that she was wearing a white blouse – which did not remind him of Jessie Mary – and that she had a scarlet bow at her neck.

"Yes, sir?" A mouse-like human being slipped from the back of the shop to the middle point of the counter. "Yes, sir?" it repeated, with an accent on the query. The girl at the desk took no notice.

Macgregor approached. "I was wantin' a pencil," he said in the tone of one requesting a pint of prussic acid.

"A pencil!" exclaimed the mouse-like human being, as though she had a dim recollection of hearing of such a thing long, long ago. "A pencil – oh, certainly," she added, more hopefully.

"Penny or ha'penny," murmured the girl at the desk.

"Penny or ha'penny?" demanded the mouse-like human being, almost pertly.

Men didn't expect change out of a penny! "A penny yin," said Macgregor with an attempt at indifference. He tried to look at the girl, but could not get his eyes higher than her elbow.

"A penny pencil!" The mouse-like human being assumed an expression suitable to a person who has just discovered the precise situation of the North Pole, but not the Pole itself.

"Top drawer on your left, Miss Tod," whispered the girl at the desk.

"Quite so, Christina," Miss Tod replied with dignity. There were times when she might have been accused of copying her assistant's manners. She opened the drawer, which was a deep one, peered into it, groped, and brought forth three bundles of pencils. With sudden mildness she enquired of the girl: "These? ... Those?"

"No; them!" said Christina, forgetting her grammar and grabbing the third bundle. "Wait a minute." She slipped lightly from her stool and gently edged M. Tod from the position at the counter which had been familiar to the latter for five-and-thirty years. "This," she said to Macgregor, laying the bundle in front of him, "is a special line. One dozen – price threepence." She looked over his head in a manner suggesting that it was quite immaterial to her whether he purchased the dozen or faded away on the spot.

But he had his dignity too. Producing three pennies from two pockets, he laid them on the counter, took up the bundle of pencils, said "Thank ye" to nobody in particular, and marched out. Nor did he forget to close the door behind him.

The stationer and her assistant regarded each other for several seconds.

"Dae ye think," said M. Tod slowly, "that that young man is a newspaper reporter?"

"No," replied Christina, with a sniff or two of her straight little nose.

"Or a pictur' artist?" said M. Tod, conveying the two bundles to the wrong drawer.

Christina, without a word, recovered them and put them into their proper places. She mounted her stool and whipped up a pen.

M. Tod sighed. "I never used to keep pencils at that price. They canna be vera guid."

"They're rotten."

"Oh, lassie!"

"Sell – or gang bankrupt," said Christina with enough bitter cynicism for twenty-one. "There's a penny profit on the bundle. *Ex* – cuse me." She dipped her pen.

As Macgregor was nearing his home, a prey to misery and wroth, a grinning face popped from a close-mouth.

"Haw! haw! Macgreegor! So ye're courtin', are ye?"

As the clock incontinently strikes when the hour has come, so struck Macgregor. And he struck so hard; that it was afterwards necessary he should see Willie Thomson to the latter's door. Alone again, he cast the bundle of pencils into a dark entry and made his way home.

His father opened the door, smiling a welcome. "Weel Macgreegor – "

"I'm wearied," said the boy, and passed straightway to

his room and bolted the door. Jimsie was sleeping like a log, and was, as usual, occupying most of the bed.

Macgregor stood at the old chest of drawers that served as dressing-table, his elbows planted thereon, his face in his hands. He *was* wearied.

But under his tired eyes lay a small oblong package with a covering of newspaper. The neatness of it made him think of his mother; she had a way of making next to nothing look something important in a parcel.

Presently, wondering a little, he undid the paper.

It contained one of his father's old razors.

Five minutes later he was enjoying a *real* shave. The luxury was only exceeded by the importance he felt! And only two cuts that bled worth mentioning ...

How one's life may be changed in a short couple of hours!

But Macgregor was still without regret for having flung the pencils into the dark entry.

VI

CIRCUMSTANCE rather than circumspection was accountable for the fact that Macgregor followed the elusive, winding trail of love alone. The tender adventures of our 'teens usually consist in encounters between two boys and two girls; two friends who tacitly admit that they want to meet the girls; two friends who pretend that they do not want to see the boys at any distance; and to sum up, two pairs of young human beings with but a single thought – themselves. Also it may happen, now and then, that for lack of likelier company Prince Charming goes hunting with Master Fathead, while Princess Lilian Rose lays the scent along with Miss Gooseberry, which but adds plausibility to the assumption that neither sex has the courage of its inclinations. For, to be honest, there is no cowardice like that of lad's love; no hypocrisy like that of lass's. But, surely you remember! And if so it happened that in your own day you, perforce, fared solitary to the chase, you will sympathise all the more with the unheroic hero of this slight record.

In this respect Macgregor was not fortunate in his male friends. The oldest thereof, Willie Thomson, openly contemned the female sex, not omitting his aunt; the others confined their gallantries to the breezy pastimes of pushing girls off the sidewalk, bawling pleasantries after them, and guffawing largely at their own wit or the feminine *repartee*. Their finer instincts were doubtless still dormant. The only mortals worthy of respect were sundry more or less prominent personages whose feet or fists were their fortunes. In these days the adoration of the active by the inert is, one hopes, at its zenith of inflation. Again, to put it now in metaphor, Macgregor's friends could do with a brass band in scarlet uniform all the time, but they had no use for a secret orchestra of muted strings. All of which was perfectly natural – just as natural as Macgregor's inexplicable preference for the secret orchestra. Spring comes early or late; the calendar neither foretells nor records its coming. A lad and a lass – how and when and why the one first realises that the other is more than a mere human being are questions without answers. Well, it is a mercy that the world still holds something that cannot be explained away. In one sense this boy was no more refined than his neighbours; in another they were coarser than he. Remains the fact that he followed the trail alone – or thought he did.

Willie Thomson, for one, was interested. He had been interested to the extent of grinning in Macgregor's early tenderness for little Katie, and to the extent of sniggering in his friend's bashful pursuit of Jessie Mary. But now the interest was that of the boy who discovers a nest just beyond his hand and wonders what sort of eggs he will get if, somehow, he can reach it. On the whole, Willie resented his swollen nose and cut lip less than the recent ill-disguised attempts to avoid his company. The latter rankled. Truth to tell, without Macgregor he was rather a lonely creature, a kind of derelict. No one really wanted him. He was not without acquaintances, shirkers like himself; but in the congregation of loafers is not true comradeship. Without admitting it even to himself, he still admired the boy who had faithfully championed his cause – not always virtuous – in the past, whose material possessions he had invariably shared, whose stolid sense of honour had so often puzzled his own mischievous mind, whose home he had envied despite a certain furtive dread of the woman who ruled there. Altogether it may be questioned whether Willie's grudge was directed against his old friend and not against that which had caused his old friend's defection. At all events, he began to spare Macgregor any necessity for dodging, and took to shadowing him on his solitary strolls.

On the grey Saturday afternoon of the week rendered so eventful by his first real shave, Macgregor was once more standing by the window of M. Tod's shop. He was endeavouring to prop up his courage with the recollection of the fact that a fortnight ago, at the same hour as the present, there had been no old woman behind the counter, and with the somewhat rash deduction that no old woman was there now.

He was also wondering what he could buy for a penny without making a fool of himself. The spending of a penny when there is absolutely nothing one wants to buy is not quite so simple a transaction as at first thought it may seem – unless, of course, the shop is packed with comestibles; and even then one may hesitate to choose. Besides, Macgregor was obsessed by the memory of the pencil transaction of three nights ago. Had he but kept his head then, and confined his purchase to a single pencil, he might now have had a fair excuse for requiring another. At any rate, he could have met suspicion with the explanation that he had lost the first. But who would believe that he had used, or lost, a whole dozen within the brief space of three days?

A wretched position to be in, for nothing else in the world of stationery was quite so natural and easy to ask for as a pencil – unless a – why had he not thought of it before? – a pen! Saved! He would enter boldly, as one who had every right to do so, and demand to be shown some pencils – no, pens, of course. There were many varieties of pens, he knew, even in small shops, so his selection would take time – lots of time! If only he were *sure* the old woman wasn't there.

And just then the bell rang, the door of the shop opened and closed, and the old woman herself came out. In spite of her hat Macgregor recognised her at once. She turned her face skywards to make certain that it wasn't raining, gave a satisfied smirk, which Macgregor accepted with a fearful start, though it was intended for the window and its contents, and trotted up the street.

On the wave of relief, as it were, Macgregor was carried from the window to the entrance. Yet he had no sooner opened the door with its disconcerting note of warning than he wished he had delayed a minute or two longer. To retire, however, was out of the question. He closed the door as though he were afraid of wakening a baby, and faced the counter.

The girl was there, and wearing the scarlet blouse again. Laying aside the magazine which she had just picked up, she smiled coldly and said calmly: "Good-afternoon. Nice day after the rain."

In mentally rehearsing his entrance the previous night Macgregor had, among other things, seen himself raise his brand-new bowler hat. To his subsequent shame and regret, he now omitted to perform the little courtesy. That he should forget his manners was perhaps even less surprising than that he should forget the hat itself, which gripped his head in a cruel fashion.

"Ay," he said solemnly in response to the polite greeting, and advanced to the counter.

"Not just so disagreeable as yesterday," she added, a trifle more cordially.

"Ay – na." He glanced up and down the counter. "I – I was wantin' a pencil," he said at last.

"A *pencil!*" cried Christina; then in a voice from which all the amazement had gone: "A pencil – oh, certainly."

Macgregor reddened, opened his mouth and – shut it. Why should he make a bigger fool of himself by explaining that he had meant to say "a pen?" Besides (happy thought!), the pen would be an excuse for calling another time.

Christina opened the drawer and paused, pursing her lips. Her tone was casual as she said: "I hope you found the dozen you bought lately quite satisfactory."

"Oh – ay, they were – splendid." Macgregor blushed again.

Christina smiled as prettily as any musical comedy actress selling guinea button-holes at a charity fête. She said: "I'll tell Miss Tod. She'll be delighted. It's a great saving, buying a dozen, isn't it?" Her hand went into the drawer. "Especially when one uses so many. It's hardly worth while buying a single pencil, is it?" Her hand came out of the drawer and laid a bundle in front of Macgregor. "Wonderful how they can do it for threepence!"

He stared at the bundle, his will fluttering like a bird under a strawberry net. Dash the pencils! – but she might be offended if –

"Some shops sell those pencils at a ha'penny each, I know," she went on; "and I believe some have the neck – I mean the cheek to ask a penny. Would you like me to put them in paper, sir?"

Recovering from the shock of the "sir," Macgregor shook his head, and laid three coppers on the counter.

"Thank you," said she. "Is there anything else to-day?"

Before he could answer, the door opened and an elderly man entered. At the ring of the bell Macgregor dropped the bundle; the flimsy fastening parted, and the pencils were scattered.

Christina checked an "Oh, crickey!" and turned to attend to the second customer while the first collected his purchases from the floor.

The elderly man wanted a newspaper only, but, thanks to Christina's politeness over the transaction, he went out feeling as if he had done quite a stroke of business.

"I think you should let me tie them up for you," she said to Macgregor, who was rising once more, rather red in the face.

"Thank ye," he said apologetically, handing her the pencils.

"Accidents will happen," she remarked cheerfully. "If they didn't, there would be mighty little happening. I say, there's only eleven pencils here."

"The ither rolled ablow the counter. It doesna matter," he said.

"Oh, but that won't do. See, I'll give you another now, and get the one under the counter some day – next stocktaking, maybe." She began to make a parcel, then halted in the operation. "Are you sure there's nothing else to-day, sir?"

Macgregor didn't want to go just yet, so he appeared to be thinking deeply.

"Essay paper – notebooks," she murmured "Notepaper – envelopes – indiarubber – "

"Injinrubber," said Macgregor. (He would give it to Jimsie.)

She turned and whipped a box from a shelf. "Do you prefer the red or the white – species?" she enquired, and felt glad she hadn't said "sort."

"Oh, I'm no heedin' which," he replied generously, with a bare glance at the specimens laid out for his inspection.

"All the same price – one penny per cake. The red is more flexible." By way of exhibiting its quality, she took the oblong lengthwise between her finger and thumb and squeezed. To her dismay it sprang from her grip and struck her customer on the chin.

"Oh, mercy!" she exclaimed, "I didna mean – "

Recovering the missile from the floor, he said gravely: "My! ye're a comic!"

"I'm not! I tell ye I didna mean it. Did it hurt ye?"

"No' likely! I ken ye didna try it." He smiled faintly. "If ye had tried to hit me, ye wud ha'e missed me."

"If I had tried, I wud ha'e hit ye a heap harder," she said indignantly.

"Try, then." His smile broadened as he offered her the cake. "I'll stan' still."

Christina's sporting instinct was roused. "I'll bet ye the price o' the cake I hit ye." And let fly.

It went over his left shoulder.

"Ha'e anither shot," he said, stooping to pick up the rubber.

But as swiftly as it had gone her professional dignity returned. Macgregor came back to the counter to receive a stiff: "Thank you. Do you require anything else to-day?"

His mumbled negative, his disappointed countenance reproached her.

"Of course," she said pleasantly, as she put his purchases in paper, "I cannot charge you for the indiarubber."

"Aw, cheese it!" he muttered shortly, flinging a penny on the counter.

"I beg your pardon?" – this with supreme haughtiness.

"Oh, ye needna. An' ye can keep yer injinrubber – an' yer pencils forbye!" With these words he wheeled about and strode for the door.

Christina collapsed. A customer who paid for goods and then practically threw them at her was beyond her experience and comprehension.

"Here!" she cried. "Stop a minute! I – I was jist jokin'. Come back an' get yer things. We'll no' quarrel aboot the penny."

With his fingers on the handle he paused and regarded her half angrily, half reproachfully. He wanted to say something very cutting, but it wouldn't come.

"Please," said Christina softly, dropping her eyes. "Ye'll get me into trouble if ye dinna tak' them."

"Eh?"

"Miss Tod wud be vexed wi' me for lossin' a guid customer. She wud gi'e me the sack, maybe."

"Wud she? – the auld besom!" cried Macgregor, retracing his steps.

" Oh, whisht! She's no' an auld besom. But I ken she wud be vexed." Christina sighed. "I suppose I'm to blame for – "

"It's me that's to blame," he interrupted. "Here!" he said in an unsteady whisper, "will ye shake han's?"

After a momentary hesitation she gave him her hand, saying graciously: "I've no objections, I'm sure. To tell the truth," she went on, "I am not entirely disinterested in you, sir."

Macgregor withdrew his empty hand. "I – I wish ye wudna speak like that," he sighed.

"Like what?"

"That awfu' genteel talk."

"Sorry," she said. "But it gangs doon wi' maist o' the customers. Besides, I try to keep it up to please ma aunt. But it doesna soun' frien'ly-like, does it?"

"That's why I dinna like it," he ventured.

"I see. But if ye was servin' in a shop ye wud ha'e to speak the same way."

"I'm in the pentin' trade," he informed her, with an air of importance.

"I've a nose – but I like the smell fine. Ye're no' offended, are ye?"

"I'm no' that easy offended. Is Miss Tod yer aunt?"

"Na, na; she's nae relation. Ma aunt is Mrs. James Baldwin." In the frankest fashion she gave a brief sketch of her position on the world's surface. While she spoke she seated herself on the stool, and Macgregor, without thinking about it, subsided upon the chair and leant his arm upon the counter. Ere she ended they were regarding each other almost familiarly.

Anon Macgregor furnished a small account of himself and his near relatives.

"That's queer!" commented Christina when he had finished.

"What?" he asked, anxiously.

"Ma Uncle James is a great frien' o' your Uncle Purdie. Your uncle buys a heap o' fancy things frae mine, an' he's often been in oor hoose. I hear he's worth a terrible heap o' money, but naebody wud think it. I like him fine."

"Ye wudna like ma aunt fine," said Macgregor.

"No' bein' acquaint wi' her, I canna say," Christina returned. "But I believe if it hadna been for her yer uncle wud never ha'e made his fortune at the grocery trade – "

"Her! What had she got to dae wi' 't?"

"Dear knows; but Uncle James says she egged him on to mak' money frae the day she married him. But mony a woman does that. I wud dae it masel' – no' that I'm greedy; I jist couldna endure a man that didna get on. I hate a stick-in-the-mud. It's a fac', though, that Mr. Purdie got the push-on frae his wife. An' Uncle James says he's no' near done yet: he'll be Lord Provost afore he's feenished. Ye should keep in wi' yer Uncle Purdie."

Macgregor scarcely heard her latter words. His Aunt Purdie responsible for his Uncle Purdie's tremendous success in business! The idea was almost shocking. From his earliest boyhood it had been a sort of religion with him to admire his uncle and despise his aunt. Could any good thing come out of Aunt Purdie?

"I doobt yer Uncle James doesna ken *her* extra weel," he said at last.

"Oh, ma uncle's a splendid judge o' character," she assured him. "Especially female character," she added. "That's why he married ma aunt an' adopted me. I took his name, like ma aunt did when she married him. It was a love match, in spite o' their ages. There's grander names, but nane better, nor Baldwin. In ma youth I called it Bald-yin to tease ma aunt when she was saft on him. But never heed aboot that the noo. D'ye ken what astonishes me aboot yersel'?"

"What?" asked Macgregor, startled.

"That ye're no' in the grocery trade."

"Me! What for wud I be a grocer?"

"What for are ye a penter? An' yer Uncle Purdie has nae offspring. My! if I had had a chance like you!" She heaved a sigh. "I'm sure yer uncle wud ha'e ta'en ye into his business. Ye canna be sae stupid that he wudna gi'e ye even a trial. Nae offence intended."

"I could ha'e been in the business if I had wanted," Macgregor replied, with some dignity. "He offered me a job when I left the schule. But, ye see, I aye had the notion to be a penter. I like to be movin' ma han's an' feet."

"An' what did yer parents say?"

"They canna thole Aunt Purdie. It was her that brought the message frae ma uncle – as if it was a favour. They said I was to choose for masel'."

"Pride's an awfu' thing for costin' folk cash," the girl remarked, with a shake of her head.

"Eh?"

"Naething," she replied. After a slight pause she continued: "It's no' for me to speak aboot yer parents, but I hope ye'll excuse me sayin' that ye're a bigger fool than ye look."

"Wha – what d'ye mean?"

"I didna mean to insult ye or hurt yer feelin's." Another pause. "D'ye no' want to get up in the world, man? D'ye no' want to be a millionaire – or a thoosandaire, onyway?"

"Me?"

"Ay, you!"

Across the counter he regarded her in a semi-dazed

fashion, speechless. She was rather flushed; her eyes danced with eagerness. Apparently she was all in earnest.

"Are ye gaun to be a penter a' yer life?" she demanded.

"What for no'?" he retorted with some spirit. "It's guid pay."

"Guid pay! In ten year what'll ye be makin'?"

"I couldna say. Maybe – maybe twenty-five shillin's; maybe – "

"A week?"

"Ay; of course," he said, nettled. "D'ye think I meant a month?"

"If ye was wi' yer uncle an' stickin' to yer business, I wud ha'e said 'a day'! Ma gracious goodness! if ye was pleasin' a man like that, there's nae sayin' where ye wud be in ten year."

"Ach," he said, with an attempt at lightness, "I'm no' heedin'."

Christina doubled her fist and smote the counter with such violence that he fairly jumped on his seat.

"Ye're no' heedin'! What's the use o' bein' alive if ye're no' heedin'? But ye're a' the same, you young workin' men. Yer rule is to dae the least ye can for yer wages, an' never snap at an opportunity. An' when ye get aulder ye gang on strike an' gas aboot yer rights, but ye keep dumb enough aboot yer deserts, an' – "

"Here, haud on!" cried Macgregor, now thoroughly roused. "What dae you ken aboot it? Ye're jist a lassie – "

"I've eyes an' ears."

There was a pause.

"Are ye a-a suffragist?" he asked, weakly.

"I ha'ena quite decided on that p'int. Are you in favour o' votes for females? Aweel, there's nae use answerin', for ye've never thought aboot it. I suppose, like the ither young men aboot here, ye buy yer brains every Seturday done up in the sports edition o' the evenin' paper. Oh, Christopher Columbus! that's when *I* get busy on a Seturday nicht. Footba' – footba' – footba'!"

Macgregor swallowed these remarks, and reverted to the

previous question. "What," he enquired a little loftily, "dae *you* expec' to be earnin' ten year frae the noo?"

Promptly, frankly, she replied: "If I'm no' drawin' thirty shillin's a week I'll consider masel' a bad egg. Of course, it a' depends on whether I select to remain single or itherwise."

This was too much for Macgregor. He surveyed her with such blank bewilderment that she burst out laughing.

He went red to the roots of his hair, or at any rate to the edge of his hat. "Oh, I kent fine ye was coddin' me," he said crossly, looking hurt and getting to his feet.

She stopped laughing at once. "That's the worst o' talkin' plain sense nooadays; folk think ye're only coddin'," she observed, good-humouredly. "I'm sorry I vexed ye." Impulsively she held out her hand. "I doobt we'll ha'e to shake again."

This, also, was too much for Macgregor. He seized her fingers in a grip that made her squeal.

And just then bang went the bell above the door.

Christina bit her lip and smiled through her tears as M. Tod entered the shop.

"Anything else to-day?" she enquired in her politest voice, and placed the little parcel under Macgregor's hand.

His reply was inaudible. His hand closed automatically on his purchase, his eyes met hers for the fraction of a second, and then he practically bolted.

"Young men are aye in sich a great hurry nooadays." remarked M. Tod, beginning to remove her gloves.

"He's the young man that bought the dizzen pencils the ither nicht," Christina explained, examining the joints of her right hand. "I've just been sellin' him anither dizzen."

"Dearie me! he *must* be a reporter on yin of the papers."

"He's a whale for pencils, whatever he is," Christina returned, putting straight the piles of periodicals that adorned the counter. "I doobt he wud need to report wi' his feet forbye his han's to get through a dizzen pencils in three days. It's a bit o' a mystery aboot the pencils."

"A mystery!" exclaimed M. Tod, who was just about to blow into a glove.

Christina picked the neglected penny from the counter and dropped it into the till. "It's a case o' *cherchez la femme,*" she said softly, with quite a passable accent.

"What's that?" murmured M. Tod.

"French," sighed Christina, making a jotting of her last sales, and taking a long time to do it.

M. Tod stared for a moment or two, shook her head, drew a long breath, and with the same inflated her glove.

VII

MACGREGOR was half-way home ere he comprehended the cause of the dull ache about his temples. He eased his hat and obtained relief. But there was no lid to lift from his mind, which seemed to be overcrowded with a jumble of ideas – old ideas turned topsy-turvey, some damaged, some twisted, and new ideas struggling, as it were, for existence. Moral earthquakes are not infrequent during our 'teens and twenties; by their convulsions they provide construction material for character; but the material is mixed, and we are left to choose whether we shall erect sturdy towers or jerry-buildings.

The boy was not, of course, aware that here was a crisis in his life. He was staggered and disturbed, just as he would have been had the smooth, broad street on which he walked suddenly become a narrow pass beset with rifts and boulders. The upheaval of his preconceived notions of girlhood had been sharp indeed. He had never heard a girl speak as Christina had spoken; it had never occurred to him that a girl could speak so. But while he felt hurt and vexed, he harboured no resentment; her frank friendliness had disposed of that; and while he was humbled, he was not – thanks to his modesty, or, if you prefer it, lack of cocksureness – grievously humiliated. It is not in the nature of healthy youth to let misery have all its own way.

Before he reached home he was able to extract several sips of comfort from his recent experience. He knew her name and she knew his; they had discovered a mutual acquaintance (how we love those mutual acquaintances – sometimes!); they had shaken hands twice.

He spent the evening indoors – he might have done otherwise had not Christina said something about being busy on Saturday nights. He was patient with his little brother, almost tender towards his sister. He played several games of draughts with his father, wondering between his deplorable moves when he should see Christina again. He spoke in a subdued fashion. And about nine o'clock his mother anxiously asked him whether he was feeling quite well, and offered to prepare a homely potion. One regrets to record that he returned a rough answer and went off to bed, leaving Lizzie to shake her head more in sorrow than in anger while she informed John that she doubted Macgregor was "sickenin' for something." As Macgregor had not condescended to play draughts for at least two years, John was inclined to share her fears; it did not occur to him to put down such conduct to feminine influence; and an hour later, at her suggestion, he went to his son's room and softly opened the door.

"Oh! ye're no' in yer bed yet, Macgreegor?"

"I'm jist gaun."

"What are ye workin' at?"

"Jist sharpenin' a pencil. I'll no' be lang" – impatiently.

"Are ye feelin' weel enough?"

"I'm fine. Dinna fash yersel'."

John withdrew and reported to Lizzie. She was not satisfied, and before going to bed, about eleven o'clock, she listened at Macgregor's door. All she heard was: "Here, Jimsie, I wish to peace ye wud keep yer feet to yersel'."

She opened the door. "Laddie, are ye no' sleepin' yet?"

"Hoo can I sleep wi' Jimsie jabbin' his feet in ma back?"

She entered, and going to the bed removed the unconscious Jimsie to his own portion thereof, at the same time urging him into a more comfortable position. Then she came round and laid her hand on her first-born's brow.

"Are ye sure ye're a' richt, laddie?"

"Ay, I'm fine. I wish ye wudna fash," he said shortly, turning over.

Lizzie went out, closing the door gently. On the kitchen dresser she set out the medicine bottle and spoon against emergencies.

Perhaps there is a mansion in Heaven that will always be empty – a mansion waiting to receive those who in their youth never snubbed their anxious parents. Ere the door closed Macgregor was pricked with compunction. He was sensitive enough for that. But it is the sensitive people who hurt the people they care for.

In extenuation let it be said at once that the boy was enduring a dire reaction. It now appeared that Christina's friendliness had been all in the way of business. Socially (he did not think the word, of course) Christina was beyond him. Christina, for all he knew, sat at night in a parlour, had an aunt that kept a servant (and, maybe, a gramaphone), was accustomed to young men in high collars and trousers that always looked new. Yes, she had shaken hands with him simply in order to get him to come back and buy another dozen of pencils.

He was very unhappy. He tossed from side to side until the voice of Jimsie, drowsy and peevish, declared that he had taken all the clothes. Which was practically true, though he did not admit it as he disentangled himself of the blankets and flung them all at his brother. He did not care if he froze – until he began to feel a little cold, when he rescued with difficulty a portion of the coverings from Jimsie's greedy clutch. He would not go to the shop again. But he would pass it as often as possible. He would get Willie Thomson to accompany him, and they would smoke cigarettes, and they would stop at the door when a customer was entering, and laugh very loudly. He would save up and take Jessie Mary to the dance – at least, he would think about it. After all, it might be more effective to go to the shop and buy more presents for Jessie Mary and – oh, great idea! – demand that they should be sent to her address!

The clock in the kitchen struck one. With any sympathy at all it would have struck at least five. It was like telling a person in the throes of toothache that the disease is not serious. By the way, one wonders if doctors will ever know as much about disease as patients know about pain. Speculation apart, it is a sorry business to flatter ourselves we have been suffering all night only to find that the night is but beginning. Still, there must have been something far wrong with the Robinsons' kitchen clock. Macgregor waited, but to his knowledge it never struck two. Indeed, it missed all the hours until nine.

Macgregor, however, presented himself in good time for the Sunday breakfast. His punctuality was too much for his mother, and she insisted on his taking a dose from the bottle on the dresser. Even youth is sometimes too tired to argue. "Onything for peace," was his ungracious remark as he raised the spoon to his lips.

Scotland in its harshest, bleakest period of religious observance could not have provided a more dismal Sabbath than Macgregor provided for himself. Although his mother gave him the option of staying at home, he accompanied his parents to church; although he came back with a good appetite, he refused to let himself enjoy his dinner; although he desired to take the accustomed Sunday afternoon walk with his father down to the docks (they had gone there, weather permitting, for years), he shut himself up in the solitude of his bedroom.

He spent most of the afternoon in putting points to his stock of pencils. How the operation should have occupied so much time may be explained by the fact that the lead almost invariably parted from the wood ere a perfect point was attained. Indeed, when the task was ended, he had comparatively little to show for his threepence save a heap of shavings, fragments and dust. His resentment, however, was all against M. Tod: he wished she had been of his own sex and size. He also wished she had kept an ice-cream shop, open on Sundays. – No, he didn't! Christina wouldn't like working on Sundays; besides, an awful lot of chaps hung about ice-cream shops. He wondered what church Christina attended. If he only knew, he might go there in the evening. (What our churches owe to young womanhood will never be known.) But there were scores of churches in Glasgow. It would take years to get round them – and in the end she might sit in the gallery and he under it. In the unlikely event of his again entering Miss Tod's shop, there would be no harm in asking Christina about her church and whether she sang in the choir. But stop! if she didn't sing in the choir, she might think he was chaffing her. That wouldn't do at all. Better just find out about the church, and if he didn't get a view of her on his first visit he could try again.

There appears no reason why Macgregor's spirits should have gradually risen throughout these and other equally rambling reflections; but the fact remains that they did so. By tea-time he was in a comely condition of mind. He made young Jimsie happy with the cake of rubber and presented Jeannie surreptitiously with a penny, "to buy sweeties." He seemed interested in his father's account of a vessel that had been in collision the previous day. He did not scowl when his mother expressed satisfaction with the way in which he was punishing the bread and butter, and openly congratulated herself on having administered the physic just in time. Nay, more; he offered to stay in the house with Jimsie while John and Lizzie took an evening stroll and Jeannie went with a friend to evening service. No people are quite so easily made happy as parents, and when, out of doors, John suggested that Macgregor's weekly allowance should be raised to one shilling, Lizzie actually met him half-way by promising to make it ninepence in future.

During their absence Macgregor did his utmost to amuse Jimsie, who was suffering from an incipient cold, but shortly after their return he became restless, and ere long announced (rather indistinctly) his intention of going out for "twa-three" minutes.

Lizzie was about to ask "where?" when John remarked that it was a fine night and that he would come too. Thus was frustrated Macgregor's desire to take one look at the shuttered shrine with "M. Tod" over the portal – a very foolish sort of desire, as many of us know – from experience.

In the circumstances Macgregor accepted his father's company with a fairly good grace, merely submitting that the walk should be a short one.

On the way home, at a corner, under a lamp, they came upon Willie Thomson in earnest and apparently amicable conversation with Jessie Mary. Such friendliness struck Macgregor as peculiar, for since the days of their childhood the twain had openly expressed contempt and dislike for each other, and he wondered what was "up," especially when the sight of him appeared to cause Willie, at least, considerable embarrassment. But presently the happy idea flashed upon him that Willie had suddenly become "sweet" on Jessie Mary, and would accordingly need to be dodged no longer. He felt more friendly towards Willie than for some time past. His feelings with regard to Jessie Mary were less definite, but he was sure his face had not got "extra red" under her somewhat mocking glance.

"Ye're no' as thick wi' Wullie as ye used to be," his father remarked.

"Oh, we've nae quarrel," he returned. "What did ye say was the name o' that damaged boat ye saw the day?"

He went to bed not unhappy. He would find a way of getting to know Christina better and of proving to her that the painting trade was as good as any.

VIII

"YE'VE been in business a long time, Miss Tod," said Christina on Monday afternoon, looking up from the front advertising page of a newspaper; "so I wish ye wud tell me yer honest opinion o' business in general."

M. Tod paused in the act of polishing a fancy ink-pot (she had spasms of industry for which there was no need) and stared in bewildered fashion at her assistant. "Dearie me, lassie!" she exclaimed, "ye say the queerest things! Ma honest opinion o' business? I'm sure I never thought aboot – "

"I'll put it anither way. Supposin' ye was back at the schule, an' ye was asked to define business – ye ken what define means – what wud be yer answer?"

"Is it fun ye're after?" M. Tod enquired, a trifle suspiciously.

"I was never mair serious in ma life," Christina returned rather indignantly.

"I didna mean to offend ye," the other said gently. "But ye ken fine what business is – whiles I think ye ken better nor me, though I've been at it for near six-an'-thirty years."

"I'm not offended," said Christina, dropping the vernacular for the moment. "And I merely desired to know if your definition of business was the same as mine."

It always made M. Tod a little nervous when her assistant addressed her in such correct speech. "Business," she began, and halted. She set the ink-pot on the counter, and tried to put the duster in her pocket.

"A few words will suffice," the girl remarked encouragingly, and took charge of the duster.

"Business," resumed the old woman, and quite unconsciously put her hands behind her back, "business is jist buyin' and sellin'." And she gave a little smile of relief and satisfaction.

Christina shook her head. "I suppose that's what they taught ye at the schule – jist the same as they taught me. If it wasna for their fancy departments, sich as physiology an' Sweedish drill, the schules wud be oot o' date. 'Jist buyin' an' sellin'!' – Oh, Christopher Columbus!"

M. Tod was annoyed, partly, no doubt, at discovering her hands behind her back, but ere she could express herself Christina added:

"In *ma* honest opinion business chiefly consists of folk coddin' yin anither."

M. Tod gasped. "Coddin'! D'ye mean deceivin'?"

"Na; there's a difference between coddin' an' deceivin'. Same sort o' difference as between war an' murder. An' they say that all's fair in love – I ha'e ma doobts aboot love – an' war. Mind ye, I'm no' saying' onything against coddin'. We're a' in the same boat. Some cods wi' advertisin' – see daily papers; some cods wi' talk; some cods wi' lookin' solemn an' smilin' jist at the right times. But we're a' coddin', cod, cod, coddin'! But we'll no' admit it! An' naebody wud thank us if we did."

The old woman was almost angry. "I'm sure I never codded a customer in ma life," she cried.

Christina regarded her very kindly for a second or two ere she returned pleasantly: "I wudna say but what you're an exception to the rule, Miss Tod. But ye're a rare exception. Even ma uncle – an' he's the honestest man in the world – once codded me when I was assistin' ma aunt at Kilmabeg, afore she got married. Wi' his talk an' his smiles he got me to buy things against ma better judgment – things I was sure wud never sell. If he had been dumb an' I had been blind, I would never ha'e made the purchase. But I was young then. Of course *he* didna want to cod me; it was jist a habit he had got into wi' bein' in business. But there's nae doobt," she went on calmly, ignoring M. Tod's obvious desire to get a word in, "there's nae doobt that coddin' is yin o' the secrets o' success. When ye consider that half the trade o' the world consists in sellin' things that folk dinna need an' whiles dinna want – "

"Whisht, lassie! Ye speak as if naebody had a conscience!"

"I didna mean that," was the mild reply. "It's the only thing in this world that's no' easy codded – though some folk seem to be able to do the trick. For, of course, there's a limit to coddin' in business – fair coddin', I mean. But ye've taken ma remarks ower seriously, Miss Tod."

"I never heard sich remarks in a' ma days."

"I'm sorry I've annoyed ye."

"Ye ha'ena annoyed me dearie. But I'm vexed to think ye've got sich notions in yer young heid." M. Tod sighed.

Christina sighed also, a little impatiently, and picked up the fancy ink-pot from the counter. "Hoo lang ha'e ye had this in the shop?" she enquired carelessly.

M. Tod shook her head. "Ten years, onyway. It wudna sell."

"It's marked eighteenpence."

"Ay. But when I had a wee sale, five year back, I put it among a lot of nick-nacks at threepence, an' even then it wudna sell. It's no' pretty."

"It's ugly – but that's nae reason for it no' sellin'." Christina examined the glass carefully. "It's no' in bad condition," she observed. "Wud ye part wi' it for ninepence?"

"Ninepence! I'll never get ninepence!"

"Never say die till ye're buried! Jist wait a minute." Christina went over to the desk and spent about five minutes there, while M. Tod watched her with intermittent wags of her old head.

The girl came back with a small oblong of white card. "Dinna touch it, Miss Tod. The ink's no' dry," she said warningly, and proceeded to place the inkpot and card together in a prominent position on the glass show-case that covered part of the counter. "Noo, that'll gi'e it a chance. Instead o' keepin' it in a corner as if we were ashamed o' it, we'll mak' a feature o' it for a week, an' see what happens. Ye'll get yer ninepence yet."

Christina printed admirably, and her employer had no difficulty in reading the card a yard away even without her glasses. It bore these words:

ANTIQUE
NOVEL GIFT
MERELY 9D

"If ye call a thing 'antique,' " explained Christina, "folk forget its ugliness. An' the public likes a thing wi' 'novel' on it, though they wudna believe ye if ye said it was new. An' as for 'gift' – weel, that adds to the inkpot's chances o' findin' a customer. D'ye see?"

"Ay," said the old woman. "Ye're a clever lassie, but I doobt ye'll never get ninepence."

"Gi'e me a week," said Christina, "an' if it doesna disappear in that time, we'll keep it till Christmas an' reduce it to a shillin'. But I think a week'll suffice."

M. Tod hesitated ere she gently said: "But ye'll no' try to cod onybody, dearie?"

Christina waved her hand in the direction of the card. "I'll leave the public to cod itsel'," she said. "Noo it's time ye was gettin' ready for yer walk."

It may have been that Christina, in the back of her mind, saw in Macgregor a possible customer for the ugly inkpot. At any rate, she was disappointed when the evening passed without his entering the shop; she hoped she had not spoken too plainly to him on his last visit – not but what he needed plain speaking. She was not to know until later how Macgregor's employer had unexpectedly decreed that he should work overtime that night, nor how Macgregor had obeyed joylessly despite the extra pay.

He called the following evening – and found M. Tod alone at the receipt of custom. He had yet to learn that on Tuesdays and Thursdays Christina left business early in order to attend classes. He must have looked foolish as he approached the counter, yet he had the presence of mind to ask for a ha'penny evening paper. Fortune being fickle – thank goodness! – does not confine her favour to the brave, and on this occasion she had arranged that M. Tod should be sold out of that particular evening paper. So Macgregor saved his money as well as his self-respect.

On the morrow M. Tod, who still clung to the belief that the young man wrote for the papers, reported the incident to her assistant. Possibly Christina could have given a better reason than this for her subsequent uncertainty of temper, and doubtless it was mere absent-mindedness that accounted for her leaving the sliding panel to the window a few inches open after she had thrown it wide without any apparent purpose. And it is highly probable that Macgregor would have taken advantage of the aperture had he not been again working overtime on that and on the two following nights.

So it was not until Saturday afternoon that they met once more. Macgregor held aloof from the shop until M. Tod appeared – of course she was later than usual! – and, after an anxious gaze at the sky, proceeded to toddle up the street. Then he approached the window. He was feeling fairly hopeful. His increased allowance had come as a pleasant surprise. Moreover, he had saved during the week fourpence in car-money and had spent nothing. He had fifteenpence in his pocket – wealth!

As he halted at the window, the panel at the back was drawn tight with an audible snap. For a moment he felt snubbed; then he assured himself there was nothing extraordinary in the occurrence, and prepared to enter the shop, reminding himself, firstly, that he was going to purchase a penholder, secondly, that he was not going to lose his head when the bell banged.

Christina was perched at the desk writing with much diligence. She laid down a pencil and slipped from her stool promptly but without haste.

"Good-afternoon, Mr. Robinson," she said demurely.

If anyone else in the world had called him "Mister Robinson" he would have resented it as chaff, but now, though taken aback, he felt no annoyance.

"Ay, it's a fine day," he returned, rather irrelevantly, and suddenly held out his hand.

This was a little more than Christina had expected, but she gave him hers with the least possible hesitation. For once in her life, however, she was not ready with a remark.

Macgregor having got her hand, let it go immediately, as though he were doubtful as to the propriety of what he had done.

"I've been workin' late every day this week excep' Tuesday," he said.

For an instant Christina looked pleased; then she calmly murmured: "Oh, indeed."

"Ay, every day excep' Tuesday, till nine o'clock," he informed her, with an effort.

"Really!"

He struggled against a curious feeling of mental suffocation, and said: "I was in here on Tuesday nicht. I – I didna see ye."

"I attend a shorthand class on Tuesday nights."

"Oh!" He wanted very much to make her smile, so he said; "When I didna see ye on Tuesday, I was afraid ye had got the sack."

Christina drew herself up. "What can I do for you to-day, Mr. Robinson?" she enquired with stiff politeness.

"I was jist jokin'," he cried, dismayed; " I didna mean to offend ye."

Christina's fingers played a soundless tune on the edge of the counter; her eyes gazed over his head into space. She waited with an air of weary patience.

"I was wantin' a pen – a penholder," he said at last, in a hopeless tone of voice.

"Ha'penny or penny?" she asked without moving.

"A penny yin, please," he said humbly.

She turned and twitched a card from its nail, and laid it before him. "Kindly take your choice," she said, and moved up the counter a yard or so. She picked up a novelette and opened it.

Macgregor examined and fingered the penholders for nearly a minute by the clock ere he glanced at her. She appeared to be engrossed in the novelette, but he was sure he had hurt her feelings.

"I was jist jokin'," he muttered.

"Oh, you wanted a ha'penny one." She twitched down another card of penholders, laid it before him as if – so it seemed to him – he had been dirt, and went back to her novelette.

Had he been less in love he would surely have been angry then. Had she seen his look she would certainly have been sorry.

There was a long silence while his gaze wandered, while he wondered what he could do to make amends.

And lo! the ugly inkpot caught his eye. He read the accompanying card several times; he fingered the money in his pocket; he told himself insistently that ninepence was not worth considering. Once more he glanced at the girl. She was frowning slightly over the page. Perhaps she wanted him to go.

"I'll buy that, if ye like," he said, pointing at the inkpot.

"Eh?" cried Christina, and dropped the novelette. "Beg your pardon," she went on, recovering her dignity and moving leisurely towards him, "but I did not quite catch what you observed." She was pleased that she had used the word "observed."

"I'll buy that," repeated Macgregor. "What's it for?"

"It's for keeping ink in. It's an inkpot. The price is ninepence,"

"I can read," said Macgregor, with perhaps his first essay in irony.

Christina tilted her chin. "I presume you want it for a gift," she said haughtily.

"Na; I'm gaun to pay for it."

"I meant to give away as a gift." It was rather a stupid sentence, she felt. If she had only remembered to use the word "bestow."

The boy's clear eyes met hers for a second.

"It holds a great deal of ink," she said, possibly in reply to her conscience.

"I'll buy a bottle o' ink, too, if ye like," he said recklessly, and looked at her again.

A flood of honest kindliness swamped the business instinct

of Christina. "I didna mean that!" she exclaimed, flopping into homely speech; "an' I wudna sell ye that rotten inkpot for a hundred pound!"

It will be admitted that Macgregor's amazement was natural in the circumstances. Ere he recovered from it she was in fair control of herself.

"It's as good as sold to the Rev. Mr. McTavish," she explained. Her sole foundation for the statement lay in the fact that the Rev. Mr. McTavish was to call for a small parcel of stationery about six o'clock. At the same time she remembered her duty to her employer. "But we have other inkpots in profusion," she declared.

The limit of his endurance was reached. "Oh," he stammered, "I wish ye wudna speak to me like that."

"Like what?"

"That fancy way – that genteel English."

The words might have angered her, but not the voice. She drew a quick breath and said:

"Are ye a frien' or a customer?"

"Ye – ye ken fine what I want to be," he answered, sadly.

Now she was sure that she liked him.

"Well," she said, slowly, "suppose ye buy a ha'penny penholder – jist for the sake o' appearances – an' then" – quickly – "we'll drop business." And she refused to sell him a penny one, and, indeed, anything else in the shop that afternoon.

It must be recorded, however, that an hour or so later she induced the Rev. Mr. McTavish to buy the ugly inkpot.

"It wasna easy," she confessed afterwards to please M. Tod, "an' I doobt he jist bought it to please me; but it's awa' at last, an' ye'll never see it again – unless, maybe, at a jumble sale. He was real nice aboot it, an' gaed awa' smilin'."

"I hope ye didna deceive the man," said M. Tod, trying not to look gratified.

"I told him the solemn truth. I told him it was on ma conscience to sell the inkpot afore anither day had dawned. It's no' every day it pays ye to tell the truth, is it?" The last sentence was happily inaudible to the old woman.

"But, lassie, I never intended ye to feel ye had ta'en a vow to sell the inkpot. I wud be unco vexed to think – "

Christina gave her employer's shoulder a little kindly, reassuring pat. "Na, na; ye needna fash yersel' aboot that," she said. Then, moving away; "As a matter o' fac', I had compromised myself regardin' the inkpot in – in anither direction."

Which was all Greek to M. Tod.

IX

FOR a fortnight it ran smoothly enough. There were, to be sure, occasional ripples: little doubts, little fears, little jealousies: but they passed as swiftly as they appeared.

Macgregor, having no overtime those weeks, contrived to visit the shop nightly, excepting Tuesdays and Thursdays, Christina's class nights. He paid his footing, so to speak, with the purchase of a ha'penny evening paper – which he could not well take home since his father was in the habit of making a similar purchase on the way from work. M. Tod was rarely in evidence; the evenings found her tired, and unless several customers demanded attention at once (a rare event) she remained in the living-room, browsing on novelettes selected for her by her assistant. She was given to protesting she had never done such a thing prior to Christina's advent, to which Christina was wont to reply that, while she herself was long since "fed up" with such literature, it was high time M. Tod should know something about it. Only once did the old woman intrude on the young people and prevent intimate converse; but even then Macgregor did not depart unhappy, for Christina's farewell smile was reassuring in its whimsicality, and in young love of all things seeing is believing.

It must not be supposed, all the same, that she gave him much direct encouragement; her lapses from absolute discretion were brief as they were rare. But the affections of the youthful male have a wonderful way of subsisting on crumbs which hope magnifies into loaves. Nevertheless, her kindliness was a definite thing, and under its influence the boy lost some of his shyness and gained a little confidence in himself. He had already taken a leap over one barrier of formality: he had called her "Christina" to her face, and neither her face nor her lips had reproved him; he had asked her to call him "Macgreegor" – or "Mac" if she preferred it, and she had promised to "see about it."

On this November Saturday afternoon he was on his way

to make the tremendous request that she should allow him to walk home with her when her day's work was over. He was far from sure of himself. In the reign of Jessie Mary – what an old story now! – he would not have openly craved permission, but would have hung about on the chance of meeting her alone and in pleasant humour. But he could not act so with Christina. Instinct as well as inclination prevented him. Moreover, he had been witness, on a certain evening when he had lingered near the shop – just to see her with her hat on – of the fate that befel a young man (a regular customer, too, Christina told him afterwards) who dared to proffer his escort off-hand. Christina had simply halted, turned and pointed, as one might point for a dog's guidance, and after a long moment the young man had gone in the direction opposite to that in which he had intended. To Macgregor the little scene had been gratifying yet disturbing. The memory of it chilled his courage now. But he was not the boy to relinquish a desire simply because he was afraid.

He broke his journey at a sweet-shop, and rather surprised himself by spending sixpence, although he had been planning to do so for the past week. He had not yet given Christina anything; he wanted badly to give her something; and having bought it, he wondered whether she would take it. He could not hope that the gift would affect the answer to his tremendous request.

Coming out of the sweet-shop he caught sight of the back of Willie Thomson, whom he had not seen for two weeks. Involuntarily he gave the boyish whistle, not so long ago the summons that would have called the one to the other with express speed. Now it had the reverse effect, for Willie started, half turned, and then walked quickly up a convenient side-street. The flight was obvious, and for a moment Macgregor was hurt and angry. Then with sudden sympathy he grinned, thinking, "He'll be after Jessie Mary, an' doesna want me." He was becoming quite grateful to Willie, for although he had encountered Jessie Mary several times of late, she had not reminded him of the approaching dance, and he gave Willie credit for that.

A few minutes later Macgregor stood at the counter that had become a veritable altar. Not many of us manage to greet the girls of our dreams precisely as we would or exactly as we have rehearsed the operation, and Macgregor's nerves at the last moment played him a trick.

In a cocky fashion, neither natural nor becoming, he wagged his head in the direction of the living-room and flippantly enquired: "Is she oot?"

To which Christina, her smile of welcome passing with never a flicker, stiffly replied: "Miss Tod *is* out, but may return at any moment."

"Aw!" he murmured, "I thought she wud maybe be takin' her usual walk."

"What usual walk?"

His hurt look said: "What have I done to deserve this, Christina?"

And she felt as though she had struck him. "Ye shouldna tak' things for granted," she said, less sharply. "I didna think ye was yin o' the cheeky sort."

"Me!" he cried in consternation.

"Weel, maybe ye didna mean it, but ye cam' into the shop like a dog wi' twa tails. But" – as with a sudden inspiration – "maybe ye've been gettin' a rise in yer wages. If that's the case, I'll apologise."

He shook his head. "I dinna ken what ye're drivin' at. I – I was jist gled to see ye – "

"Oh, we'll no' say ony mair aboot it. Maybe I was ower smart," she said hastily. "Kindly forget ma observations." She smiled apologetically.

"Are ye no' gaun to shake han's wi' me?" he asked, still uneasy.

"Surely!" she answered warmly. "An' I've got a bit o' news for ye, Mac." The name slipped out; she reddened.

Yet her cheek was pale compared with the boy's. "Oh!" he exclaimed under his breath. Then with a brave attempt at carelessness he brought from his pocket a small white package and laid it on the counter before her. "It – it's for you," he said, forgetting his little speech about wanting to give her something and hoping she would not be offended.

Christina was not prepared for such a happening; still, her wits did not desert her. She liked sweets, but on no account was she going to have her acceptance of the gift misconstrued. She glanced at Macgregor, whose eyes did not meet hers; she glanced at the package; she glanced once more at Macgregor, and gently uttered the solitary word:

"Platonic?"

"Na," he replied. "Jujubes."

Christina bit her lip.

"D'ye no' like them?" he asked anxiously.

The matter had got beyond her. She put out her hand and took the gift saying: "Thank ye, Mac; they're ma favourite sweeties. But – ye're no' to dae it again."

"What kin' o' sweeties did ye think they was?" he asked breaking a short silence.

"Oh, it's o' nae consequence," she lightly replied. "D'ye no' want to hear ma bit o' news?"

" 'Deed, ay, Christina." Now more at ease, he settled himself on the chair by the counter.

"Weel, – ye'll excuse me no' samplin' the jujubes the noo; it micht be awkward if a customer was comin' – weel, yer Uncle Purdie was visitin' ma uncle last night, an' what d'ye think I did?"

"What?"

"I asked him for a job!"

"A job!" exclaimed Macgregor. "In – in yin o' his shops?"

"Na; in his chief office."

"My! ye've a neck – I mean, ye're no' afraid."

"Ye dinna get muckle in this world wi'oot askin' for it."

"What did he say?" the boy enquired, after a pause.

"He said the job was mine as sune as I was ready to tak' it. Ye see, I tell't him I didna want to start till I had ma shorthand an' typewritin' perfec'. That'll tak' me a few months yet."

"I didna ken ye could typewrite."

"Oh, I've been workin' at it for near a year, but I can only get practisin' afore breakfast an' whiles in the evenin'. Still,

I think I'll be ready for the office aboot the spring, if no' earlier."

Macgregor regarded her with sorrow mingled with admiration. "But what way dae ye want to leave here?" he cried, all at once realising what the change would mean to him.

"There's nae prospects in a wee place like this. Once I'm in a big place, like yer uncle's, I'll get chances. I want to be yer uncle's private secretary – "

"Ye're ower young."

"I didna say in six months." Her voice changed. "Are ye no' pleased, Mac?"

"Hoo can I be pleased when ye're leavin' here? Can ye no' stop? Ye're fine where ye are. An' what'll Miss Tod dae wantin' ye?"

"I'll get uncle to find her another girl – a pretty girl, so that ye'll come here for yer stationery, eh?"

"If ye leave, I'll never come here again. Could ye no' get a job behind the counter in yin of ma uncle's shops?" – clutching at a straw.

"I'll gang furder in the office. If I was a man I daresay I wud try the shop. If I was you, Mac, I wud try it."

"I couldna sell folk things."

"In a big business like yer uncle's there's plenty work besides sellin'. But I suppose ye'll stick to the pentin'."

"Ay," he said shortly.

"Weel, I suppose it's nane o' ma business," she said good-humouredly. "But, bein' a frien', I thought ye wud ha'e been pleased to hear ma news."

Ere he could reply a woman came in to purchase notepaper. Possibly Christina's service was a trifle less "finished" than usual; and she made no attempt to sell anything that was not wanted. Macgregor had a few minutes for reflection, and when the customer had gone he said, a shade more hopefully:

"Ye'll no' be kep' as late at the office as here. Ye'll ha'e yer evenin's free, Christina."

"I'll ha'e mair time for classes. I'm keen on learnin'

French an' German. I ken a bit o' French already; a frien' o' ma uncle's, a Frenchman, has been gi'ein' me lessons in conversation every Sunday night for a while back. It'll be useful if I become a secretary."

"Strikes me," said Macgregor, gloomily, "ye've never ony time for fun."

"Fun?"

"For walkin' aboot an' – an' that."

"Oh, ye mean oot there." She swung her hand in the direction of the street. "I walk here in the mornin' – near a mile – an' hame at night; an' I've two hours free in the middle o' the day – uncle bargained for that when he let me come to Miss Tod. As for loafin' aboot on the street, I had plenty o' the street when I was young, afore ma aunt took me to bide wi' her at Kilmabeg. The street was aboot the only place I had then, an' I suppose I wud be there yet if ma aunt hadna saved me. D'ye ken, Mac," she went on almost passionately, "it's no' five years since I wanted a decent pair o' shoes an' a guid square meal... Oh, I could tell ye things – but anither time, maybe. As for spendin' a' yer spare time on the street, when ye've ony other place to spend it, it's – weel, I suppose it's a matter o' taste; but if I can dae onything wi' ma spare time that'll mak' me independent later on, I'm gaun to dae it. That's flat!" Suddenly she laughed. "Are ye afraid o' me, Mac?"

"No' likely!" he replied, with rather feeble indignation. "But whiles ye're awfu' – queer."

At that she laughed again. "But I'm no' so badly off for fun, as ye call it, either," she resumed presently. "Noo an' then uncle tak's auntie an' me to the theatre. Every holiday we gang to the coast. An' there's always folk comin' to the hoose – "

"Auld folk?"

"Frae your age upwards. An' next year, when I put up ma hair, I'll be gettin' to dances. Can ye waltz?"

Macgregor gave his head a dismal shake. "I – I doobt ye're ower high-class," he muttered hopelessly. "Ye'll no' be for lookin' at me next year."

"No' if ye wear a face like a fiddle. I like to look at cheery things. What's up wi' ye?"

"Oh, naething. I suppose ye expec' to be terrible rich some day."

"That's the idea."

"What'll ye dae wi' the money? I suppose ye dinna ken."

"Oh, I ken fine," she returned, with an eager smile. "I'll buy auntie a lovely cottage at the coast, an' uncle a splendid motor car, an' masel' a big white steam yacht."

"Ye're no' greedy," he remarked a little sulkily.

"That'll be merely for a start, of course. I'll tak' ye a trip roun' the world for the price o' a coat o' pent to the yacht. Are ye on? Maybe ye'll be a master-penter by then."

"I – I'll never be onything – an' I'm no' carin'," he groaned.

"If ye lie doon in the road ye'll no' win far, an' ye're likely to get tramped on, forbye. What's wrang wi' ye the day?" she asked kindly.

"Ye – ye jist mak' me miserable," he blurted out, and hung his head.

"Me!" she said innocently. "I'm sure I never meant to dae that. I'm a hard nut, I suppose; but no' jist as hard as I seem. Onything I can dae to mak' ye happy again?"

The door opened, the bell banged, and a man came in and bought a weekly paper.

"Weel?" said Christina when they were alone.

"Let me walk hame wi' ye the nicht," said Macgregor, who ought to have felt grateful to the chance customer whose brief stay had permitted him to get his wits and words together.

"Oh!" said Christina.

"I'll wait for ye as long as ye like."

Some seconds passed ere Christina spoke. "I'm not in the habit of being escorted – " she began.

"For ony sake dinna speak like that."

"I forgot ye wasna a customer. But, seriously, I dinna think it wud be the thing."

"What way, Christina?"

"Jist because, an' for several other reasons besides. My! it's gettin' dark. Time I was lightin' up." She struck a match, applied it to a long taper, and proceeded to ignite the jets in the window and above the counter. Then she turned to him again.

"Mac."

Something in her voice roused him out of his despair. "What, Christina?"

"If ye walk hame wi' me, I'll expect ye to come up an' see ma aunt an' uncle. Ye see, I made a sort o' bargain wi' them that I wudna ha'e ony frien's that they didna ken aboot."

Macgregor's expression of happiness gave place to one of doubt. "Maybe they wudna like me," he said.

"Aweel, that's your risk, of course. But they'll no' bite ye. I leave the shop at eight." She glanced at her little silver watch. "Mercy! It's time I was puttin' on the kettle. Miss Tod'll be back in a jiffy. Ye best gang, Mac."

"I'll be waitin' for ye at eight," he said, rising. "An' it's awfu' guid o' ye, Christina, though I wish ye hadna made that bargain – "

"Weel, I like to be as honest as I can – ootside o' business. If ye dinna turn up, I'll forgive ye. Noo – "

"Oh I'll turn up. It wud tak' mair nor your aunt an' uncle – "

"Tits, man!" she cried impatiently, "I'll be late wi' her tea. Adieu for the present." She waved her hand and fled to the living-room.

Macgregor went home happy in a subdued fashion. He found a letter awaiting him. It was from Grandfather Purdie; it reminded him that his seventeenth birthday was on the coming Monday, contained a few kindly words of advice, and enclosed a postal order for ten shillings. Hitherto the old man's gift had been a half-crown, which had seemed a large sum to the boy. But ten shillings! – it would be hard to tell whether Macgregor's feeling of manliness or of gratitude was the greater.

Mrs. Robinson was not a little disturbed when her son failed to hand over the money to her to take care of for him, as had been the custom in the past, and her husband had some difficulty in persuading her to "let the laddie be in the meantime."

Macgregor had gone to his room to make the most elaborate toilet possible.

"You trust him, an' he'll trust you," said John. "Dinna be aye treatin' him like a wean."

"It's no' a case o' no' trustin' him," she returned a little sharply. "Better treat him like a wean than let him think he's a man afore his time."

"It's no' his money in the bank that tells what a chap's made o', Lizzie. Let us wait an' see what he does wi' it. Mind ye, it's his to dae what he likes wi'. Wait till the morn, an' then I'll back ye up in gettin' him to put a guid part o' it, onyway, in the bank. No' that I think ony backin' up'll be necessary. If he doesna want to put it in the bank, he'll dae it to please us. I'll guarantee that, wife."

"If I had your heart an' you had ma heid," she said with a faint smile, "I daresay we wud baith be near perfec', John. Aweel, I'm no' gaun to bother the laddie noo. But" – seriously – "he's been oot an awfu' lot at nicht the last week or twa."

"Courtin'," said John, laughing.

"Havers!" she retorted. "He's no' the sort."

"Neither was I," said John, "an' look at me noo!"

And there they let the subject drop.

At seven o'clock Macgregor left the house. At the nearest post-office he had his order converted into coin. In one of his pockets he placed a couple of shillings – for Jeannie and Jimsie. He had no definite plans regarding the balance, but he hoped his mother would not ask for it. Somehow its possession rendered the prospect of his meeting with the Baldwins a thought less fearsome. He would tell Christina of his grandfather's gift, and later on, perhaps, he would buy – he knew not what. All at once he wished he had a *great* deal of money – wished he were clever – wished he could talk like Christina, even in the manner he hated – wished vague but beautiful things. The secret aspirations of lad's love must must surely make the angels smile – very tenderly.

He reached the trysting place with a quick heart, a moist brow, and five and twenty minutes to spare.

X

FROM five to seven o'clock on Saturdays M. Tod and her assistant did a fairly brisk trade in newspapers; thereafter, as Christina often thought, but refrained from saying, it was scarcely worth while keeping the shop open. A stray customer or two was all that might be expected during the last hour, and Christina was wont to occupy herself and it by tidying up for Sunday, while M. Tod from the sitting-room bleated her conviction, based on nothing but a fair imagination and a bad memory, that the Saturday night business was not what it had been twenty years ago. The old woman invariably got depressed at the end of the week; she had come to grudge the girl's absence even for a day.

Christina was counting up some unsold periodicals, chattering cheerfully the while on the ethics of modern light literature. The door opened with a suddenness that suggested a pounce, and a young woman, whom Christina could not recollect having seen before, started visibly at the bang of the bell, recovered herself, and closed the door carefully. It was Christina's habit to sum up roughly the more patent characteristics of new customers almost before they reached the counter. In the present case her estimate was as follows: "Handsome for the money; conceited, but not proud."

"Good-evening," she said politely.

"Evenin'," replied the other, her dark eyes making a swift survey of the shop. She threw open her jacket, already unbuttoned, disclosing a fresh white shirt, a scarlet bow and a silver belt. Touching the belt, she said: "I think this was got in your shop."

Christina bent forward a little way. "Perhaps," she said pleasantly. "I couldn't say for certain. We've sold several of these belts, but of course we haven't the monopoly."

It may have been that the young woman fancied she was being chaffed. Other customers less unfamiliar with Christina had fancied the same thing. At all events her tone sharpened.

"But I happen to ken it was got here."

"Then it *was* got here," said Christina equably. "Do you wish to buy another the same? I'm sorry we're out of them at present, but we could procure one for you within – "

"No, thanks. An' I didna buy this one, either. It was bought by a young gentleman friend of mines."

"Oh, indeed!" Christina murmured sympathetically. Then her eyes narrowed slightly.

"I came to see if you could change it," the young woman proceeded. "It's miles too wide. Ye can see that for yersel'."

"They are worn that way at present," said Christina, with something of an effort.

"Maybe. But I prefer it tight-fittin'. Of course I admit I've an extra sma' waist."

"Yes – smaller than they are worn at present."

"I beg your pardon!"

"Granted," said Christina absently. She was trying to think of more than one male customer to whom she had sold a belt. But there had been only one. The dark eyes of the young woman glimmered with malignant relish.

"As I was sayin'," she said. "I prefer it tight-fittin'. I've a dance on next week, an' as it is the belt is unsuitable, an' the young man expec's me to wear it. Of course I couldna tell him that it didna fit me. So I thought I would jist ask ye to change it wi'oot lettin' on to him." She gave a self-conscious giggle.

"I see," said Christina, dully. "But I'm afraid there's only the one size in those belts, and, besides, we can't change goods that have been worn for a month."

"Oh, so ye mind when ye sold it!" said the other maliciously. "Ye've a fine memory, Miss! But though I've had it for a month – it was part o' his birthday present, ye ken – I've scarcely worn it – only once or twice, to please him."

There was a short silence ere Christina spoke. "If you are bent on getting the belt made tight-fitting, a jeweller would do it for you, but it would cost as much as the belt is worth," she said coldly. "It's a very cheap imitation, you know," she added, for the first time in her business career decrying her own wares.

It was certainly a nasty one, but the young woman almost succeeded in appearing to ignore it.

"So ye canna change it – even to please ma young man?" she said mockingly.

"No," Christina replied, keeping her face to the foe, but with difficulty.

Said the foe: "That's a pity, but I daresay I'll get over it." She moved to the door and opened it. She smiled, showing her teeth. (Christina was glad to see they were not quite perfect.) "A sma' waist like mines is whiles a misfortune," she remarked, with affected self-commiseration.

Christina set her lips, but the retort *would* come. "Ay," she said viciously; "still, I suppose you couldn't grow tall any other way."

But the young woman only laughed – she could afford to laugh, having done that which she had come to do – and departed to report the result of her mission to the youth known as Willie Thomson.

"Wha was that, dearie?" M. Tod called from the living-room.

Christina started from an unlovely reverie. "Merely a female," she answered bitterly, and resumed counting the periodicals in a listless fashion.

The poison bit deep. The cheek of him to suggest walking home with *her* when he was going to a dance with that tight-laced girl next week! No doubt he admired her skimpy waist. He was welcome to it and her – and her bad teeth. And yet he had seemed a nice chap. She had liked him for his shyness, if for nothing else. But the shy kind were always the worst. He had very likely been taking advantage of his shyness. Well, she was glad she had found him out before he could walk home with her. And possibly because she was glad, but probably because she was quite young at heart, tears came to her eyes...

When ten minutes had passed, M. Tod, missing the cheerful chatter, toddled into the shop.

"What's wrang, dearie? Preserve us! Ha'e ye been cryin'?"

"Cryin'!" exclaimed Christina with contempt. "But I think I'm in for a shockin' cauld in ma heid, so ye best keep awa' frae me in case ye get the infection. A cauld's a serious thing at your time o' life." And she got the feebly protesting old woman back to the fireside, and left her there.

At eight o'clock Macgregor saw the window lights go out and the shop lights grow dim. A minute later he heard an exchange of good-nights and the closing and bolting of a door. Then Christina appeared, her head a little higher even than usual.

He went forward eagerly. He held out his hand and – it received his gift of the afternoon unopened.

"I've changed my mind. I'll bid you good-night and good-bye," said Christina, and walked on.

Presently he overtook her.

"Christina, what's up?"

"Kindly do not address me any more."

"Any more? – Never? – What way? – "

She was gone.

He dashed the little package into the gutter and strode off in the opposite direction, his face white, his lip quivering.

If Macgregor seemed in the past to have needed a thorough rousing, he had it now. For an hour he tramped the streets, his heart hot within him, the burden of his thoughts – "She thinks I'm no' guid enough."

And the end of the tramp found him at the door of the home of Jessie Mary. For a wonder, on a Saturday night at that hour, she was in. She opened the door herself.

At the sight of the boy something like fear fell upon her. For what had he come thus boldly?

He did not keep her in suspense. "Will ye gang wi' me to that dance ye was talkin' aboot?" he asked abruptly, adding, "I've got the money for the tickets."

A curse, a blow even, would have surprised her less.

"Will ye gang, Jessie?" he said impatiently.

For the life of her she could not answer at once.

Said he: "If it's Wullie ye're thinkin' o' I'll square him."

"Wullie!" she exclaimed, a cruel contempt in the word.

"Weel, if naebody else is takin' ye, will ye gang wi' me?"

"Dae – dae ye want me, Macgreegor?"

"I'm askin' ye."

She glanced at him furtively, but he was not looking at her; his hands were in his pockets, his mouth was shaped to emit a tuneless whistle. She tried to laugh, but made only a throaty sound. It seemed as if a stranger stood before her, one of whom she knew nothing save his name. And yet she liked the stranger and wanted much to go to the dance with him.

The whistling ceased.

"Are ye gaun wi' somebody else?" he demanded, lifting his face for a moment.

It was not difficult to guess that something acute had happened to him very recently. Jessie Mary suddenly experienced a guilty pang. Yet why Macgregor should have come back to her now was beyond her comprehension. Yon yellow-haired girl in the shop could not have told him anything – that was certain. And though she had not really wanted him back, now that he had come she was fain to hold him once more. Such thoughts made confusion in her mind, out of which two distinct ideas at last emerged: she did not care if she had hurt the yellow-haired girl; she could not go to the dance on Macgregor's money.

So gently, sadly, she told her lie; "Ay, there's somebody else, Macgreegor." Which suggests that no waist is too small to contain an appreciable amount of heart and conscience.

A brief pause, and Macgregor said drearily:

"Aweel, it doesna matter. I'll awa' hame." And went languidly down the stairs.

"It doesna matter." The words haunted Jessie Mary that night, and it was days before she got wholly rid of the uncomfortable feeling that Macgregor had not really wanted her to go to the dance, and that he had, in fact, been "codding" her.

Whereas, poor lad, he had only been "codding" himself,

or, at least, trying to do so. By the time he reached the bottom step he had forgotten Jessie Mary.

Once more he tramped the streets.

At home Lizzie was showing her anxiety, and John was concealing his.

When, at long last, he entered the kitchen, he did not appear to hear his mother's "Whaur ha'e ye been, laddie?" or his father's "Ye're late, ma son." Their looks of concern at his tired face and muddy boots passed unobserved.

Having unlaced his boots and rid his feet of them more quietly than usual, he got up and went to the table at which his mother was sitting.

He took all the money – all – from his pockets and laid it before her.

"There's a shillin' each for Jeannie an' Jimsie. I'm no' needin' the rest. I'm wearied," he said, and went straightway to his own room.

John got up and joined his wife at the table. "Did I no' tell ye," he cried, triumphantly, " that Macgreegor wud dae the richt thing?"

Lizzie stared at the little heap of silver and bronze.

"John," she whispered at last, and there was a curious distressed note in her voice, "John, d'ye no' see? – he's gi'ed me ower much!"

XI

AS a rule tonics are bitter, and their effects very gradual, often so gradual as to be hardly noticeable until one's strength is put to some test. While it would be unfair to deny the existence of "backbone" in Macgregor, it is but just to grant that the "backbone" required stiffening. And it is no discredit to Macgregor that the tincture of Christina's hardier spirit which, along with her (to him) abundant sweetness, he had been absorbing during these past weeks, was the very tonic he needed, the tonic without which he could not have acted as he did on the Monday night following his dismissal.

Of this action one may say, at first thought, that it was simply the outcome of an outraged pride. Yet Macgregor's pride was at best a drowsy thing until a girl stabbed it. It forced him to Jessie Mary's door, but there failed him. Throughout the miserable Sunday it lay inert, with only an occasional spasm. And though he went with it to the encounter on Monday, he carried it as a burden. His real supporters were Love and Determination, and the latter was a new comrade, welcome, but not altogether of his own inspiring.

He did not go to the shop, for he had neither money nor the petty courage necessary to ask it of his parents. On the pavement, a little way from the door, he waited in a slow drizzle of rain. He had no doubts as to what he was going to do and say. The idea had been with him all day, from early in the morning, and it *had* to be carried out. Perhaps his nerves were a little too steady to be described as normal.

When eight o'clock struck on a neighbouring tower, he did not start or stir. But across the street, peering round the edge of a close-mouth, another boy jerked his head at the sound. Willie Thomson was exceedingly curious to know whether Saturday night had seen the end of the matter.

Christina, for no reason that she could have given, was

late in leaving the shop; it was twenty minutes past the hour when she appeared.

She approached quickly, but he was ready for her.

"No!" she exclaimed at the sight of him.

He stepped right in front of her. She was compelled to halt, and she had nothing to say.

He faced her fairly, and said – neither hotly nor coldly, but with a slight throb in his voice:

"I'll be guid enough yet." With a little nod as if to emphasise his words, and without taking his eyes from her face, he stood aside and let her go.

Erect, he followed her with his eyes until the darkness and traffic of the pavement hid her. Then he seemed to relax, his shoulders drooped slightly, and with eyes grown wistful he moved slowly down the street towards home. Arrived there he shut himself up with an old school dictionary.

Dull work, but a beginning… .

"Guid enough yet." Christina had not gone far when through all her resentment the full meaning of the words forced itself upon her. "Oh," she told herself crossly, "I never meant him to take it that way." A little later she told herself the same thing, but merely impatiently. And still later, lying in the dark, she repeated it with a sob.

As for the watcher, Willie Thomson, he set out without undue haste to inform Jessie Mary that once more Macgregor had been left standing alone on the pavement. Somehow Willie was not particularly pleased with himself this evening. Ere his lagging feet had borne him half way to the appointed place he was feeling sorry for Macgregor. All at once he decided to spy no more. It would be rather awkward just at present to intimate such a decision to Jessie Mary, but he could "cod" her, he thought, without much difficulty, by inventing reports in the future. Cheered by his virtuous resolutions, he quickened his pace.

Jessie Mary received him in the close leading to her abode. She was in an extraordinarily bad temper, and cut short his report almost at the outset by demanding to know when he intended repaying the shilling he had borrowed a fortnight previously.

"Next week," mumbled Willie, with that sad lack of originality exhibited by nearly all harassed borrowers.

Whereupon Jessie Mary, who was almost a head the taller, seized him by one ear and soundly cuffed the other until with a yelp he broke loose and fled into the night, never to know that he had been punished for that unfortunate remark of Macgregor's – "it doesna matter." Yet let us not scoff at Jessie Mary's sense of justice. The possessors of greater minds than hers, having stumbled against a chair, have risen in their wrath and kicked the sofa – which is not at all to say that the sofa's past has been more blameless than the chair's. Life has a way of settling our accounts without much respect for our book-keeping.

Jessie Mary felt none the better of her outbreak. She went to bed wishing angrily that she had taken Macgregor at his word. The prospects of obtaining an escort to the dance were now exceedingly remote, for only that afternoon she had learned that the bandy-legged young man in the warehouse whom she had deemed "safe at a pinch," and who was the owner of a dress suit with a white vest, had invited another girl and was actually going to give her flowers to wear.

Willie went to bed, too, earlier than usual, and lay awake wondering, among other things, whether his aching ear entitled him to a little further credit in the matter of his debt to Jessie Mary – not that any length of credit would have made payment seem possible. For Willie was up to the neck in debt, owing the appalling sum of five shillings and ninepence to an old woman who sold newspapers, paraffin oil and cheap cigarettes, and who was already threatening to go to his aunt for her money – a proceeding which would certainly result in much misery for Willie. He was "out of a job" again; but it isn't easy to get work, more especially when one prefers to do nothing. To some extent Macgregor was to blame for his having got into debt with the tobacconist, for if Macgregor had not stopped smoking, Willie would not have needed to buy nearly so many cigarettes. Nevertheless, Willie's thoughts did not dwell long or bitterly on that point. Rather did they dwell on Macgregor himself. And after a while Willie drew up his legs and pulled the insufficient bedclothes over his head and lay very still. This he had done since he was a small boy, when lonesomeness got the better of him, when he wished he had a father and mother like Macgregor's.

And, as has been hinted, neither was Christina at ease that night.

Indeed, it were almost safe to say that of the four young people involved in this little tragi-comedy, Macgregor, yawning over his old school dictionary, was the least unhappy.

XII

ON the fifth night, at the seventh page of words beginning with a "D," Macgregor closed the dictionary and asked himself what was the good of it all. His face was hot, his whole being restless. He looked at his watch – a quarter to eight. He got up and carefully placed the dictionary under a copy of "Ivanhoe" on the chest of drawers. He would go for a walk.

He left the house quietly.

In the kitchen Lizzie, pausing in her knitting, said to John: "That's Macgreegor awa' oot."

"It'll dae him nae harm," said John. "He's becomin' a great reader, Lizzie."

"I dinna see why he canna read ben here. It's cauld in his room. What's he readin'?"

"The book he got frae his Uncle Purdie three year back."

"Weel, I'm sure I'm gled if he's takin' an interest in it at last."

"Oh, 'Ivanhoe' 's no' a bad story," remarked John. "Whiles it's fair excitin'."

Said Jimsie from the hearthrug: "He doesna seem to enjoy it much, Paw."

"Weel, it's no' a funny book."

"It's time ye was in yer bed, Jimsie," said Mrs. Robinson. "It's ower late for ye."

"Aw, the wean's fine," said John.

Jeannie laid down her sewing. "Come on, Jimsie, an' I'll tell ye a wee story afore ye gang to sleep."

"Chaps ye!" Jimsie replied, getting up.

When the two had gone, Lizzie observed casually: "It's the first nicht Macgreegor's been oot this week."

"Weel, ye should be pleased, wumman." John smiled.

A pause.

"I wonder what made him gi'e up a' his siller on Seturday nicht."

"Same here. But I wudna ask him," said John, becoming grave. "Wud you?"

She shook her head. "I tried to, on Sunday, but someway I couldna. He's changin'."

"He's growin' up, Lizzie."

"I suppose ye're richt," she said reluctantly, and resumed her knitting.

From the darkest spot he could find on the opposite pavement Macgregor saw Christina come out of the shop, pass under a lamp, and disappear. He felt sorely depressed during the return journey. The dictionary had failed to increase either his knowledge or his self-esteem. He wondered whether History or Geography would do any good; there were books on these subjects in the house. He realised that he knew nothing about anything except his trade, and even there he had to admit that he had learned less than he might have done. And yet he had always wanted to be a painter.

The same night he started reading the History of England, and found it a considerable improvement on the Dictionary. He managed to keep awake until the arrival of Julius Cæsar. Unfortunately he had taken the book to bed, and his mother on discovering it in the morning indiscreetly asked him what he had been doing with it. "Naething special," was his reply, indistinctly uttered, and here ended his historical studies, though for days after Lizzie left the book prominent on the chest of drawers.

The day being Saturday, the afternoon was his own. Through the rain he made his way furtively to a free library, but became too self-conscious at the door, and fled. For the sum of threepence a picture house gave him harbourage, and save when the scenes were very exciting he spent the time in trying not to wonder what Christina would think of him, if she thought at all. He came forth ashamed and in nowise cheered by the entertainment.

In the evening he went once more to watch her leave the

shop. M. Tod came to the door with her, and they stood talking for a couple of minutes, so that he had more than a glimpse of her. And a spirit arose in him demanding that he should attempt something to prove himself, were it only with his hands. It was not learning, but earning, that would make him "guid enough yet"; not what he could say, but what he could do. There would be time enough for speaking "genteel English" and so on after – well, after he had got up in the world.

For a moment he felt like running after Christina and making her hearken to his new hope, but self-consciousness prevailed and sent him homewards.

"Hullo!" From a close came a husky voice, apologetic, appealing.

"Hullo, Wullie!" Macgregor stopped. He was not sorry to meet Willie; he craved companionship just then, though he had no confidence to give.

"Are ye for hame?"

"Ay."

"I – I'll come wi' ye, if ye like, Macgreegor?"

"Come on then."

Willie came out, and they proceeded along the street without remark until Macgregor enquired –

"Where are ye workin' the noo, Wullie?"

"I'm no' workin'. Canna get a job. Dae ye ken o' onything?"

"Na. What kin' o' job dae ye want?"

"Onything," said Willie, and added quickly, "an' I'll stick to it this time, if I get the chance."

After a short pause – "My fayther got ye a job before," said Macgregor.

"I ken. But I wud stick – "

"Honest?"

Willie drew his hand across his throat.

"Weel," said Macgregor, "I'll tell ma fayther an' ye can gang an' see him at the works on Monday."

"I'll be there. Ye're a dacent chap, Macgreegor."

Neither seemed to have anything more to say to the other, but their parting was cordial enough.

Next day, Sunday, was wet and stormy, and there was no afternoon stroll of father and son to the docks. John was flattered by Macgregor's ill-concealed disappointment – it was like old times. Perhaps he would not have been less flattered had he known his boy's desire to tell him out of doors a thing that somehow could not be uttered in the house. Macgregor spent the afternoon in studying secretly an old price-list of Purdie's Stores.

The following night, while returning from the errand of previous nights, he again encountered Willie.

"So ma fayther's gaun to gi'e ye a job. He tell't me it was fixed."

"Ay," said Willie, "but he canna tak' me on for a fortnicht."

"Weel, that's no lang to wait."

For a few seconds Willie was mute; then he blurted out – "I'm done for!"

"Done for!" exclaimed Macgregor, startled by the despair in the other's voice. "What's wrang, Wullie?"

"I'm in a mess. But it's nae use tellin' ye. Ye canna dae onything."

"Is't horses?" Macgregor asked presently.

"Naw, it's no' horses!" Willie indignantly replied.

How virtuous we feel when accused of the one sin we have not committed!

The next moment he clutched Macgregor's arm. "Come in here, an' I'll tell ye." He drew his companion into a close. "I – I couldna tell onybody else."

From the somewhat incoherent recital which followed Macgregor finally gathered that the old woman to whom Willie owed money had presented her ultimatum. If Willie failed to pay up that night she would assuredly not fail to apply to his aunt first thing in the morning.

"Never heed, Wullie," said Macgregor, taking his friend's arm, and leading him homewards. "Yer aunt'll no' kill ye."

"I wish to – she wud!" muttered Willie with a vehemence that shocked his friend. "She's aye been ill to live wi', but it'll be a sight harder noo."

"Wud the auld wife no' believe ye aboot gettin' a job in a fortnicht? She wudna? Aweell, she'll believe me. Come on, an' I'll speak to her for ye."

But the "auld wife" was adamant. She had been deceived with too many promises ere now. At last Macgregor, feeling himself beaten, disconsolately joined Willie and set out for home. Neither spoke until Macgregor's abode was reached. Then Macgregor said:

"Bide here till I come back," and ran up the stair. He knew his father was out, having gone back to the works to experiment with some new machinery. He found his mother alone in the kitchen.

"Mither," he said with difficulty, "I wish ye wud gi'e me five shillin's o' ma money."

He could not have startled her more thoroughly.

"Five shillin's, laddie! What for?"

"I canna tell ye the noo."

"But – "

"It's no' for – for fun. If ye ask me, I'll tell ye in a secret this day fortnicht. Please, mither."

She got up and laid her hands on his shoulder and turned him to the full light of the gas. He looked at her shyly, yet without flinching. And abruptly she kissed him, and as abruptly passed to the dresser drawer where she kept her purse.

Without a word she put the money in his hand. Without a word he took it, nodded gravely, and went out. In one way Lizzie had done more for her boy in these three minutes than she had done in the last three years.

Macgregor had a sixpence in his pocket, and he added it to the larger coins.

"She can wait for her thruppence," he said, giving the money to the astounded Willie. "Awa' an' pay her. I'll maybe see ye the morn's nicht. So long!" He walked off in the direction opposite to that which Willie ought to take.

But Willie ran after him; he was pretty nearly crying. "Macgreegor," he stammered, "I'll pay ye back when I get ma first wages. An' I'll no' forget – oh, I'll never forget. An' I'll dae ye a guid turn yet!"

"Ye best hurry in case she shuts her shop," said Macgregor, and so got rid of him.

While it is disappointing to record that Willie has thus far never managed to repay Macgregor in hard cash, though he has somehow succeeded in retaining the employment found for him by John, it is comforting to know that his promise to do Macgregor a good turn was more than just an emotional utterance. When, on the following Wednesday and Friday nights, he stealthily tracked Macgregor to the now familiar watching place, his motives were no longer curious or selfish, but benevolent in the extreme. Not that he could bring himself to sympathise with Macgregor in the latter's devotion to a mere girl, for, as a matter of fact, he regarded his friend's behaviour as "awfu' stupid"; but if Macgregor was really "saft" on the girl, it behoved him, Willie, to do what he could to put an end to the existing misunderstanding.

On the Friday night he came regretfully to the conclusion that the "saftness" was incurable, and he accordingly determined to act on the following afternoon. By this time his knowledge of the movements of M. Tod and her assistant was practically as complete as Macgregor's, so that he had no hesitation in choosing the hour for action. He had little fear of Macgregor's coming near the shop in daylight.

So, having witnessed the exit of M. Tod, he crossed the street, and examined the contents of the window, as he had seen Macgregor do so often. He was not in the least nervous. The fact that he was without money did not perturb him: it would be the simplest thing in the world to introduce himself and his business by asking for an article which stationers' shops did not supply. A glance at a druggist's window had given him the necessary suggestion.

On entering he was seized with a most distressing cough, which racked him while he closed the door and until he reached the counter.

"A cold afternoon," Christina remarked in a sympathetic tone.

"Ay. Ha'e ye ony chest protectors?" he hoarsely enquired.

For the fraction of a second only she hesitated. "Not exactly," she replied. "But I can recommend this." From under the counter she brought a quire of brown paper. "It's cheaper than flannel and much more sanitary," she went on. "There's nothing like it for keeping out the cold. You've only got to cut out the shape that suits you." She separated a sheet from the quire and spread it on the counter. "Enough there for a dozen protectors. Price one penny. I'll cut them out for you, if you like."

"The doctor said I was to get a flannel yin," said Willie, forgetting his hoarseness. "Ha'e ye ony nice ceegarettes the day, miss?"

"No."

"Will ye ha'e ony on Monday?"

"No."

"When d'ye think ye'll ha'e some nice ceegarettes?"

Christina's eyes smiled. "Perhaps," she said solemnly, "by the time you're big enough to smoke them. Anything else to-day?"

"Ye're no' sae green," he said, with grudging admiration.

"No," said she; "it's only the reflection." She opened the glass case and took out an infant's rattle. "Threepence!"

Willie laughed. "My! ye're a comic!" he exclaimed.

"Children are easily amused."

There was a short pause. Then Willie, leaning his arms on the edge of the counter, looked up in her face and said:

"So you're the girl that's mashed on Macgreegor Robi'son." He grinned.

A breath of silence – a sounding smack.

Willie sprang back, his hand to his cheek. Christina, cheeks flaming, eyes glittering, teeth gleaming, hands clenched, drew herself up.

"Get oot o' this!" she cried. "D'ye hear me! Get oot – "

"Ay, I hear ye," said Willie resentfully, rubbing his cheek. "Ye're ower smart wi' yer han's. I meant for to say – "

"Be quiet!"

" – you're the girl Macgreegor's mashed on – an' I – "

Christina stamped her foot. "Clear oot, I tell ye!"

" – I wudna be Macgreegor for a thoosan' pounds! Keep yer hair on, miss. I'll gang when it suits me. Ye've got to hear – "

"I'll no' listen." She put her hands to her ears.

"Thon girl, Jessie Mary, took a rise oot o' ye last week, an' it was me that put her up to it. Macgreegor gi'ed her the belt, richt enough, but that was afore he got saft on you – "

"Silence! I cannot hear a word you say," declared Christina, recovering herself and her more formal speech, though her colour, which had faded, now bloomed again.

"I'll cry it loud, if ye like, so as the folk in the street can hear. But ye can pretend ye dinna hear," he said ironically. "I'm no' heedin' whether ye hear or no'."

"I wish you would go away, you impertinent thing!"

"Macgreegor – " he began.

Once more she covered her ears.

"Macgreegor," proceeded Willie, with a rude wink, "never had ony notion o' takin' Jessie Mary to the dance. She was jist coddin' ye, though I daursay she was kin' o' jealous because ye had cut her oot. So I think ye should mak' it up wi' Macgreegor when ye get the chance. He's awfu' saft on ye. I wudna be him for a – "

"Go away!" said Christina. "You're simply wasting your breath."

"Dinna let on to Macgreegor that I tell't ye," he continued, unmoved, "an' if Jessie Mary tries it on again, jist yer put yer finger to yer nose at her."

"If you don't go at once, I'll – "

"Oh, ye canna dae onything, miss. I'll forgi'e ye for that scud ye gi'ed me, but I wud advise ye no' to be so quick wi' yer han's in future, or ye'll maybe get into trouble." He turned towards the door. "I daursay ye ken fine that Macgreegor watches ye leavin' the shop every nicht – "

"What *are* you talking about?"

"Gi'e him a whistle or a wave the next time. There's nae use in bein' huffy."

"That's enough!"

Willie opened the door. "An' ye best hurry up, or ye'll maybe loss him. So long. I'll no' tell him I seen ye blushin'."

Christina opened her mouth, but ere she could speak, with a grin and a wink he was gone. She collapsed upon the stool. She had never been so angry in her life – at least, so she told herself.

XIII

JOHN ROBINSON and his son sat on a pile of timber at the docks. Dusk was falling, and the air that had been mild for the season was growing chill.

John replaced his watch in his pocket. "It's comin' on for tea-time. Are ye ready for the road, Macgreegor?"

"Ay," said the boy, without stirring.

For two hours he had been struggling to utter the words on which he believed his future depended.

"Weel," said John, getting out his pipe preparatory to lighting it on passing the gate, "we best be movin'."

It was now or never. Macgregor cleared his throat.

"The pentin' trade's rotten," he said in a voice not his own.

"Eh?" said John, rather staggered by the statement which was without relevance to any of the preceding conversation. "What's rotten aboot it?"

"Everything."

"That's the first I've heard o' 't. In fac', I'm tell't the pentin' trade is extra brisk the noo."

"That's no' what I meant," Macgregor forced himself to say. "I meant it was a rotten trade to be in."

John gave a good-humoured laugh. "Oh, I see! Ye dinna like the overtime! Aweel, that's nateral at your age, Macgreegor" – he patted his son's shoulder – "but when ye're aulder, wi' a wife an' weans, maybe, ye'll be gled o' overtime whiles, I'm thinkin'."

"It's no the overtime," said Macgregor.

"What is't, then? What's wrang wi' the trade?" The question was lightly put.

"There's – there's nae prospec's in it for a man."

"Nae prospec's! Hoots, Macgreegor! there's as guid prospec's in the pentin' as in ony ither trade. Dinna fash yer heid aboot that – no' but what I'm pleased to ken ye're thinkin' aboot yer prospec's, ma son. But we'll speak aboot it on the road hame."

"I wish," said Macgregor, with the greatest effort of all, "I wish I had never gaed into it. I wish I had gaed into Uncle Purdie's business."

John sat down again. At last he said: "D'ye mean that Macgreegor?"

"Ay, I mean it."

For the first time John Robinson felt disappointed – in a vague fashion, it is true, yet none the less unpleasantly disappointed – in his son.

"But ye've been at the pentin' for three year," he said a little impatiently.

"I ken that, fayther."

"An' ye mind ye had the chance o' gaun into yer uncle's business when ye left the schule?"

"Ay."

"But ye wud ha'e naething but the pentin'."

Macgregor nodded.

"Maybe ye mind that yer Aunt Purdie was unco offended, for it was her notion – at least, it was her that spoke aboot it – an' she declared ye wud never get a second chance. D'ye no' mind Macgreegor?"

"I mind aboot her bein' offended, but I dinna mind aboot – the ither thing," Macgregor answered dully.

"But *I* mind it, for she was rale nesty to yer mither at the time. In fac', I dinna ken hoo yer mither stood her impidd-ence. An', in a way, it was a' ma fau't, for it was me that said ye was to choose the trade that ye liked best – an' I thocht I was daein' the richt thing, because I had seen lads spiled wi' bein' forced into trades they didna fancy. Ay, I thocht I was daein' the richt thing – An' noo ye're tellin' me I did the wrang thing."

"Fayther, it's me that's to blame. I – I didna mean to vex ye."

"Aweel, I dinna suppose ye did," said John sadly. "But for the life o' me I canna see hoo ye can hope to get into yer uncle's business at this time o' day ... But we'll be keepin' yer mither waitin'."

He rose slowly and Macgregor joined him. At the gate

John apparently forgot to light his pipe. They were half way home ere he spoke.

He put his hand round his son's arm. "Ye're no' to think, Macgreegor, that I wud stan' in yer road when ye want to better yersel'. No' likely! I never was set on bein' a wealthy man masel', but naethin' wud mak' me prooder nor to see you gang up in the world; an' I can say the same for yer mither. An' I can see that ye micht gang far in yer uncle's business, for yer uncle was aye fond o' ye, an' I think ye could manage to please him at yer work, if ye was tryin'. *But* – ye wud need yer aunt's favour to begin wi', an' that's the bitter truth, an' she's no' the sort o' body that forgets what she conseeders an affront. Weel, it'll need some thinkin' ower. I'll ha'e to see what yer mither says. An' ye best no' expec' onything. Stick to the pentin' in the meantime, an' be vera certain afore ye quit the trade ye're in. That's a' I can say, ma son."

Macgregor had no words then. Never before had his father seriously spoken at such length to him. His heart was heavy, troubled about many things.

Eight o'clock on Monday night saw him at the accustomed spot; on Wednesday night also he was there. If only Christina had been friends with him he would have asked her what he ought to do. Yet the mere glimpse of her confirmed him in his desire to change his trade. On the Wednesday night it seemed to him that she walked away from the shop much more slowly than usual, and the horrid thought that she might be giving some other "man" a chance to overtake her assailed him. But at last she was gone without that happening.

On the way home he encountered Jessie Mary. She greeted him affably, and he could not but stop.

"Lovely dance on Friday. Ye should ha'e been there. Ma belt was greatly admired," she remarked.

"Was it?"

"I think I've seen the shop where ye bought it," she said, watching his face covertly.

"It's likely," he replied, without emotion.

Jessie Mary was relieved; evidently he was without knowledge of her visit to the shop. Now that the world was going well with her again she bore no ill-will, and was fain to avoid any. For at the eleventh hour – or, to be precise, the night before the dance – she had miraculously won back the allegiance of the young man with the exquisite moustache, who served in the provision shop, and for the present she was more than satisfied with herself.

So she bade Macgregor good-night, a little patronisingly perhaps, and hurried off to reward her recovered swain with the pleasant sight of herself and an order for a finnan haddie.

Macgregor was still in the dark as to whether his father had mentioned to his mother the subject of that conversation at the docks. John had not referred to it again, and the boy was beginning to wonder if his case was hopeless.

On the Friday night, however, just when he was about to slip from the house, his mother followed him to the door. Very quietly she said:

"When ye come in, Macgreegor, I want ye to tell me if ye're still set on leavin' the pentin'. Dinna tell me noo. Tak' yer walk, an' think it ower, seriouslike. But dinna be late, laddie."

She went back to the kitchen, leaving him to shut the door.

It was not much after seven o'clock, but he went straightway in the direction of M. Tod's shop. For the first time in what seemed an age, he found himself at the familiar, glittering window. And lo! the glazed panel at the back was open a few inches. Quickly he retreated to the edge of the pavement, and stood there altogether undecided. But desire drew him, and gradually he approached the window again.

Christina was sitting under the lamp, at the desk, her pretty profile bent over her writing, her fair plait falling over the shoulder of her scarlet shirt. She was engaged in pencilling queer little marks on paper, and doing so very rapidly. Macgregor understood that she was practising shorthand.

No doubt she would be his uncle's private secretary some day, while he –

All at once it came to him that no one in the world could answer the great question but Christina. If the thing didn't matter to Christina, it didn't matter to him; it was for her sake that he would strive to be "guid enough yet," not for the sake of being "guid enough" in itself. Besides, she had put the idea into his head. Surely she would not refuse to speak to him on that one subject.

Now all this was hardly in accordance with the brave and independent plan which Macgregor had set out to follow – to wit, that he would not attempt to speak to Christina until he could announce that he was a member of his uncle's staff. Yes, love is the great maker of plans – also, the great breaker.

Coward or not, it took courage to enter the shop.

Christina looked up, her colour deepening slightly.

"Hullo," she said coolly, though not coldly.

It was not a snub anyway, and Macgregor walked up to the counter. He came to the point at once.

"Wud ye advise me to try an' get a job frae ma uncle?" he said, distinctly enough.

"Me?" The syllable was fraught with intense astonishment.

"Ye advised me afore to try it," he said, fairly steadily.

"Did I?" – carelessly.

It was too much for him. "Oh, Christina!" he whispered reproachfully.

"Well, I'm sure it's none of my business. I thought you preferred being a painter."

The pity was that Christina should have just then remembered the existence of such a person as Jessie Mary, also the fact of her own slow walk from the shop the previous night. Yet she had forgotten both when she opened the panel at the back of the window a few inches. And perhaps she was annoyed with herself, knowing that she was not behaving quite fairly.

He let her remark concerning his preference for the painting pass, and put a very direct question.

"What made ye change yer mind aboot me that night?"

"What night?" she asked flippantly, and told herself it was the silliest thing she had ever uttered.

She had gone too far – she saw it in his face.

"I didna think ye was as bad as that," he said in a curiously hard voice, and turned from the counter.

Quick anger – quick compunction – quick fear – and then: "Mac!"

He wheeled at the door. She was holding out her hand. Her smile was frail.

"Are ye in earnest?" he said in a low voice, but he did not wait for her answer.

She drew away her hand, gently. "Dinna ask me ony questions," she pleaded. "I – I didna really mean what I said that night, or this night either. I think I was off my onion" – a faint laugh – "but I'm sorry I behaved the way I did. Is that enough?"

It was more than enough; how much more he could not say. "I've missed ye terrible," he murmured.

Christina became her practical self. "So ye're for tryin' yer uncle's business – " she began.

"If he'll gi'e me the chance."

"Weel, I'm sure I wish ye the best o' luck."

"Then ye think I ought to try?" This with great eagerness.

"If ye've made up yer mind it's for the best," she answered cautiously.

He had to be satisfied with that. "Will I let ye ken if it comes off?"

She nodded. Then she glanced at her watch.

"Can – can I get walkin' hame wi' ye, Christina?" It was out before he knew.

She shook her head. "Uncle said he wud come for me; he had some business up this way. If ye wait a minute, ye'll see him. I'll introduce ye. He'll be interested seein' ye're a nephew o' Mr. Purdie."

"Oh, I couldna. I best hook it. But, Christina, I can come to-morrow, eh?"

She laughed. "I canna prevent ye. But I'll no' be here in

the afternoon. Uncle's takin' auntie an' me to a matinée, an' I'll no be back much afore six."

"Weel, I'll meet ye at eight an' walk hame wi' ye."

"Will ye?"

"Oh, Christina, say 'ay.' "

"I'll consider it."

And he had to be satisfied with that, too, for here the noisy door opened to admit a tall, clean-shaven, pleasant-featured man of middle-age.

"Hullo, uncle!" cried Christina.

Macgregor fled, but not without gaining a quick smile that made all the difference in the world to him.

Ten minutes later he hurried into the home kitchen.

"Mither, I've decided to leave the pentin'." The moment he said it his heart misgave him, and the colour flew to his face. But he need not have doubted his parents.

"Weel, ma son," said John soberly, "we'll dae the best we can wi' yer Aunt Purdie."

"Jist that," said Lizzie.

And that was all.

An urgent piece of work had to be done the following afternoon, and he was later than usual, for a Saturday, in getting home. He found his mother preparing to go out, and his father looking strangely perplexed.

"She's gaun to see yer Aunt Purdie," said John in a whisper.

Macgregor looked from one to the other, hesitated, and went over to Lizzie. He put his hand on her arm.

"Mither, ye're no' to gang. I – I'll gang masel'."

Then, indeed, Lizzie Robinson perceived that her boy was in danger of becoming a man.

XIV

TO press the little black button at the door of his aunt's handsome west-end flat was the biggest thing Macgregor had ever done. As a small boy he had feared his Aunt Purdie, as a schoolboy he had hated her, as a youth he had despised her; his feelings towards her now were not to be described, but it is certain that they included a well-nigh overpowering sense of dread; indeed, the faint thrill of the electric bell sent him back a pace towards the stair. His state of perspiration gave place to one of miserable chillness.

A supercilious servant eyed his obviously "good" clothes and bade him wait. Nevertheless, a sting was what Macgregor needed just then; it roused the fighting spirit. When the servant returned, and in an aloof fashion – as though, after all, it was none of her business – suggested that he might enter, he was able to follow her across the hall, with its thick rugs and pleasantly warm atmosphere, to the drawing-room, without faltering. Less than might have been expected the grandeur of his surroundings impressed – or depressed – him, for in the course of his trade he had grown familiar with the houses of the rich. But he had enough to face in the picture without looking at the frame.

Mrs. Purdie was seated at the side of the glowing hearth, apparently absorbed in the perusal of a charitable society's printed list of donations.

"Your nephew, ma'am," the servant respectfully announced and retired.

Mrs. Purdie rose in a manner intended to be languid. Macgregor had not seen the large yet angular figure for two years. With his hat in his left hand he went forward holding out his right. A stiff, brief handshake followed.

"Well, Macgregor, this is quite an unexpected pleasure," she said, unsmiling, resuming her seat. "Take a chair. It is a considerable period since I observed you last." Time could not wither the flowers of language for Mrs. Purdie. "You are getting quite a big boy. How old are you now? Are your parents in good health?" She did not wait for answers to these inquiries. "I am sorry your uncle is not at home. His commercial pursuits confine him to his new and commodious premises even on Saturday afternoons." (At that moment Mr. Purdie was smoking a pipe in the homely parlour of Christina's uncle, awaiting his old friend's return from the theatre.) "His finance is exceedingly high at present." With a faint smack of her lips she paused, and cast an inquiring glance at her visitor.

Macgregor saw the ice, so to speak, before him. The time had come. But he did not go tapping round the edge. Gathering himself together, he leaped blindly.

In a few ill-chosen words he blurted out his petition.

Then there fell an awful silence. And then – he could hardly believe his own ears!

There are people in the world who seem hopelessly unloveable until you – perforce, perhaps – ask of them a purely personal favour. There may even be people who leave the world with their fountains of goodwill still sealed simply because no one had the courage or the need to break the seals for them. Until to-day the so-called favours of Aunt Purdie had been mere patronage and cash payments.

Even now she could not help speaking patronisingly to Macgregor, but through the patronage struggled a kindliness and sympathy of which her relations so long used to her purse-pride, her affectations, her absurdities, could never have imagined her capable. She made no reference to the past; she suggested no difficulties for the present; she cast no doubts upon the future. Her nephew, she declared, had done wisely in coming to her; she would see to it that he got his chance. It seemed to Macgregor that she promised him ten times all he would have dreamed of asking. Finally she bade him stay to dinner and see his uncle; then, perceiving his anxiety to get home and possibly, also, his dread of offending her by expressing it, she invited him for the following Sunday evening, and sent him off with a full heart and a light head.

He burst into the kitchen, bubbling over with his wonderful news. During its recital John gave vent to noisy explosions of satisfaction, Jeannie beamed happily, Jimsie stared at his transformed big brother, and Lizzie, though listening with all her ears, began quietly to prepare her son's tea.

"An' so she treated ye weel, Macgreegor," said John, rubbing his hands, while the speaker paused for words.

"She did that! An' I'm to get dooble the wages I'm gettin' the noo, an' I've to spend the half o' them on night classes, for, ye see, I'm to learn *everything* aboot the business, an' then – "

Said Lizzie gently: "Wud ye like yer egg biled or fried, dearie?"

It was nearly eight o'clock when he reached the shop, and he decided to wait at a short distance from the window until Christina came out. He was not going to risk interruption by the old woman or a late customer; he would tell his wonderful tale in the privacy of the busy pavement, under the secrecy of the noisy street. Yet he was desperately impatient, and with every minute after the striking of the hour a fresh doubt assailed him.

At last the lights in the window went out, and the world grew brighter. Presently he was moving to meet her, noting dimly that she was wearing a bigger hat than heretofore.

She affected surprise at the sight of him, but not at his eagerly whispered announcement:

"I've got it!"

"Good for you," she said kindly, and refrained from asking him, teasingly, where he thought he was going. "It was lovely at the theatre," she remarked, stepping forward.

"Dae ye no' want to hear aboot it?" he asked disappointed, catching up with her.

"Of course," she said cheerfully. "Was yer uncle nice?"

"It was ma aunt," he explained somewhat reluctantly, for he feared she might laugh. But she only nodded understandingly, and, relieved, he plunged into details.

"Ye've done fine," she said when he had finished – for

the time being, at anyrate. "I'm afraid it'll be you that'll be wantin' a private secretary when I get that length."

"Dinna laugh at me," he murmured reproachfully.

"Dinna be ower serious, Mac," she returned. "Ye'll get on a' the better for bein' able to tak' a joke whiles. I'm as pleased as Punch aboot it."

He was more pleased, if possible. "If it hadna been for you, Christina, I wud never ha'e had the neck to try it," he said warmly.

"I believe ye!" she said quaintly.

"But it's the truth – an' I'll never forget it."

"A guid memory's a gran' thing! An' when dae ye start wi' yer uncle?"

"Monday week."

"That's quick work. Ye've beat me a' to sticks. Dinna get swelled heid!"

"Christina, I wish ye wudna – "

"I canna help it. It's the theatre, I suppose. Oh, I near forgot to tell ye, yer uncle was in when we got hame frae the theatre. I hadna time to speak to him, for I had to run back to the shop. Hadna even time to change ma dress. I think yer uncle whiles gets tired o' bein' a rich man an' livin' in a swell house. Maybe *you'll* feel that way someday."

He let her run on, now and then glancing wistfully at her pretty, animated face. The happiness, the triumph, he had anticipated were not his. But all the more they were worth working for.

So they came to the place where she lived.

"Come up," she said easily; "I tell't auntie I wud maybe bring ye up for supper."

Doubtless it was the shock of gratification as much as anything that caused him to hang back. She had actually mentioned him to her aunt!

"Will ma uncle be there?" he stammered at last.

"Na, na. Ye'll see plenty o' *him* later on!"

"Maybe yer aunt winna be pleased – "

"Come on, Mac! Ye're ower shy for this world!" she laughed encouragingly.

They went up together.

Christina had a latch-key, and on opening the door, said:

"Oh, they haven't come home yet. Out for a walk, I suppose. But they'll be home in a minute. Come in. There's a peg for your hat."

She led the way into a fire-lit room and turned up the gas. Macgregor saw a homely, cosy parlour, something like his grandfather's at Rothesay, but brighter generally. A round table was trimly laid for supper. In the window a small table supported a typewriter and a pile of printed and manuscript books, the sight of which gave him a sort of sinking feeling.

"Sit down," she said, indicating an easy-chair. "Auntie and uncle won't be long."

He took an ordinary chair, and tried hard to look at his ease.

As she took off her hat at the mirror over the mantelpiece she remarked: "You'll like uncle at once, and you'll like auntie before long. She's still a wee bit prim."

He noticed that her speech had changed with entering the house, but somehow the "genteel English" did not seem so unnatural now. He supposed he would have to learn to speak it, too, presently.

"But she is the best woman in the world," Christina continued, patting her hair, "and she'll be delighted about you going into your uncle's business. I think it was splendid of you managing your aunt so well."

Macgregor smiled faintly. "I doobt it was her that managed me," he said. "But Christina, I'll no' let her be sorry – nor – nor you either."

"Oh, I'm sure you'll get on quickly." she said, gravely, bending to unbutton her long coat.

"I intend to dae that," he cried, uplifted by her words. "Gi'e me a year or twa, an' I'll show ye!"

She slipped out of the coat, and stood for a moment, faintly smiling, in her best frock, a simple thing of pale grey lustre relieved with white, her best black shoes, her best thread stockings, her heavy yellow plait over her left shoulder.

The boy caught his breath.

"Just a minute," she said, and left the room to put away her coat and hat.

Macgregor half turned in his chair, threw his arms upon the back and pressed his brow to his wrist.

So she found him on her return.

"Sore head, Mac?" she asked gently, recovering from her surprise, and going close to him.

"Let me gang," he whispered; "I – I'll never be guid enough."

The slight sound of a key in the outer door reached the girl's ears. She gave her eyes an impatient little rub.

She laid a hand on his shoulder.

"Cheer up!" she said, almost roughly, and stooping quickly, she touched her lips to his hair, so lightly, so tenderly, that he was not aware.

Wee Macgreegor Enlists

Arms And The Maid

THROUGH the gateway flanked by tall recruiting posters came rather hurriedly a youth of no great stature, but of sturdy build and comely enough countenance, including bright brown eyes and fresh complexion. Though the dull morning was coldish, perspiration might have been detected on his forehead. Crossing the street, without glance to right or left, he increased his pace; also, he squared his shoulders and threw up his head with an air that might have been defiance at the fact of his being more than an hour late for his day's work. His face, however, betrayed a certain spiritual emotion not suggestive of anticipated trouble with employer or foreman. As a matter of fact, the familiar everyday duty had ceased to exist for him, and if his new exaltation wavered a little as he neared the warehouse, fifteen minutes later, it was only because he would have to explain things to the uncle who employed him, and to other people; and he was ever shy of speaking about himself.

So he hurried through the warehouse without replying to the chaffing inquires of his mates, and ran upstairs to his uncle's office. He was not afraid of his uncle; on the other hand, he had never received or expected special favour on account of the relationship.

Mr. Purdie was now a big man in the grocery trade. He had a cosy private room with a handsome desk, a rather gorgeous carpet and an easy-chair. He no longer attended at the counter or tied up parcels – except when, alone on the premises late in the evening, he would sometimes furtively serve imaginary customers, just for auld lang syne, as he excused to himself his absurd proceeding.

"But what kep' ye late, Macgreegor?" he inquired, with a futile effort to make his good-humoured, whiskered visage assume a stern expression. "Come, come, oot wi' it! An 'unce o' guid reasons is worth a pun' o' fair apologies."

"The recruitin' office," said Macgregor, blushing, "wasna open till nine."

"The recruitin' office! What – what – guidsake, laddie! dinna tell me ye've been thinkin' o' enlistin'!"

"I've enlisted."

Mr. Purdie fell back in his chair.

"The 9th H.L.I.," said Macgregor, and, as if to improve matters if possible, added, "Glesca Hielanders – Kilts."

The successful grocer sat up, pulled down his waistcoat and made a grimace which he imagined to be a frown. "Neither breeks nor kilts," he declared heavily, "can cover deceit. Ye're under age, Macgreegor. Ye're but eichteen!"

"Nineteen, Uncle Purdie."

"Eh? An' when was ye nineteen?"

"This mornin'."

Mr. Purdie's hand went to his mouth in time to stop a guffaw. Presently he soberly inquired what his nephew's parents had said on the matter.

"I ha'ena tell't them yet."

"Ah, that's bad. What – what made ye enlist?"

Macgregor knew, but could not have put it in words.

"Gettin' tired o' yer job here?"

"Na, Uncle Purdie."

"H'm!" Mr. Purdie fondled his left whisker. "An' when – a – ha'e ye got to – a – jine yer regiment?"

"The morn's mornin'. I believe we're gaun into camp immediately."

"Oho! So ye'll be wantin' to be quit o' yer job here at once. Weel, weel, if ye feel it's yer duty to gang, lad, I suppose it's mines to let ye gang as cheery as I can. But – I maun tell yer aunt." Mr. Purdie rose.

Macgregor smiled dubiously. "*She'll* no' be pleased onyway."

"Aw, ye never can tell what'll please yer aunt. At least, that's been ma experience for quarter o' a century. But it'll be best to tell her – through the 'phone, of course. A handy invention the 'phone. Bide here till I come back."

In a few minutes he returned suppressing a smile.

"I couldna ha'e presumed frae her voice that she was delighted," he reported; "but she commanded me to gi'e ye five pound for accidental expenses, as she calls them, an' yer place here is to be preserved for ye, an' yer wages paid, even supposin' the war gangs on for fifty year."

With these words Mr. Purdie placed five notes in his astonished nephew's hand and bade him begone.

"Ye maun tell yer mither instanter. I canna understan' what way ye didna tell her first."

"I – I was feart I wud maybe be ower wee for the Glesca Hielanders," Macgregor explained.

"Ye seem to me to be a heid taller since yesterday. Weel, weel, God bless ye an' so forth. Come back an' see me in the efternune."

Macgregor went out with a full heart as well as a well-filled pocket. It is hardly likely that the very first "accidental expense" which occurred to him could have been foreseen by Aunt Purdie – yet who shall discover the secrets of that august lady's mind?

On his way home he paused at sundry shop windows – all jewellers'. And he entered one shop, not a jeweller's, but the little stationery and fancy goods shop owned by Miss M. Tod, and managed, with perhaps more conscience than physical toil, by the girl he had been courting for two years without having reached anything that could be termed a definite understanding, though their relations were of the most friendly and confidential nature.

"Mercy!" exclaimed Christina, at his entrance at so unusual an hour; "is the clock aff its onion, or ha'e ye received the sack?"

He was not quick at answering, and she continued: "Ye're ower early, Mac. Yer birthday present'll no be ready till the evenin'. Still, here's wishin' ye many happies, an' may ye keep on improvin'."

He smiled in a fashion that struck her as unfamiliar.

"What's up, Mac?" she asked, kindly. "Surely ye ha'ena cast oot wi' yer uncle?"

"I've enlisted," he softly exploded.

She stared, and the colour rose in her pretty face, but her voice was calm. "Lucky you!" said she.

He was disappointed. Involuntarily he exclaimed: "Ye're no a bit surprised!"

"What regiment?"

He told her, and she informed him that he wouldn't look so bad in a kilt. He announced that he was to report himself on the morrow, and she merely commented, "Quick work."

"But, Christina, ye couldna ha'e guessed I was for enlistin'," he said, after a pause.

"I was afraid – I mean for to say, I fancied ye were the sort to dae it. If I had kent for sure, I wud ha'e been knittin' ye socks instead o' a silly tie for yer birthday."

"Ha'e ye been knittin' a tie for *me*?"

"Uh-ha – strictly platonic, of course."

She had used the word more than once in the past, and he had not derived much comfort from looking it up in the dictionary. But now he was going – he told himself – to be put off no longer. Seating himself at the counter, he briefly recounted his uncle's kindness and his aunt's munificence. Then he attempted to secure her hand.

She evaded his touch, asking how his parents had taken his enlistment. On his answering –

"Dear, dear!" she cried, with more horror than she may have felt, "an here ye are, wastin' the precious time in triflin' conversation wi' me!"

"It's you that's daein' the triflin'," he retorted, with sudden spirit; "an' it's your fau't I'm here noo instead o' at hame."

"Well, I never!" she cried. "I believe I gave ye permission to escort me from these premises at 8 p.m.," she proceeded in her best English, which he hated, "but I have not the slightest recollection of inviting ye to call at 10 a.m. However, the 8 p.m. appointment is hereby cancelled."

"Cancel yer Auntie Kate!" he rejoined, indignant. "Hoo can ye speak like that when dear knows when I'll see ye again?"

"Oh, ye'll no be at the Front for a week or so yet, an' we'll hope for the best. Still, I'll forgive ye, seein' it's yer nineteenth birthday. Only, I'm thinkin' yer parents'll be wantin' ye to keep the hoose the nicht."

Macgregor's collar seemed to be getting tight, for he tugged at it as he said: "I'll tell them I'm gaun oot to see *you*."

"That'll but double the trouble," she said, lightly.

Their eyes met, and for the first time in their acquaintance, perhaps, hers were first to give way.

"Christina," he said, abruptly, "I want to burst that five pound."

"Ye extravagant monkey!"

"On a – a ring."

"A ring! Ha'e ye enlisted as a colonel?" But her levity lacked sparkle.

As for Macgregor, he had dreamed of this moment for ages. "Ye'll tak' it, Christina?" he whispered. "Gi'e me yer size – a hole in a bit pasteboard ... " Speech failed him.

"Me?" she murmured – and shook her head. "Ye're ower young, Mac," she said, gently.

"I'm a year aulder nor you ... Christina, let's get engaged afore I gang – say ye will!"

She moved a little way up the counter and became engrossed in the lurid cover of a penny novel. He moved also until he was directly opposite.

"Christina! ... Yer third finger is aboot the same as ma wee yin."

"Ay; but ye needna remind me o' ma clumsy han's."

"Play fair," he said. "Will ye tak' the ring?"

"I dinna ken, Mac."

But her hand was in his.

Too soon they heard Miss Tod stirring in the back room.

"If ye spend mair nor a pound on a ring," said Christina, "I'll reconsider ma decision!"

"Ye've decided!" he almost shouted.

"No yet," she said, with a gesture of dismissal as Miss Tod entered.

Breaking It Gently

THE quest of the right ring occupied the whole of the forenoon, and Macgregor reached his home in bare time for the family dinner. He desired to break his news as gently as possible, so, after making, to his mother's annoyance, a most wretched meal, he said to his father, who was lighting his pipe, in a voice meant to be natural:

"I got five pound frae Aunt Purdie the day."

"Ye what!" Mr. Robinson dropped the match, and shouted to his wife, who, assisted by their daughter, was starting to wash up. "Lizzie! Did ever ye hear the like? Macgreegor's got five pound frae his Aunt Purdie! Dod, but that's a braw birthday –"

"She said it was for accidental expenses," stammered the son.

Lizzie turned and looked at him. "What ails ye the day, laddie?"

"Uncle Purdie's gaun to keep ma place for me," he floundered.

"Keep yer place for ye!" cried John. "What's a' this aboot accidental expenses? Ha'e ye got hurt?"

Mrs. Robinson came over and laid a damp hand on her boy's shoulder. "Macgreegor, ye needna be feart to tell us. We can thole it." She glanced at her husband, and said, in a voice he had not often heard: "John, oor wee Macgreegor has growed up to be a sojer" – and went back to her dishes.

Later, and just when he ought to be returning to his work, Mr. Robinson, possibly for the mere sake of saying something, requested a view of the five pounds.

"Ay," seconded Lizzie, cheerfully, whilst her hand itched to grab the money and convey it to the bank, "let's see them, laddie." And sister Jeannie and small brother Jimsie likewise gathered round the hero.

With a feeble grin, Macgregor produced his notes.

"He's jist got three!" cried Jimsie.

"Whisht, Jimsie!" whispered Jeannie.

"Seems to ha'e been a bad accident already!" remarked John, laughing boisterously.

"John," said Lizzie, "ye'll be late. Macgreegor'll maybe walk a bit o' the road wi' ye."

They were well on their way to the engineering works, where Mr. Robinson was foreman, when Macgregor managed to say:

"I burst the twa pound on a ring."

"Oho!" said John, gaily; then solemnly, "What kin' o' a ring, Macgreegor?"

"An engagement yin," the ruddy youth replied.

Mr. Robinson laughed, but not very heartily. "Sae lang as it's no a waddin' ring... Weel, weel, this is the day for news." He touched his son's arm. "It'll be the young lass in the stationery shop – her that ye whiles see at yer Uncle Purdie's hoose – eh?"

"Hoo did ye ken?"

"Oh, jist guessed. It's her?"

"Maybe... She hasna ta'en the ring yet."

"But ye think she will, or ye wudna ha'e tell't me. Weel, I'm sure I wish ye luck, Macgreegor. She's a bonny bit lass, rael clever, I wud say, an' – an' gey stylish."

"She's no that stylish – onyway, no stylish like Aunt Purdie."

"Ah, but ye maunna cry doon yer Aunt Purdie – "

"I didna mean that. But ye ken what I mean, fayther."

"Oh, fine, fine," Mr. Robinson replied, thankful that he had not been asked to explain precisely what *he* had meant. "She bides wi' her uncle an' aunt, does she no?" he continued, thoughtfully. "I'm wonderin' what they'll say aboot this. I doobt they'll say ye're faur ower young to be thinkin' o' a wife."

It was on Macgregor's tongue to retort that he had never thought of any such thing, when his father went on –

"An' as for yer mither, it'll be a terrible surprise to her. I suppose ye'll be tellin' her as sune's ye get back?"

"Ay... Are ye no pleased about it?"

"Me?" Mr. Robinson scratched his head. "Takin' it for

granted that ye're serious aboot the thing, I was never pleaseder. Ye can tell yer mither that, if ye like."

Macgregor was used to the paternal helping word at awkward moments, but he had never valued it so much as now. As a matter of fact, he dreaded his mother's frown less than her smile. Yet he need not have dreaded either on this occasion.

He found her in the kitchen, busy over a heap of more or less woolly garments belonging to himself. Jimsie was at afternoon school; Jeannie sat in the little parlour knitting as though life depended thereby.

He sat down in his father's chair by the hearth and lit a cigarette with fingers not quite under control.

"I'll ha'e to send a lot o' things efter ye," Lizzie remarked. "This semmit's had its day."

"I'll be gettin' a bit leave afore we gang to the Front," said Macgregor, as though the months of training were already nearing an end.

"If ye dinna get leave sune, I'll be up at the barracks to ha'e a word wi' the general."

"It'll likely be a camp, mither."

"Aweel, camp or barracks, see an' keep yer feet cosy, an' dinna smoke ower mony ceegarettes." She fell to with her needle.

At the end of a long minute, Macgregor observed to the kettle: "I tell't fayther what I done wi' the twa pound."

"Did ye?"

"Ay. He – he was awfu' pleased."

"Was he?"

Macgregor took a puff at his cold cigarette, and tried again. "He said I was to tell ye he was pleased."

"Oh, did he?"

"Never pleaseder in his life."

"That was nice," commented Lizzie, twirling the thread round the stitching of a button.

He got up, went to the window, looked out, possibly for inspiration, and came back with a little box in his hand.

"That's what I done," he said, dropped it on her sewing, and strolled to the window again.

After a long time, as it seemed, he felt her gaze and heard her voice.

"Macgreegor, are ye in earnest?"

"Sure." He turned to face her, but now she was looking down at the ring.

"It'll be Mistress Baldwin's niece," she said, at last.

"Hoo did ye ken?"

"A nice lass, but ower young like yersel'. An' yet" – she lifted her eyes to his – "ye're auld enough to be a sojer. Does she ken ye've enlisted?"

He nodded, looking away. There was something in his mother's eyes ...

"Aweel," she said, as if to herself, "this war'll pit auld heids on some young shouthers." She got up, laid her seam deliberately on the table, and went to him. She put her arm round him. "Wi' yer King an' yer Country an' yer Christina," she said, with a sort of laugh, "there winna be a great deal o' ye left for yer mither. But she's pleased if you're pleased – this time, at ony rate." She released him. "I maun tell Jeannie," she said, leaving the kitchen.

Jeannie came, and for once that sensible little person talked nonsense. In her eyes, by his engagement, her big brother had simply out-heroed himself.

"Aw, clay up, Jeannie," he cried at last, in his embarrassment. "Come on oot wi' me, an' I'll stan' ye a dizzen sliders."

First Blood

MACGREGOR, his countenance shining with lover's anticipation and Lever's soap, was more surprised than gratified to find Willie Thomson awaiting him at the close-mouth. For Willie, his oldest, if not his choicest friend, had recently jeered at his intention of becoming a soldier, and they had parted on indifferent terms, though Willie had succeeded in adding to a long list of borrowings a fresh item of twopence.

Willie and prosperity were still as far apart as ever, and even Willie could hardly have blamed prosperity for that. He had no deadly vices, but he could not stick to any job for more than a month. He was out of work at present. Having developed into a rather weedy, seedy-looking young man, he was not too proud to sponge on the melancholy maiden aunt who had brought him up, and whose efforts at stern discipline during his earlier years had seemingly proved fruitless. Macgregor was the only human being he could call friend.

"Ye're in a hurry," he now observed, and put the usual question: "Ha'e ye a fag on ye?"

Macgregor obliged, saying as kindly as he could, "I'll maybe see ye later, Wullie."

"Thon girl again, I suppose."

"So long," said Macgregor, shortly.

"Haud on a meenute. I want to speak to ye. Ha'e ye done it?"

"Ay, this mornin'... An' I'm gey busy."

"Ye should leave the weemen alane, an' then ye wud ha'e time to spare."

"What ha'e ye got to speak aboot?" Macgregor impatiently demanded, though he was in good time for his appointment.

"I was thinkin' o' enlistin'," said Willie.

"Oh!" cried his friend, interested. "Ye've changed yer mind, Wullie?"

"I've been conseederin' it for a while back. Ye needna think *you* had onything to dae wi' it," said Willie.

"Ye've been drinkin' beer," his friend remarked, not accusingly, but merely by way of stating a fact.

"So wud you, if ye had ma aunt."

"Maybe I wud," Macgregor sympathetically admitted.

"But ye couldna droon her in twa hauf pints. Ach, I'm fed up wi' her. She startit yatterin' at me the nicht because I askit her for saxpence; so at last I tell't her I wud suner jine Kitchener's nor see her ugly face for anither week."

"What did she say?"

"Said it was the first guid notion ever I had."

"Weel," said Macgregor eagerly, after a slight pause, "since ye're for enlistin', ye'd best dae it the nicht, Wullie."

"I suppose I micht as weel jine your lot," said Willie, carelessly.

Macgregor drew himself up. "The 9th H.L.I. doesna accep' onything that offers."

"I'm as guid as you – an' I'm bigger nor you."

"Ye're bigger, but ye're peely-wally. Still, Wullie, I wud like fine to see ye in ma company."

"Ye've got a neck on ye! *Your* company! ... Aweel, come on an' see me dae it."

In the dusk Macgregor peered at his watch. It told him that the thing could not be done, not if he ran both ways. "I canna manage it, Wullie," he said, with honest regret.

"Then it's off," the contrary William declared.

"What's off?"

"I've changed ma mind. I'm no for the sojerin'."

At this Macgregor bristled, so to speak. He could stand being "codded," but already the Army was sacred to him.

"See here, Wullie, will ye gang an' enlist noo or tak' a hammerin'?"

"Wha'll gi'e me the hammerin'?"

"Come an' see," was the curt reply. Macgregor turned back into the close and led the way to a small yard comprising some sooty earth, several blades of grass and a couple of poles for the support of clothes lines. A little light came from windows above. Here he removed his jacket, hung it carefully on a pole, and began to roll up his sleeves.

"It's ower dark here," Willie complained. "I canna see."

"Ye can feel. Tak' aff yer coat."

Willie knew that despite his inches he was a poor match for the other, yet he was a stubborn chap. "What business is it o' yours whether I enlist or no?" he growled.

"Will ye enlist?"

"I'll see ye damp first!"

"Come on, then!" Macgregor spat lightly on his palms. "I've nae time to waste."

Willie cast his jacket on the ground. "I'll wrastle ye," he said, with a gleam of hope.

"Thenk ye; but I'm no for dirtyin' ma guid claes. Come on!"

To Willie's credit, let it be recorded, he did come on, and so promptly that Macgregor, scarcely prepared, had to take a light tap on the chin. A brief display of thoroughly unscientific boxing ensued, and then Macgregor got home between the eyes. Willie, tripping over his own jacket, dropped to earth.

"I wasna ready that time," he grumbled, sitting up.

Macgregor seized his hand and dragged him to his feet, with the encouraging remark, "Ye'll be readier next time."

In the course of the second round Willie achieved a smart clip on his opponent's ear, but next moment he received, as it seemed, an express train on the point of his nose, and straightway sat down in agony.

"Is't bled, Wullie?" Macgregor presently inquired with compunction as well as satisfaction.

"It's near broke, ye – !" groaned the sufferer, adding, "I kent fine ye wud bate me."

"What for did ye fecht then?"

"Nane o' your business."

"Weel, get up. Yer breeks'll get soakit sittin' there." The victor donned his jacket.

"Ma breeks is nane o' your business neither."

"Ach, Wullie, dinna be a wean. Get up an' shake han's. I've got to gang."

"Gang then! Awa' an' boast to yer girl that ye hut a man on his nose behind his back – "

"Havers, man! What's wrang wi' ye?"

"I'll tell ye what's wrang wi' you, Macgreegor Robi'son!" Willie cleared his throat noisily. "Listen! Ye're ower weel aff. Ye've got a dacent fayther an' mither an' brither an' sister; ye've got a dacent uncle; ye've got a dacent girl... An' what the hell ha'e I got? A rotten aunt! Maybe she canna help bein' rotten, but she is – damp rotten! She wud be gled, though she wud greet, if I got a bullet the morn. There ye are! That's me!"

"Wullie!" Macgregor exclaimed, holding out his hand, which the other ignored.

"I'm rotten, tae," he went on, bitterly. "Fine I ken it. But I never had an equal chance wi' you. I'm no blamin' ye. Ye've aye shared me what ye had. I treated ye ill aboot the enlistin'. But I wasna gaun to enlist to please you, nor ma aunt, neither." He rose slowly and picked up his shabby jacket. "But, by – , I'll enlist to please masel'!" He held out his hand. "There it is, if ye want it, Macgreegor... Ha'e ye a match? Weel, show a licht. Is ma nose queer-like?"

"Ay'" Macgregor unwillingly replied, and, with inspiration, added consolingly, "But it was aye that, Wullie."

The Ring

"WHA was chasin' ye?" Christina inquired, as Macgregor came breathless to the counter, which she was tidying up for the night.

"I was feart I was gaun to be late," he panted.

"I wud ha'e excused ye under the unique circumstances," she said graciously. "Sit doon an' recover yer puff."

He took the chair, saying: "It was Wullie Thomson. He's awa' to enlist."

"Wullie Thompson! Weel, that's a bad egg oot the basket. Hoo did ye manage it, Mac?"

"It wasna me," Macgregor replied, not a little regretfully. "He's enlistin' to please hissel'. He says he's fed up wi' his aunt."

"She's been feedin' him up for a lang while, puir body. But ye're a queer lad," she said softly, "the way ye stick to a fushionless character like him. I was tellin' Miss Tod," she continued, "aboot – "

"Oor engagement!" he burst out, scarlet.

"Whist, man! – ye've a wild imagination! – aboot ye enlistin'. She's been in a state o' patriotic tremulosity ever since. Dinna be surprised if she tries for to kiss ye."

"I wud be mair surprised," said Macgregor, with unexpected boldness, "if you tried it."

"Naething could exceed ma ain amazement," she rejoined, "if I did."

"I've got the ring," he announced, his hand in his pocket.

"Order! Remember, I'm still at the receipt o' custom – three bawbees since seeven o'clock."

"I hope ye'll like it," he said, reluctantly withdrawing his hand empty. "Miss Tod canna hear us, can she?"

"Ye never can tell what a spinster'll hear when she's interested. At present she's nourishin' hersel' on tea – her nineteenth cup for the day; but she'll be comin' shortly to embrace ye an' shut the shop. I micht as weel get on ma hat … An' what did yer parents say to ye?"

"They said ye was an awfu' nice, clever, bonny, handsome lassie – "

"Tit, tit! Aboot the enlistin', I meant. But I'll no ask ye that. They wud be prood, onyway."

"Ma uncle's raised ma wages, an' they're to be payed a' the time I'm awa'."

"Shakespeare! That's a proper uncle to ha'e! But dinna be tempted to stop awa' till ye're a millionaire. Oh, here's Miss Tod. Keep calm. She'll no bite ye."

The little elderly woman who entered had made the acquaintance of Macgregor in his early courting days, especially during the period wherein he had squandered his substance in purchases of innumerable and unnecessary lead pencils, etcetera, doubtless with a view to acquiring merit in her eyes as well as in her assistant's.

She now proceeded to hold his hand, patting it tenderly, while she murmured "brave lad" over and over again, to his exquisite embarrassment.

"But ye'll bate the nesty Rooshians, dearie – I *meant* for to say the Prooshians, Christina – an' ye'll come marchin' hame a conductor or an inspector, or whatever they ca' it, wi' medals on yer breist an' riches in yer purse – "

"An' rings on his fingers an' bells – "

"Noo, noo, lassie, ye're no to mak' fun o' me! Whaur's his case?"

Christina handed her an aluminium cigarette case – the best in the shop – and she presented it to Macgregor, saying: "Ye're no to gang an' hurt yer health wi' smokin'; but when ye tak' a ceegarette, ye'll maybe gi'e a thocht to an auld body that'll be rememberin' ye, baith mornin' an' nicht."

"If he smokes his usual, he'll be thinkin' o' ye every twinty meenutes," remarked the girl, and drawing on her gloves, she came round to the door in order to close an interview which threatened to become lugubrious for all parties.

"Everybody's terrible kind," Macgregor observed, when he found himself alone with Christina on the pavement. "Will ye look at the ring noo?"

She shook her head and stepped out briskly.

After a little while he revived. "I hope ye'll like it, Christina. It's got pearls on it. I hope it'll fit ye." A long pause. "I wish ye wud say something."

"What'll I say?"

"Onything. I never heard ye dumb afore."

"Maybe I'm reformin'."

"Christina!"

"That's ma name, but ye needna tell everybody."

"Dinna tease. We – we ha'e awfu' little time. Tak' aff yer glove an' try the ring. Naebody'll notice. Ye can look at it later on."

"I'm no in the habit o' acceptin' rings frae young men."

"But – but we're engaged."

"That's news, but I doobt it's no official."

"At least we're near engaged. Say we are, Christina."

"This is most embarrassing, Mr. Robinson."

"Aw, Christina!" said the boy, helplessly.

She let him remain in silent suspense for several minutes, until, in fact, they turned into the quiet street of her abode. Then she casually remarked:

"Ma han's gettin' cauld wantin' its glove, Mac."

He seized it joyfully and endeavoured to put the ring on. "It's ower wee!" he cried, aghast.

"That's ma middle finger."

It fitted nicely. Triumphantly he exclaimed: "*Noo* we're engaged!"

She had no rejoinder ready.

"Ye can tak' ma arm, if ye like," he said presently, just a little too confidently.

"I dinna feel in danger o' collapsin' at present," she replied, regarding the ring under the lamp they were passing. "Ye're an extravagant thing!" she went on. "I hope ye got it on appro."

"What – dae ye no like it?"

"I like the feel o' it," she admitted softly, "an' it's real bonny; but ye – ye shouldna ha'e done it, Mac." She made as if to remove the ring.

He caught her hand. "But we're engaged!"

"Ye're ower sure o' that," she said a trifle sharply.

He stared at her.

"Firstly, I never said I wud tak' the ring for keeps," she proceeded. "Secondly, ye ha'ena seen ma uncle yet – "

"I'm no feart for him – if ye back me up. Him an' yer aunt'll dae onything ye like."

"Thirdly, ye ha'e never …" She broke off as they reached the close leading to her home.

"What ha'e I no done, Christina?"

"Never heed… Leave go ma finger."

"Will ye keep the ring?"

"Hoo can I keep the ring when ye ha'e never …" Again the sentence was not completed. She freed her hand and stepped within the close.

"Tell me, an' I'll dae it, Christina," he cried.

She shook her head, smiling rather ruefully.

"Tell me," he pleaded.

"I canna – an' maybe ye wouldna like me ony better if I could." She took off the ring and with a wistful glance at it offered it to him.

He took it, and before she knew, it was on her finger again.

"Ye've jist *got* to keep it!" he said, desperately. "An' Christina, I – I'm gaun to kiss ye!"

"Oh, mercy!"

But he had none…

"Are we engaged or no?" he whispered at last.

"Let me get ma breath."

"Hurry up!"

She laughed, though her eyes were wet. "Oh, dear," she murmured,"I never thought I wud get engaged wi'oot a – a …"

"A what?"

Suddenly she leaned forward and touched his cheek. "Dinna fash yersel', Mac. Bein' in war-time, I suppose the best o' us has got to dae wi'oot some luxury or ither – sich as a proper High-Class Proposal."

In Uniform

THERE happened to be a little delay in providing the later batches of recruits with the garb proper to their battalion, and it was the Monday of their third week in training when Privates Robinson – otherwise Macgregor – and Thomson saw themselves for the first time in the glory of the kilt. Their dismay would doubtless have been overwhelming had they been alone in that glory; even with the numerous comrades in similar distress they displayed much awkwardness and self-consciousness. During drill Willie received several cautions against standing in a semi-sitting attitude, and Macgregor, in his anxiety to avoid his friend's error, made himself ridiculous by standing on his toes, with outstretched neck and fixed, unhappy stare.

As if to intensify the situation, the leave for which they had applied a few days previously was unexpectedly granted for that evening. Before he realized what he was saying, Macgregor had inquired whether he might go without his kilt. Perhaps he was not the first recruit to put it that way. Anyway, the reply was a curt "I don't think."

"I believe ye're ashamed o' the uniform," said Willie, disagreeable under his own disappointment at the verdict.

"Say it again!" snapped Macgregor.

Willie ignored the invitation, and swore by the great god Jings that he would assuredly wear breeks unless something happened. The only thing that may be said to have happened was that he did not wear breeks.

As a matter of fact, Macgregor, with his sturdy figure, carried his kilt rather well. The lanky William, however, gave the impression that he was growing out of it perceptibly, yet inevitably.

Four o'clock saw them started on their way, and with every step from the camp, which now seemed a lost refuge, their kilts felt shorter, their legs longer, their knees larger, their person smaller. Conversation soon dried up. Willie whistled tunelessly through his teeth; Macgregor kept his jaw set and occasionally and inadvertently kicked a loose stone. Down on the main road an electric car bound for Glasgow hove in sight. Simultaneously they started to run. After a few paces they pulled up, as though suddenly conscious of unseemliness, and resumed their sober pace – and lost the car.

They boarded the next, having sacrificed twelve precious minutes of their leave. Of course, they would never have dreamed of travelling "inside" – and yet ... They ascended as gingerly as a pretty girl aware of ungainly ankles surmounts a stile. Arrived safely on the roof, they sat down and puffed each a long breath suggestive of grave peril overcome. They covered their knees as far as they could and as surreptitiously as possible.

Presently, with the help of cigarettes, which they smoked industriously, they began to revive. Their lips were unsealed, though conversation could not be said to gush. They did their best to look like veterans. An old woman smiled rather sadly, but very kindly, in their direction, and Macgregor reddened, while Willie spat in defiance of the displayed regulation.

As the journey proceeded, their talk dwindled. It was after a long pause that Willie said:

"Ye'll be fore hame as sune as we get to Glesca – eh?"

"Ay... An' you'll be for yer aunt's – eh?"

"Ay," Willie sighed, and lowering his voice, said: "What'll ye dae if they laugh at ye?"

"They'll no laugh," Macgregor replied, some indignation in his assurance.

"H'm! ... Maybe *she'll* laugh at ye."

"Nae fears!" But the confident tone was overdone. Macgregor, after all, was not quite sure about Christina. She laughed at so many things. He was to meet her at seven, and of late he had lost sleep wondering how she would receive his first appearance in the kilt. He dreaded her chaff more than any horrors of war that lay before him.

"Aw, she'll laugh, sure enough," croaked Willie. "I wud ha'e naething to dae wi' the weemen, if I was you. Ye canna trust them," added this misogynist of twenty summers.

Macgregor took hold of himself. "What'll ye dae if yer aunt laughs?" he quietly demanded.

"Her? Gor! I never heard her laugh yet – excep' in her sleep efter eatin' a crab. But by Jings, if she laughs at me, I – I'll gang oot an' ha'e a beer!"

"But ye've ta'en the pledge."

"To – ! I forgot aboot that. Weel, I – I'll wait an' see what she's got in for the tea first... But she *canna* laugh. I'll bet ye a packet o' fags she greets."

"I'll tak' ye on!"

It may be said at once that the wager was never decided, for the simple reason that when the time came Willie refused all information – including the fact that his aunt had kissed him. Which is not, alas, to say that his future references to her were to be more respectful than formerly.

At three minutes before seven Macgregor stood outside Miss Tod's little shop, waiting for the departure of a customer. It would be absurd to say that his knees shook, but it is a fact that his spirit trembled. Suspended from a finger of his left hand was a small package of Christina's favourite sweets, which unconsciously he kept spinning all the time. His right hand was chiefly occupied in feeling for a pocket which no longer existed, and then trying to look as if it had been doing something entirely different. He wished the customer would "hurry up"; yet when she emerged at last, he was not ready. He was miserably, desperately afraid of Christina's smile, and just as miserably, desperately desirous to see it again.

Solemnly seven began to toll from a church tower. He pulled himself up. After all, why should she laugh? And if she did – well...

Bracing himself, he strode forward, grasped the rattling handle and pushed. The little signal bell above the door went off with a monstrous "ding" that rang through his spine, and in a condition of feverish moistness he entered, and, halting a pace within, saw in blurred fashion, and seemingly at a great distance, the loveliest thing he knew.

Christina did smile, but it was upon, not at, him. And she said lightly, and by no means unkindly:

"Hullo, Mac! ... Ye've had yer hair cut."

From sheer relief after the long strain, something was bound to give way. The string on his finger snapped and the package, reaching the floor, gaily exploded.

Mrs. McOstrich Entertains

"I'M fed up wi' pairties," was Macgregor's ungracious response when informed at home of the latest invitation. "I dinna ask for leave jist for to gang to a rotten pairty."

"Ay, ye've mair to dae wi' yer leave," his father was beginning, with a wink, when his mother with something of her old asperity, said:

"Macgreegor, that's no the way to speak o' pairties that folk gi'e in yer honour. An' you, John, should think shame o' yersel'. Ye should baith be sayin' it's terrible kind o' Mistress McOstrich to ask ye what nicht wud suit yer convenience."

Macgregor regarded his mother almost as in the days when he addressed her as "Maw" – yet not quite. There was a twinkle in his eye. Evidently she had clean forgotten he had grown up! Possibly she detected the twinkle and perceived her relapse, for she went on quickly –

"Though dear knows hoo Mistress McOstrich can afford to gi'e a pairty wi' her man's trade in its present condeetion."

"She's been daft for gi'ein' pairties since ever I can mind," Mr. Robinson put in, "an' the Kaiser hissel' couldna stop her. Still, Macgreegor, she's an auld frien', an' it wud be a peety to offend her. Ye'll be mair at hame there nor ye was at yer Aunt Purdie's swell affair. Dod, Lizzie, thon was a gorgeous banquet! I never tasted as much nor ett as little; I never heard sich high-class conversation nor felt liker a nap; I never sat on safter chairs nor looked liker a martyr on tin tacks."

Macgregor joined in his father's guffaw, but stopped short, loyalty revolting. Aunt Purdie had meant it kindly.

"Tits, John!" said Lizzie, "ye got on fine excep' when ye let yer wine jeelly drap on the carpet."

"Oho, so there was wine in 't! I fancied it was inebriated-like. But the mistak' I made was in tryin' to kep it when it was descendin'. A duke wud jist ha'e let it gang as if a wine jeelly was naething to him. But, d'ye ken, wife, I was unco uneasy when I discovered the bulk o' it on ma shoe efter we had withdrew to the drawin' room – "

"Haud yer tongue, man! Macgreegor, what nicht'll suit ye?"

"If ye say a nicht, I'll try for it; but I canna be sure o' gettin' a late pass." He was less uncertain when making appointments with Christina.

And Mr. Robinson once more blundered and caused his son to blush by saying: "He wud rayther spend the evenin' wi' his intended – eh, Macgreegor?"

"But she's to be invited!" Lizzie cried triumphantly. "So there ye are!"

"Ah, but that's no the same," John persisted, "as meetin' her quiet-like. When I was courtin' you, Lizzie, did ye no prefer – "

Lizzie ignored her man – the only way. "What aboot Friday, next week?"

"If we're no in Flanders afore then," reluctantly replied the soldier of seven weeks' standing.

Happily for Mrs. McOstrich's sake Macgregor was able to keep the engagement, and credit may be given him for facing the wasted evening with a fairly cheerful countenance. Perhaps Christina, with whom he arrived a little late, did something to mitigate his grudge against his hostess.

Mrs. McOstrich was painfully fluttered by having a real live kiltie in her little parlour, which was adorned as heretofore with ornaments borrowed from the abodes of her guests. Though Macgregor was acquainted with all the guests, she insisted upon solemnly introducing him, along with his betrothed to each individual with the formula: "This is Private Robi'son an' his intended."

While Macgregor grinned miserably, Christina, the stranger, smiled sweetly, if a little disconcertingly.

Then the party settled down again to its sober pleasures. Macgregor possessed a fairly clear memory of the same company in a similar situation a dozen years ago, but the only change which now impressed itself upon him was that Mr. Pumpherston had become much greyer, stouter, shorter of breath, and was no longer funny. And, as in the past, the prodigious snores of Mr. McOstrich, who still followed his trade of baker, sounded at intervals through the wall without causing the company the slightest concern, and were likewise no longer funny.

After supper, which consisted largely of lemonade and pastries, the hostess requested her guests, several being well-nigh torpid, to attend to a song by Mr. Pumpherston. No one (excepting his wife) wanted to hear it, but the Pumpherston song had become traditional with the McOstrich entertainments. One could not have the latter without the former.

"He's got a new sang," Mrs. Pumpherston intimated, with a stimulating glance round the company, "an' he's got a tunin' fork, forbye, that saves him wrastlin' for the richt key, as it were. Tune up, Geordie!"

Mr. Pumpherston deliberately produced the fork, struck it on his knee, winced, muttered "dammit," and gazed upwards. Not so many years ago Macgregor would have exploded; to-night he was occupied in trying to find Christina's hand under the table.

"Doh, me, soh, doh, soh, me, doh," hummed the vocalist.

Christina, who had been looking desperately serious, let out a small squeak and hurriedly blew her nose. Macgregor regarded her in astonishment, and she withdrew the little finger she had permitted him to capture.

"It's a patriotic sang in honour," Mrs. Pumpherston started to explain –

"Ach, woman!" cried her spouse, "ye've made me loss ma key." He re-struck the fork irritably, and proceeded to inform the company – "It's no exac'ly a new sang, but – "

"Ye'll be lossin' yer key again, Geordie."

With a sulky grunt, Mr. Pumpherston once more struck his fork, but this time discreetly on the leg of his chair, and in his own good time made a feeble attack on "Rule, Britannia."

"This is fair rotten," Macgregor muttered at the third verse, resentful that his love should be apparently enjoying it.

"Remember ye're a sojer," she whispered back, "an' thole." But she let him find her hand again.

The drear performance came to an end amid applause sufficient to satisfy Mrs. Pumpherston.

"Excep' when ye cracked on 'arose,' ye managed fine," she said to her perspiring mate, and to the hostess. "What think ye o' that for a patriotic sang, Mistress McOstrich?"

"Oh, splendid – splendid!" replied Mrs. McOstrich with a nervous start. For the last five minutes she had been lost in furtive contemplation of her two youthful guests, her withered countenance more melancholy even than usual.

Ten o'clock struck, and, to Macgregor's ill-disguised delight, Christina rose and said she must be going.

Mrs. McOstrich accompanied the two to the outer door. There she took Christina's hand, stroked it once or twice, and let it go.

"Macgreegor has been a frien' o' mines since he was a gey wee laddie," she said, "an' I'm rael prood to ha'e had his intended in ma hoose. I'll never forget neither o' ye. If I had had a laddie o' ma ain, I couldna ha'e wished him to dae better nor Macgreegor has done – in every way." Abruptly she pressed something into Christina's hand and closed the girl's fingers upon it. "Dinna look at it noo," she went on hastily. "It's yours, dearie, but ye'll gi'e it to Macgreegor when the time comes for him to – to gang. Ma grandfaytheṛ was a dandy in his way, an' it's a' he left me, though I had great expectations."

Gently she pushed the pair of them forth and closed the door.

At the foot of the stair, under a feeble gas-jet, Christina opened her hand, disclosing an old-fashioned ring set with a blood-stone.

"Ye never tell't me she was like that," the girl said softly, yet a little accusingly.

"I never thought," muttered he, truthfully enough.

Willie Stands Up

IT is not the most roughly nurtured of us who will rough it the most cheerfully. Willie Thomson, of harsh and meagre upbringing, was *the* grumbler of his billet. He found fault with the camp fare, accommodation and hours in particular, with the discipline in general. Yet, oddly enough, after a fortnight or so, he seemed to accept the physical drill at 7 a.m. with a sort of dour satisfaction, though he never had a good word to say for it.

His complaints at last exasperated Macgregor, who, on a certain wet evening, when half the men were lounging drearily within the billet, snapped the question:

"What the blazes made ye enlist?"

The answer was unexpected. "You!"

"Ye're a leear!"

With great deliberation Willie arose from the bench on which he had been reclining. He spat on the floor and proceeded to unbutton his tunic.

"Nae man," he declared, as if addressing an audience, "calls me that twicet!"

"Wudna be worth his while," said his friend, carelessly.

"I challenge ye to repeat it."

The tone of the words caused Macgregor to stare, but he said calmly enough: "Either ye was a leear the nicht ye enlisted, or ye're a leear noo. Ye can tak' yer ch'ice."

"An' you can tak' aff yer coat!"

"I dinna need to undress for to gi'e ye a hammerin', if that's what ye're efter. But I'm no gaun to dae it here. We'd baith geet into trouble."

"Ye're henny," said Willie.

Macgregor was more puzzled than angry. Here was Willie positively asking for a punching in public!

"What's wrang wi' ye, Wullie?" he asked in a lowered voice. "Wait till we get oor next leave. The chaps here'll jist laugh at ye."

"It'll maybe be you they'll laugh at. Come on, ye cooard!"

By this time the other fellows had become interested, and one of them, commonly called Jake, the oldest in the billet, came forward.

"What's up, Grocer?" he inquired of Macgregor, who had early earned his nickname thanks to Uncle Purdie's frequent consignments of dainties, which were greatly appreciated by all in the billet.

"He's aff his onion," said Macgregor, disgustedly.

"He says I'm a leear," said Willie, sullenly.

Jake's humorous mouth went straight, not without apparent effort.

"Weel," he said slowly, judicially, "it's maybe a peety to fecht aboot a trifle like that, an' we canna permit kickin', clawin' an' bitin' in this genteel estayblishment; but seein' it's a dull evenin', an' jist for to help for to pass the time, I'll len' ye ma auld boxin' gloves, an' ye can bash awa' till ye're wearit. Sam!" he called over his shoulder, "fetch the gloves, an' I'll see fair play ... I suppose, Grocer, ye dinna want to apologeeze".

Macgregor's reply was to loosen his tunic. He was annoyed with himself and irritated by Willie, but above all he resented the publicity of the affair.

With mock solemnity Jake turned to Willie. "In case o' yer decease, wud ye no like to leave a lovin' message for the aunt we've heard ye blessin' noo an' then?"

"To pot wi' her!" muttered Willie.

A high falsetto voice from the gathering audience cried: "Oh, ye bad boy, come here till I skelp ye!" – and there was a general laugh, in which the hapless object did not join.

"Ach, dinna torment him," Macgregor said impulsively.

While willing hands fixed the gloves on the combatants the necessary floor space was cleared. There were numerous offers of the services of seconds, but the self-constituted master of ceremonies, Jake, vetoed all formalities.

"Let them dae battle in their ain fashion," said he. "It'll be mair fun for us. But it's understood that first blood ends it. Are ye ready, lads? Then get to wark. Nae hittin' ablow the belt."

By this time Macgregor was beginning to feel amused. The sight of Willie and himself in the big gloves tickled him.

"Come on, Wullie," he called cheerfully.

"Am I a leear?" Willie demanded.

"Ye are! – but ye canna help it."

"I can if I like!" yelled Willie, losing his head. "Tak' that!"

A tremendous buffet with the right intended for Macgregor's nose caught his forehead with a sounding whack.

Thus began an extraordinary battle in which there was little attempt at dodging, less at guarding and none at feinting. Each man confined his attentions to his opponent's face and endeavoured to reached the bull's eye, as it were, of the target, though that point was not often attained, and never with spectacular effect. Ere long, however, Macgregor developed a puffiness around his left eye while Willie exhibited a swelling lip. Both soon were pouring out sweat. They fought with frantic enthusiasm and notable waste of energy.

The audience laughed itself into helplessness, gasping advice and encouragement to each with a fine lack of favouritism.

"Wire in, wee yin! Try again, pipe-shanks! Weel hit, Grocer! That had him, Wullie! – ye'll be a corporal afore yer auntie! Haw, Mac, that was a knock-oot, if it had struck! Cheer up, Private Thomson; gi'e him the kidney punch on his whuskers! Guid stroke, Grocer! – fair on his goods entrance! We'll be payin' for to see ye in pictur' hooses yet – the Brithers Basher! Gor, this is better nor a funeral! Keep it up, lads!" And so forth.

But it was far too fast to last. A few minutes, and both were utterly pumped. As though with mutual agreement, they paused panting. Neither had gained any visible advantage.

"Nae blood yet," remarked some one in tones of regret mingled with hope.

"Never heed," interposed Jake, humanely. "Tak' aff their gloves. They've done enough. We'll ca' it a draw – or to be conteenued in oor next dull evenin' – whichever they like. I hope you twa lads 'll never learn scienteefic boxin'. There's ower little fun in the warld nooadays."

Neither offered any resistance to the removal of the gloves.

"Shake han's, lads," said Jake.

To Macgregor's surprise, Willie's hand was out before his own.

"I'm a leear if ye like," said Willie, still panting, "but I can stan' up to ye noo!"

"So ye can," Macgregor admitted – a little reluctantly perhaps, for he had long been used to being the winner.

"If I wasna teetotal," Willie added in a burst of generosity, "I wud stan' ye a drink."

Correspondence

Macgregor to Christina

MY DEAR CHRISTINA, –

I was looking for your letter the whole of yesterday, but it did not come till this morning at 8.35 a.m., and I am sorry to say it is not near as nice as I expected. Some parts is niceish, but others is rotten. What for do you ask me if I have spotted many pretty girls here, when you know I would not be for taking the troubble of spoting any girl in the world but you, and besides they are all terrible ugly here. Yesterday I seen 2 that made me feel sick. Willie said they was on for being picked up, and he give a wink at one of them, and she put out her tongue at him, but no more happened. They was quite young girls, though hiddeous, but Willie did not seem to mind their faces ["mugs" scored out].

Willie is greatly changed since the last few weeks. You would scarcely know him, he is that fond of exercises. He is near as strong as me. They are telling him he will be a corporal before his aunt, and he gets huffy. He spoke too much about his aunt at the beginning, cursing and swearing like, and now he can't get away from it, poor sole. It is a pity she does not send him some small presents now and then. He is awful jealous of the chaps that get things from home; you can tell it by his face and the bad language he uses about the billet and the Zeppelins for 2 hours after. So just for fun, when I was writing to Uncle Purdie, I said please send the next parcel addressed to Pte. Wm. Thomson. Willie got it last night. He never let on he was pleased, but he was. He was freer nor I expected him to be with the groceries, but he eat a tin of salmon all by his lone, and in the middle of the night, at 3.15 a.m., he was took horrid bad, and 7 of the chaps made him take their private meddicines, and he could not turn out for physical exercise in the morning, but is now much better, and has made a good tea, and is eating 1lb. cokernut lozenges at this very minute.

I have no more news. But, dear Christina, I am not well pleased with your letter at all. I am quite disconsoled about it. It makes me feel like wet cold feet that has no hopes of ever getting dry and cosy again. When I seen yourself last Friday night I was not feared for anything, for you was that kind and soft-hearted, and you laughed that gentle and pretty, and your words did sound sweet even when they was chaffing-like. But now I am fearing something has gone wrong. Are you offended? I did not mean to do so. Have you got tired of me? I would think *yes* at once, if you was the common sort of girl, but you are the honest sort that would tell me straight, and not with hints in a letter. So if you are not offended, I think you must have catched a cold in your head, or got something wrong with your inside. Colds in the head is very permanent [?prevalent] in the billet for the present, and the chaps with them are ready to bite your nose off if you say a word to them.

Dear, dear Christina, please tell me what is the matter. I will not sleep well till I hear from you. The stew for dinner to-day was better than the stew yesterday, but I could not take my usual. I am fed up with anxiousness. Kindly write by return. Why do you never put any X X X in your letters? Do you want me to stop putting them in mine?

Your aff. intended,

M. ROBINSON.

P.S. – It is not to be the Dardanelles, but we are likely going to Flanders next week. Excuse writing and spelling as usual. X X X Please write at once.

Christina to Macgregor

DEAR SIR, –

Your esteemed favour duly to hand and contents noted. I deeply regret that my last communication did not meet with your unmitigated approval, but oh, dear wee Mac, I could not write a lovey-dovey letter to save my only neck. In my youth, when penny novels were my sole mental support, I used to see myself pouring forth screeds of beauteous remarks to an adoring swine 6½ ft. high × 2¾ ft. broad. But now it can't be done. Still, I am sorry if my letter hurt you. It was never meant to do that, lad. You must learn to take my chaff and other folks' unseriously. Honest, if I had been really thinking of you along with other girls, I would not have mentioned it. I'm not that sort of girl, and I'm not the sort that gets cold in the head, either, thanking you all the same for kind enquiries. But I'm by no means faultless. I get what the novelists call flippant when I am feeling most solemn. I was a bit down-hearted when I wrote last, for your letter had said "Dardanelles." Now you say "Flanders," which is no better, but I am not going to cry this time. Surely they won't send you away so soon, dear.

Glad to hear Willie is greatly changed, and I hope he will keep on changing, though I could never admire a man that ate a whole tin of salmon in once. I'm sure the two girls were not so dreadfully plain as you report. Had they got their hair up? Girls don't usually put out their tongues at young men after their hair is up, so I presume they were *very* young. It was like you to ask your uncle to send Willie the parcel.

Miss Tod is not so brisk just now. The doctor says she must either drink less tea or become a chronic dyspeptomaniac. She prefers the latter. Poor old thing, her joys are few and simple! Trade is not so bad. A new line in poetical patriotical postcards is going well. The poetry is the worst yet.

I am sending you some cigarettes with my uncle's best wishes and a pair of socks with mine. Perhaps you have enough socks from home already. If so, give them to W. T., and ask him from me to practise blushing. He can begin by winking at himself in a mirror thrice daily.

When are you going to get leave again? Miss Tod says I can get away at 6, any night I want to. No; I don't want you to stop putting those marks in your letters. If you can find one in this letter, you may take it, and I hope it will make you half as happy as I want you to be. Good-night.

CHRISTINA.

The Fat Girl

NEVER a day passed without its camp rumour. If Macgregor was disposed to be over-credulous, his friend Willie was sceptical enough for two.

"I hear we're for the Dardanelles next week," the former observed one afternoon.

Willie snorted. "What the – wud they send us yins to the Dardanelles afore we ken hoo to fire a rifle?"

"I heard it for a fac'," Macgregor returned imperturbably. "They want us yins for begnet wark, no for snipin'."

"Begnet wark! I'll bet ye fifty fags I get a dizzen Turks on ma begnet afore ye get twa on yours!"

Macgregor let the boastful irrelevance pass. "I wonder," he said, thoughtfully, "if we'll get extra leave afore we gang."

"Plenty o' leave! Keep yer mind easy, Macgreegor. It's a million in gold to a rotten banana we never get a bash at onybody. It's fair putrid to think o' a' the terrible hard wark we're daein' here to nae purpose. I wisht I was deid! Can ye len' us a bob?"

"I ha'ena got it, Wullie; honest."

Willie sadly shook his head. "That moll o' yours," said he, "is awfu' expensive. Ye've nae notion o' managin' weemen. Listen, an' I'll tell ye something. Ye mind last Monday? Weel, I had a late pass, that nicht, an' I thocht I wud miss seein' ma aunt's ugly for wance – though it meant missin' a guid meal forbye. So when I got to Glesca I picked up thon fat girl we used to fling rubbish at when we was young. An', by Jings, she was pleased an' prood! She stood me ma tea, includin' twa hot pies, an' she gi'ed me a packet o' fags – guid quality, mind ye! – an' she peyed for first-class sates in a pictur' hoose! That's hoo to dae it, ma lad!" he concluded complacently.

"An' what did you gi'e her?" Macgregor inquired, after a pause.

"Ma comp'ny, likewise some nice fresh air fried in

naething, for I took her for a short walk. I could manage wi' ninepence."

"Ach, I didna think ye was as mean as that, Wullie! Was – was she guid-lookin'?"

"I didna notice her face a great deal; but she's a beezer for stootness. I'm gaun to meet her again on ma next leave. If I tell her we've orders for the Dardanelles, there's nae guessin' what she'll dae for me."

"She maun be unco saft," Macgregor commented pityingly.

"Maybe the kilt had something to dae wi' it," Willie modestly allowed. "They a' adore the kilt. Can ye no spare saxpence ... weel, thruppence?"

"I could spare ye a bat on the ear, but I'll tell ye what I'll dae. I've got some money comin' the morn, an' I'll present ye wi' twa bob, if ye'll tak' yer oath to spend them baith on gi'ein' the fat yin a treat."

Willie gasped. "D'ye think I'm completely mad?"

"There's something wrang wi' ye when ye can sponge aff a girl, even supposin' she's fat. So ye can tak' ma offer or a dashed guid hammerin' when the first chance comes."

"Dinna be sae free wi' yer hammerin's, ma lord! Remember, it was a draw the last time."

"I wasna angry, an' I had gloves on."

Willie considered for a moment and decided to compromise.

"I'll burst a bob on her to please ye."

"Twa – or a hammerin'."

"But what – guid is the siller gaun to dae me, if I squander it a' on her? Ye micht as weel fling it in the Clyde. *She's* no wantin' that sort o' kindness frae me. She prefers a bit cuddle."

"Did ye cuddle her?" Macgregor asked with an interest indifferently concealed.

"Some o' her. But she's earnin' guid money at the – "

"I dinna suppose she wud ha' treated ye excep' she had mair money nor brains."

"She wud pairt wi' her last farden for ma sake!"

"Ach, awa' an' eat grass! It's weel seen that men are scarce the noo."

"Mind wha ye're insultin'!"

"I'm gaun up to the billet." Macgregor said, shortly, and walked off.

Presently, Willie, a new idea in his busy brain, overtook him.

"Macgreegor, if ye len' me thruppence the noo, I'll ca' it a bargain aboot the twa bob."

He got the pennies then, and on the following day a florin, upon which he took a solemn oath. But as he fingered the silver later he smiled secretly and almost serenely. If the fat girl had stood him a substantial meal, cigarettes and a picture entertainment for nothing, what might not he expect as a return for the squandering of two shillings?

As for Macgregor, his motives were probably not unmixed: the pleasure which he foresaw for the poor, fat girl was contingent on the agony of Willie while spending good money on a person other than himself.

However, Willie was not long in securing a late pass, and went upon his jaunt in an apparently chastened state of mind, though in the best possible humour.

He returned in the worst possible.

"Twa bob clean wasted," he grunted, squatting down by Macgregor's bed. "I wish to – I had flung it in the Clyde when we was crossin' the brig."

"What gaed wrang?" inquired Macgregor, rubbing his eyes. "Did she no like yer treat?"

"I'll warrant she did!"

"What did ye buy her wi' the twa bob?"

Willie sniffed at his recollections. "Like a – goat," said he, "I askit her what she wud like best for twa bob, me thinkin' naterally she wud say a feed to stairt wi'. I was ready for a feed masel'. But she squeezed ma airm an' shoved her big face intil mines, an' said she wud like a sooveneer best. To blazes wi' sooveneers! An' she dragged me awa' to a shop, an' I had to buy her a silly-like wee tie that cost me eichteen-pence-ha'penny; an' then she wanted a lang ride on the caur, an' that burst fivepence; an' she nabbed the remainin' bawbee for a keepsake." The reciter paused as if from exhaustion.

"Hurry up!" said Macgregor encouragingly. "What did she gi'e you?"

"A – kiss up a – close! To pot wi' kissin'! An' then she said she was afraid her mither wud be waitin' the ham an' egg supper for her, so she wud need to run, an' she was vexed she couldna meet me again because she had been hearin' I was a terrible bad character. An' then, takin' advantage o' ma surprise, she done a bunk... An' if ever I ha'e ony mair truck wi' weemen, may I be – "

"She wasna as saft as I fancied she was," remarked Macgregor in an uncertain voice. "So ye wud jist gang to yer aunt's for yer supper, efter a'?"

"Ay! An' the auld cat was oot at a prayer-meetin'. I ha'ena had a bite in ma mooth since denner-time. Ha'e ye onything o' yer uncle's handy?"

"I can gi'e ye a wee tin o' corned beef, Wullie. Ye ken whaur to find it."

"Least ye can dae," Willie growled. "Thenk Goad it was your money!"

"I'm thinkin' I've got guid value."

"What?"

"Guid nicht!" And stuffing some blanket into his mouth, Macgregor rolled over and quaked with imprisoned mirth.

The Alarm

IT came, as Christina would have expressed it in her early days, like a "blot from the blue." On a certain fine morning, while battalion drill was in progress, a mounted officer dashed upon the scene and was forthwith engaged in earnest conversation with the colonel. The news was evidently urgent, and it was received with an obvious gravity. A thrill ran through the ranks; you would have fancied you heard breaths of anticipation.

A minute later the companies were making for camp at the double. Arrived there they were instructed to repair to billets and, with all speed, pack up. And presently ammunition was being served out, a hundred rounds to each man; and, later, "iron" rations.

"We're awa' noo!" gasped Macgregor, recovering forcibly from Willie's greedy clutch a pair of socks knitted by Christina.

"Ay, we're awa'; an' I'll bet ye we're for Flanders," said Willie, no less excited.

"Dardanelles!" shouted Macgregor, above the din that filled the billet.

"Flanders!" yelled Willie, wildly, and started to dance – unfortunately upon a thin piece of soap.

"Dardanelles!" Macgregor repeated as he gave his friend a hand up.

"Oh – !" groaned Willie, rubbing the back of his head. "But what'll ye bet?"

"What ha'e ye got?"

"I'll bet ye thruppence – the thruppence ye lent me the day afore yesterday."

"Done! If ye win, we'll be quits; if ye loss – "

"Na, na! If I win, ye'll ha'e to pay me – "

"Ach, I've nae time to listen to ye. I've twa letters to write."

"Letters! What aboot the bet?"

"Awa' an' chase yersel'! Are ye no gaun to drap a line to yer aunt?"

"No dashed likely! She's never sent the postal order I asked her for. If I had got it, I wud ha'e payed what I'm owin' ye, Macgreegor. By heavens, I wud! I'll tak' ma oath I – "

"Aweel, never heed aboot that," Macgregor said, soothingly. "Send her a post caird an' let me get peace for three meenutes."

"Ye canna get peace in this," said Willie, with a glance round the tumultuous billet.

"I can – if ye haud yer silly tongue." Macgregor thereupon got his pad and envelopes (a gift from Miss Tod), squatted on his bed, and proceeded to gnaw his pencil. The voice of the sergeant was heard ordering the men to hurry up.

"I'll tell ye what I'll dae," said Willie, sitting down at his friend's elbow. "I'll bet ye a' I owe ye to a bob it's Flanders. Ye see, I'll maybe get shot, an' I dinna want to dee in debt. An' I'll send the auld cat a caird wi' something nice on it, to please ye… Eh?"

"Aw, onything ye like, but for ony sake clay up! Shift!" cried the distracted Macgregor.

"Weel gi'e's a fag … an' a match," said Willie.

He received them in his face, but merely grinned as he languidly removed himself.

The two scrawls so hastily and under such difficulties produced by Macgregor are sacred. He would never write anything more boyish and loving, nor yet more manly and brave, than those "few lines" to his mother and sweetheart. There was no time left for posting them when the order came to fall in, but he anticipated an opportunity at one of the stations on the journey south.

Out in the sunshine stood the hundreds of lads whose training had been so brief that some carried ammunition for the first time. There were few grave faces, though possibly some of the many grins were more reflected than original. Yet there was a fine general air of eagerness, and at the word "attention" the varied expressions gave place to one of determination.

Boom! boom! boom! … Boom! boom! boom! Dirl and

skirl; skirl and dirl! So to the heart-lifting, hell-raising music of pipes and drums they marched down to the railway.

At the station it seemed as though they had been expected to break all records in military entraining. There was terrific haste and occasional confusion, the latter at the loading of the vans. The enthusiasm was equalled only by the perspiration. But at last everything and nearly everybody was aboard, and the rumour went along that they had actually broken such and such a battalion's record.

Private Willi[illegible] Thomson, however, had already started his in[illegible]ere were eight in the compart- m[illegible]upid[illegible]d to secure a corner seat. [illegible] corp af[illegible]o Dover," he bleated. [illegible] as eve[illegible] bein' a corporal," [illegible] d'ye ken it'll be [illegible]

[illegible]ir wagers. I've a [illegible]g Macgregor – [illegible]e're boun' for [illegible]

[illegible]he question. He [illegible]rgotten to say to [illegible]t the ring she was [illegible] was going, but he [illegible]

[illegible] we're for Flanders! The Ninth [illegible] – "

A sudden silence! What the – was that? Surely not – ay, it was! – an order to detrain!

And soon the whisper went round that they were not bound for anywhere – unless the – old camp. The morning's alarm and all that followed had been merely by way of practice.

At such a time different men have different feelings, or, at least, different ways of expressing them. Jake laughed philosophically and appeared to dismiss the whole affair. Willie swore with a curious and seemingly unnecessary bitterness, at frequent intervals, for the next hour or so. Macgregor remained in a semi-stunned condition of mind until the opportunity came for making a little private bonfire of the two letters; after which melancholy operation he straightway recovered his usual good spirits.

"Never heed, Wullie," he said, later; "we'll get oor chance yet."

Willie exploded. "What for did ye get me to mak' sic a – cod o' masel'?"

"Cod o' yersel'? Me?"

"Ay, you! – gettin' me to send a caird to ma – aunt! What for did ye dae it?"

Macgregor stared. "But ye didna post it," he began.

"Ay, but I did. I gi'ed it to a man at the station."

"Oh! … Weel, ye'll just ha'e to send her anither."

"That'll no mak' me less o' a cod."

"What way? What did ye write on the caird?"

Willie hesitated, muttered a few curses, and said slowly yet savagely: –

" 'Off to Flanders, wi' – wi' kind love' – *oh, dammit*!"

An Invitation

AFTER considering the matter at intervals for about thirty years, Miss Tod, Christina's employer, decided to take a short change of air by accepting the long-standing invitation of an old and aged friend who dwelt in the country. The hour of departure arriving, she shed tears, expressed the fear that she was going to her death, embraced the girl, handed her the keys of the premises, and requested her to make any use she pleased of the rather stuffy living-room behind the shop.

Christina had no notion of accepting the offer until, an hour or two later, the idea struck her that it would be fun to give a little tea party for Macgregor and Willie Thomson. She knew Willie but slightly, but though her respect was no greater than her knowledge, she had kept a softish corner for him since the day, two years ago, when he had gone out of his way to inform her, impudently enough, that his friend Macgregor was *not* courting a certain rather bold and attractive damsel called Jessie Mary.

So she wrote forthwith to Macgregor and enclosed the following invitation, in her neatest writing, for his friend: –

Miss Christina Baldwin
requests the unspeakable
pleasure of Pte. William
Thomson's company
to T. T. Tea
on the first evening possible
(Sunday excepted) at 5.30
precisely till 7 prompt.

Menu.

Sandwiches, Sausage Rolls,
Hot Cookies, Cream Dittos,
Macaroons, Cheesecakes,
Currant Cakes, Jam Puffs,
Imperial (*née* German)
Biscuits,

And

NO BREAD.

God Save the King!

P.S. – Miss C. B. will expect

Pte. W. T. to Ask a Blessing.

It took time and patience on Macgregor's part to persuade his friend that the missive was not a "cod"; but once convinced of its genuineness, Willie took the business seriously. He swore, however, to have nothing to do with the matter of the P.S. Nevertheless, in moments of solitude, his lips might have been observed to move diligently, and it is possible that he was mentally rehearsing "For what we are about to receive, etc." His written acceptance was a model in its way.

"Coming with thanks. – Yours truly, W. THOMSON."

By the same post he wrote to his aunt – for cash; but her reply consisting of a tract headed with a picture of a young man in the remnants of a bath towel dining in a pig-sty, he was compelled once more to appeal to Macgregor, who fortunately happened to be fairly flush. He expended the borrowed shilling on a cane and a packet of Breath Perfumers for himself, and for Christina a box of toffee which, being anhungered while on sentry duty the same night, he speedily devoured with more relish than regret.

Unless we reckon evenings spent in Macgregor's home in the small boy period, and a funeral or two, Willie's experience of tea parties was nil. Despite his frequently expressed contempt for such "footerin' affairs," he was secretly flattered by Christina's invitation. At the same time, he suffered considerable anguish of mind on account of his ignorance of the "fancy behaviour" which he deemed indispensable in the presence of a hostess whom he considered "awfu' genteel." With reluctance, but in sheer desperation, he applied to his seldom-failing friend.

"What the blazes," he began with affected unconcern, "dae ye dae at a tea pairty?"

"Eat an' jaw," came the succinct reply.

"But what dae ye jaw aboot?"

"Onything ye like – as long as ye leave oot the bad language."

"I doobt I'll no ha'e muckle to say," sighed Willie.

"She'll want to hear aboot the camp an' so on," Macgregor said, by way of encouragement.

"But that'll be piper's news to her. You've tell't her – "

"I've never had the time."

Willie gasped. "What the – dae you an' her jaw aboot?"

"Nane o' your business!"

"Haw, haw!" laughed Willie, mirthlessly. "My! but ye're a spoony deevil! – nae offence intendit." The apology was made hastily owing to a sudden change in Macgregor's expression and colour.

Macgregor lit a cigarette and returned his well-stocked aluminium case to his pocket.

The silence was broken by Willie.

"Savin' up?"

"Ay."

"It's a dashed bad habit, Macgreegor. Dinna let it grow on ye. If naebody saved up, everybody wud be weel aff... Aweel, what maun be maun be." And, groaning, Private Thomson drew forth a packet which his friend had "stood" him the previous day. "Regairdin' this tea pairty," he resumed, "are ye supposed to eat a' ye can an' leave what ye canna – if there's onything to leave?"

"She'll expect ye to eat a' ye can."

"It's easy seen she doesna ken me."

"Oh, she'll be prepared for the warst, Wullie," said Macgregor, his good-humour returned. "I can shift a bit masel' when I'm in form."

Whereat Willie's countenance was illuminated by a happy thought. "I'll bet ye a tanner I'll shift mair nor you!"

Macgregor laughed and shook his head. "If you an' me was gaun oor lane to a restewrant, I wud tak' ye on; but – "

"Aw, ye mean it wudna be the thing at a tea pairty?"

"Hardly."

"Weel, weel," said Willie, with sorry resignation, "honest money's ill to earn. It wud ha'e been a snip for me. Ha'e ye a match?" Having lit up: "Tell us what else I maunna dae at the pairty."

Macgregor scratched his head. "If it had been a denner pairty," he said slowly, thinking doubtless of Aunt Purdie's, "I could ha'e gi'ed ye a queer list; but ye canna gang faur wrang at a tea pairty."

"I dinna want to gang an inch wrang."

"Weel, then, for instance, some folk objec's to a chap sookin' his tea frae his saucer – "

"I'll note that. Fire awa'!"

"An' if a cream cookie bursts – "

"Dae they burst whiles?"

"Up yer sleeve, as a rule," said Macgregor very solemnly.

"Guid Goad! I'll pass the cream cookies."

"But they're awfu' tasty."

"Are they? ... Weel, what dae ye dae if it bursts?"

"Never let bug."

"Ay, but – but what aboot the cream?"

"Best cairry an extra hanky an' plug yer sleeve wi' it."

After a dismal pause, Willie inquired: "Could ye no get her to leave the cream cookies oot o' her programme, Macgreegor?"

Macgregor looked dubious. "She's gey saft on them hersel', an' she micht be offendit if we refused them. Of course they dinna scoot up the sleeve every time."

"Oh!" – more hopefully.

"Whiles they explode doon the waistcoat – I mean tunic."

"That's enough!" wailed Willie. "If the Clyde was handy, I wud gang an' droon masel!"

On the third day following, they obtained late passes. Willie's uneasiness was considerable, yet so was his vanity. He affected an absurdly devil-may-care deportment which so stirred Macgregor's sense of pity that he had thoughts of taking back what he had said about the cream cookies. But at the last moment his bootlace snapped...

Willie's toilet was the most careful he had ever made, and included an application of exceeding fragrant pomade pilfered from his corporal's supply and laid on thickly enough to stop a leak. Finally, having armed himself with his new cane and put seven Breath Perfumers and a cigarette in his mouth, he approached the stooping Macgregor and declared himself ready for the road.

"What's that atrocious smell?" demanded Macgregor, with unwonted crustiness.

For once in his life Willie had no answer at hand, and for once he blushed.

A Tea-party

CHRISTINA was serving a customer when her two guests entered the shop. Unembarrassed she beamed on both and signed to Macgregor to go "right in." So Macgregor conducted his friend, who during the journey had betrayed increasing indications of "funk," into the absent owner's living-room, which Christina had contrived to make brighter looking than for many a year.

At the sight of the laden table Willie took fright and declared his intention of doing an immediate "slope." "Ye didna tell me," he complained, "there was to be a big compn'y."

Macgregor grabbed him by the arm. "Keep yer hair on, Wullie. There'll be naebody but the three o' us. There's nae scrimp aboot Christina," he added with pride.

"I believe ye!" responded the reassured guest. "Gor, I never seen as much pastries in a' ma born days – no but what I'm ready to dae ma bit."

Just then Christina entered, remarking:

"It's an awfu' job tryin' to sell what a person doesna want to a person that wants what ye ha'ena got; but I done it this time. Evenin', Mac. Mr. Thomson, I am delighted to meet ye."

"Aw," murmured Willie helplessly.

"Dinna terrify him," Macgregor whispered.

"Sorry," she said with quick compunction. "I'm gled to see ye, Wullie. Sit doon an' feel at hame. The kettle's jist at the bile. See, tak' Miss Tod's chair. She'll like to think that a sojer sat in it. She'll never ha'e been as near to a man. I was askin' her the ither nicht if she had ever had a lad. The answer was in the negative."

"Maybe," Macgregor suggested, "she didna like to tell ye the truth."

Christina smiled gently, saying, "Ye've a lot to learn aboot us females, Mac."

"By Jings, ye're richt there!" Willie exploded, and immediately subsided in confusion.

"Ay," she agreed placidly; "he's no a connoisseur like you, Wullie. Talkin' o' females, hoo's yer aunt keepin'?"

"Rotten – at least she was fine the last time I seen her ugly."

"The decay seems to ha'e been rapid. But, seriously, it's a peety ye canna love yer aunt better – "

"Love her! Oh, help!" The "p" was sounded just in time, and Willie glanced at Macgregor to see whether he had noticed the stumble.

Macgregor, however, had forgotten Willie – unless, perhaps to wish him a hundred miles away. Christina was wearing a new white blouse which showed a little bit of her neck, with a bow of her favourite scarlet at the opening.

"D'ye ken what ma aunt done to me the ither day?" Willie proceeded, craving for sympathy. "I was terrible hard up, an' I wrote her a nice letter on a caird wi' a view o' Glesca Cathedral on it, includin' the grave-yaird – cost me a penny; an' what dae ye think she sent me back? A bl – oomin' trac'!"

At that moment the kettle boiled, and Christina, exclaiming "Oh, mercy!" sprang to the hearth. Over her shoulder she said in a voice that wavered slightly:

"That was hard cheese, Wullie, but ye maun send her a cheerier-like caird next time. I'll stand ye an optimistic specimen afore ye leave the shop."

"Thenk ye! A – of course we'll ha'e to draw the line at picturs o' folk dookin' in the sad sea waves or canoodlin' on the shore – "

Christina, teapot in one hand, kettle in the other, burst out laughing.

"Mind ye dinna burn yersel'!" cried Macgregor, starting into life.

"Haud the kettle, Mac," said she. "It's no fair o' Wullie to be sae funny."

"I wasna funny!" Willie protested.

"It's yer notion o' the optimistic that tickled me," she said. "Pour, Mac; I'm steady noo. But ye're quite richt, Wullie. We canna be ower discreet when cash is involved.

I'll get some high-class cairds for ye to inspect till the tea's infused."

Macgregor would dearly have liked to follow her into the shop.

"She's a clinker," observed Willie under his breath.

"Eh?"

"Naething."

Which was all the conversation during the absence of the hostess.

She returned with a tray. Willie was tempted by a card with the "V. C." emblazoned on it, but feared it would look "swanky" on his part. Though hampered by the adverse criticisms of Macgregor, who naturally wanted to hold Christina's hand under cover of the table as long as possible, he succeeded at last in choosing one entitled "The Soldier's Return," depicting a bronzed youth running to embrace an old lady awaiting him in a cottage porch.

"If that doesna touch the spot," said Christina, "I'm a duchess."

They sat down to tea.

Much to Willie's relief, Christina apparently forgot all about a blessing. Anxious to please, he expressed admiration at the abundance of good things.

"I like to see a table groanin'," said the hospitable hostess.

"There'll be mair nor the table groanin' afore lang," observed Macgregor.

They all laughed like happy people, especially Willie, until with a start he remembered the cream cookies and his omission to bring an extra hanky. All the same, he proceeded to enjoy himself pretty heartily, and did the agreeable to the best of his ability, furnishing sundry anecdotes of camp life which were as new to Macgregor as they probably were to himself. At last –

"Try a cream cookie," said Christina.

But he could not face it. "Cream," he said mournfully, "doesna agree wi' me. The last time I had cream – ma aunt had got it in for her cat that had the staggers – I lay in agony for three days an' three nichts an' several 'oors into the bargain. Ma aunt feared I was gaun to croak ma last."

Macgregor made a choking sound, while Christina gravely hoped that the cat had also recovered, and passed the macaroons.

"Thenk ye," said Willie, and readily resumed operations. But he was not a little disgusted to note presently that Christina and Macgregor enjoyed their cream cookies without the slightest mishap.

His geniality was not fully restored until, at the end of the meal, Christina laid a box of superior cigarettes between her two guests.

"May I drap deid in five meenutes," he declared, "if ever I was treated like this afore! Macgreegor, ye're jist a damp lucky deevil!"

"Oh, whisht!" said Christina smiling.

"Ye should get a girl, Wullie," Macgregor remarked with the air of an old married man.

"I ha'ena your luck, ma lad. If I was trustin' a girl, I'll bet ye a bob she wud turn oot to be yin o' the sort that pinches a chap's wages afore they're warmed in his pooch, an' objec's to him smokin' a fag, an' tak's the huff if he calls her fig-face."

"I'm afraid ye're a pessimist," Christina said. "I used to dae a bit in that line masel'. Ma favourite motto was: 'Cheer up – ye'll soon be deid!' But I got past that, an' so will you."

With a sardonic smile Willie shook his head and took another cigarette; and just then Christina had to go to attend to a customer.

Willie turned to his friend. "Thon was a dirty trick aboot the cookies. I've a guid mind to bide here as lang as you."

"I didna think ye wud hae been feart for a cookie, Wullie. Of course, I'll never tell her."

"Weel, I accep' yer apology. Can ye len' us thruppence? I want to purchase some War Loan... By Jings, ye're no a bad sort, Macgreegor... Hoo dae ye think I behaved masel'?"

"No that bad."

"Weel, I want ye to tell her I ha'ena enjoyed masel' sae

much since ma Uncle Peter's funeral, ten year back."

"Tell her yersel'."

Willie pocketed a few of the superior cigarettes, and rose. "It's sax-thirty," he said. "Her an' you'll be nane the waur o' hauf an' 'oor in private. See? So long! She's a clinker!"

And before Macgregor realized it, Willie had bolted through the shop and into the street.

Christina returned, her eyes wide. "What gaed wrang wi' him, Mac?"

"Come here an' I'll tell ye."

Miss Tod Returns

"IT was awfu' dacent o' Wullie to clear oot," Macgregor remarked happily, as he moved his chair close to the one on which Christina had just seated herself.

Christina's chin went up. "It wud ha'e been dacenter o' him to ha'e waited till the time he was invited to wait."

"But he meant weel. I'm sure he didna want to gang, but he fancied it wud be nice to let you an' me ha'e a – a ..."

"I beg yer pardon?"

"Ach, ye ken what I mean. He fancied we wud enjoy a wee whiley jist by oorsel's."

"Speak for yersel'! I'm thinkin' it was exceedingly rude o' him to slope wi'oot tellin' me he had enjoyed his tea."

"He asked me to tell ye that he hadna enjoyed hissel' sae weel since his uncle's funeral, ten year back."

Christina gave a little sniff. "That's a nice sort o' compliment. Funeral, indeed!"

"Christina! what's vexin' ye?"

"Wha said I was vexed?"

"I've seen ye lookin' happier."

"Are ye a judge o' happiness?"

"I ken when I'm no happy – an' that's the noo. But I warn ye, I'm no gaun to stick it!"

"What's made ye unhappy?" she coldly inquired.

"You!"

"Dear me!" – ironically.

"Ay, jist dear you!" And with these words he caught her round the shoulders and kissed her.

Breathless and rather ruffled she exclaimed, "If ye dae that again, I'll – "

He did it again.

"Ye're gettin' terrible forward," she said, half angry, half amused.

"High time!"

She regarded him with amazement.

Suddenly he said: "Ye're as much mines as I'm yours. Deny it, if ye can."

For perhaps the first time in her life Christina temporized. "Can ye sweer ye didna arrange wi' Wullie to leave early?"

"Eh?"

The note of innocence satisfied her. "Weel," she said graciously, "I forgive ye."

"What for?"

"Takin' liberties."

Her lips wavered to a smile and he could not refrain from kissing them once more.

"Here, hauf time!" she cried, and burst out laughing.

"This is the best yet," he said jubilantly. "Three goals in twa meenutes! In future I'll kiss ye as often as I like."

"We'll see aboot that... The sojerin' has changed ye a lot," she added thoughtfully.

"D'ye no like the improvement?"

"I'll tell ye when I observe it. Noo sit still an' behave yersel', an' tell me the latest camp rumours."

Just then the bell over the door in the shop went off.

"Oh, dash yer customers!" said Macgregor.

Christina was moving from the room when –

"Are ye there, dearie?" called a familiar female voice.

"Holy Moses!" she whispered. "It's Miss Tod, hame three days afore her time."

"Oh, criffens!" gasped Macgregor. "What'll I dae?"

"Ye can either hide in the coal bunker, or bide whaur ye are – like a sojer. She'll no devour ye."

Christina then ran out to receive her employer, which she did without embarrassment.

"What a peety ye're ower late for ma wee tea-pairty. An' hoo are ye?" Macgregor heard her saying.

"Aw, I was sweirt to disturb ye wi' yer frien's, lassie," replied Miss Tod, who had been advised by postcard of Christina's doings, "but I *couldna* bide in thon place anither nicht."

"Dear, dear!" the girl said sympathizingly. "Did ye no get on wi' yer auld frien', or did the poultry attack ye? Come ben, come ben. There's jist Macgreegor left, an' he hasna consumed absolutely everything. I'll get ye a cup o' fresh tea in a jiffy."

Smiling faintly but kindly, Miss Tod greeted Macgregor, apologized for disturbing him, and subsided into her old chair.

"Oh, I'm thenkfu' to be hame," she sighed, while Christina flew to her hospitable duties. "Ye've got the room awfu' nice, dearie."

"Does the smell o' the ceegarettes annoy ye?" inquired Macgregor, now more at ease, though still ashamed of his recent panic.

"Na, na; it's jist deleecious," she protested, "efter the smell o' the country."

"Did ye no like the country, Miss Tod?"

"Maybe I could ha'e endured it till the week was up, if it hadna been for ma auld frien'. Ye see, the puir body couldna speak or think o' onything excep' airyplanes fleein' through the air an' drappin' bombs on her dwellin' hoose an' her hen-hoose, no forgettin' her pig-hoose. Mornin', noon an' nicht, she kep' speirin' at me if I was prepared to meet ma Maker, maybe wantin' a leg. Oh, I was rale vexed for her, I tell ye, but when she took the mattress aff ma bed to protect her sewin' machine frae bombs, I says to masel': 'If I've got to dee, I wud like to dae it as comfortable as I can, an' I'm sure ma Maker'll no objec' to that' ... an' so, at last, I jist tied up ma things in the broon paper, an' said I had enjoyed masel' fine, but was anxious aboot the shop – a terrible falsehood, dearie! – an' gaed to catch the sax o'clock train, an' catched the yin afore it... An' here I am. I wud ha'e let ye enjoy yer pairty in peace, but what wi' the forebodin's o' ma auld frien' an' the scent o' the hens an' pigs, I could thole nae longer."

"In short," Christina brightly remarked, "ye was completely fed up. Weel, weel, ye'll sune forget aboot yer troubles in the joys o' pursuin' pastries. We'll fetch the table close to ye so as ye can fall to wi'oot unduly streetchin' yer neck. Mac, get busy! Toast this cookie."

"She's a great manager," Miss Tod said, smiling to Macgregor. "But she'll mak' ye a rael guid wife when ye come back frae the wars – "

"Oh, whisht, Miss Tod!" cried Christina. "Ye'll cause him to blush." Which was rather a mean way of diverting attention from her own complexion.

However, at that moment the bell rang, and exclaiming, "Anither boom in trade!" she darted into the shop.

The customer seemed to be in a great hurry, for almost immediately she reappeared in the sitting-room. She was smiling and carried a small package in her hand.

"Guess wha it was," said she.

"The meenister," replied Miss Tod, who for some mysterious reason always guessed the reverend gentleman, who happened to be a customer.

"On the contrary," said Christina.

"Wullie Thomson," said Macgregor, suddenly remembering the borrowed threepence.

"Up dux! Ye deserve a sweetie." She presented the bag, open. "What sort are they?"

He laughed and answered – "War Loan Lozengers."

Aunt Purdie Intervenes

THE battalion was not an hour returned from the longest, hottest, dustiest and most exhausting route march yet experienced. Macgregor was stretched on his bed, a newspaper over his face, when an orderly shook him and shoved a visiting card into his hand.

"She's waitin' ootside," he said and, with a laugh, departed.

Macgregor rubbed his eyes and read:

MRS. ROBERT PURDIE.
13, *King's Mansions, W.* *3rd Wednesday.*

"Oh, criffens!" he groaned. "Ma aunt!" And proceeded with more haste than alacrity to tidy himself, while wondering what on earth she had come for.

Willie, scenting profit in a rich relation, though not his own, proffered his company, which was rather curtly refused. Nevertheless, he followed his friend.

Macgregor joined his aunt in the blazing sunshine. Her greeting was kindly if patronizing.

"Sorry to keep ye waitin', Aunt Purdie," he said respectfully. "If I had kent ye was coming' – "

"I understood a good soldier was always prepared to any emergency – "

"Excep' when he's aff duty, mistress." This from Willie, who had taken up his position a little way behind Macgregor, an ingratiating grin on his countenance.

Aunt Purdie drew up her tall, gaunt, richly-clad figure and examined Private Thomson through eye-glasses on a long tortoise-shell handle.

"Macgregor, who is this gentleman?"

"It's jist Wullie Thomson." said Macgregor, annoyed but reluctant to hurt his friend's feelings. "D'ye no mind him?"

"I have a very exclusive memory for faces... Dear me, he is going away!"

It was so. Either the glasses, or being called a gentleman, or both, had been too much even for Willie.

"Is the colonel in the vicinity?" Aunt Purdie demanded, recalling Macgregor's wondering gaze from the retreating figure.

"I couldna say. He's liker to be in a cauld bath."

"You have, of course, informed him who your uncle is?"

"Me an' the colonel ha'ena done much hob-nobbin' as yet," Macgregor said, smiling.

"His mother used to obtain her groceries from your uncle. If you could have presented the colonel to me – well, never mind. I presume the major is on the *quee vive.*"

"He'll be ha'ein' a wash an' brush up, I wud say."

"But why are you not being drilled or digging up trenches or firing guns –"

"We're a' deid men this efternune. Had a big rout mairch the day."

"Oh, indeed! Well, when does the band play?"

"The baun's burstit wi' the rout mairch. It couldna blaw the ash aff a ceegarette. I'm rael sorry –"

"I would like to inspect the apartments you live in. Pray conduct me –"

"Some o' the chaps is cleanin' theirsel's. If ye like, I'll tell them to hurry up or get ablow the blankets."

"Certainly not!" said Mrs. Purdie with decision. "Is there no tea-room adjacent?"

"Jist the canteen. I doobt I couldna tak' ye inside, but I could fetch ye oot a drink – something T. T., I suppose?"

She waved the offer away. "Is there nothing to be perceived or observed in this camp?" she inquired with some impatience.

Her nephew scratched his head. "Weel," he said at last, "there's the view frae this end, an' there's the view frae the ither end. I'm sorry ye've come when there's naething daein',"

"So am I. However, it is not the time to indulge in discriminations. Your uncle thought it was better for me to come than to write a letter."

"Is onything wrang wi' ma uncle?" Macgregor asked anxiously.

"Barring an invidious bunion, he is in his usual health. But we are going to Aberdeen to-morrow, for a fortnight, and we have invited your intended to come with us. She – "

"Christina! But she canna gang awa' to Aberdeen when – " He stopped short, at a loss. He had an appointment with Christina for the following evening. Surely –

"I arranged with Miss Tod this morning. Christina will be writing to you, I presume."

"She – she's gaun wi' ye?"

"Certainly – D. V., of course."

"For a – a fortnicht?"

"The change will be good for her. You must not be selfish. Your uncle was afraid you might be put out: that is why I came to explain. But apart from the beneficial change, Christina, as I observed to your uncle, ought to see the world while she is young." Macgregor answered nothing. Possibly he did not catch her latter remarks. Christina going away for a fortnight, and he might be ordered abroad at any moment!

"Come," said his aunt, kindly enough, "don't be huffy."

Mercifully, just then an officer passed. In the action of saluting Macgregor regained self-control.

"I hope ye get guid weather at Aberdeen," he managed to say, and his aunt admired him even more than at the hour of his enlistment.

"Yer uncle an' me jist wishes ye was free to jine us," she said with unwonted warmth and homeliness of accent. Her hand went to the fastening of her purse, and hesitated. No! Something told her this was not the moment for a gift, however splendid.

"Well, I must be going," she remarked, stiffening again. "Kindly conduct me to the exit. I thought there would have been more to inspire the mind in this place... Good-bye. We will take good care of Christina."

Never in his life had Macgregor been so deeply hurt and angered – not even in the old days by Aunt Purdie, who was not now the object of his resentment.

Willie, who always tried to make the best of things, insults not excepted, approached presently with a hopeful appeal for a loan.

"Gang to blazes!" was the response.

Willie could scarce believe his ears. "Macgreegor! did she no cough up onything?"

Macgregor walked on.

"An' she fancies hersel' for a – swell!" exclaimed Willie viciously.

"Anither word an' I'll knock the face aff ye!"

It was Willie's turn to feel resentment.

In the evening came a note from Christina, hurriedly written. She was terribly busy getting ready for the morning train. It was most kind of Mrs. Purdie. Her own uncle must have let drop to Mr. Purdie that a summer outing this year was not possible, and Mr. Purdie must have told Mrs. Purdie... Of course, she, Christina, would never have dreamed of going away otherwise. But the time would soon pass, Mac, and she intended to enjoy it thoroughly...

If only she had left out that last sentence! But what true lover has not been stabbed by something very like it in his time?

The Fat Girl Again

MACGREGOR dropped his reply to Christina's unsatisfactory note into the pillar-box and, half wishing he had destroyed it instead, rejoined the faithful Willie Thomson. He still looked so gloomy that Willie once more demanded to be told what the – was "up" with him. Receiving no response, Willie remarked:

"If ye tak' a face like that to yer girl, she'll be wantin' to play a tune on it."

Macgregor held his peace. They had just arrived in Glasgow, but without a trace of the usual eagerness on his part.

"I believe," said Willie, with an inspiration, "her an' you ha'e cast oot."

"Clay up! She's awa' her holidays."

"Save us! Awa' her holidays!" cried Willie, uttering, unawares, his friend's bitterest thought –"an' we may get oor mairchin' orders ony meenute! Weel, weel, preserve me frae the female sect! I suppose ye'll be for gi'ein' yer ain folk a treat for a change."

"They're a' at Rothesay, at Granpaw Purdie's," Macgregor returned shortly, now half glad that he had let the letter go.

It was not a harsh letter, yet neither was it a humble one. In effect, it informed Christina that she was welcome to disport herself even though the writer lay dead in a trench. While intended to be freezing, it had been written in considerable heat, physical and mental.

"Then what are ye gaun to dae the nicht?" Willie pursued, his mind simmering with curiosity. Macgregor had been very queer since his aunt's visit of the previous afternoon, and the arrival of a letter, eagerly grabbed, had by no means mitigated the queerness. Willie was convinced that something had gone wrong between Macgregor and Christina. He would not be sorry to see the engagement broken. Macgregor would have more time and cash to spend on his friends. On the other hand, Christina was undoubtedly a "clinker" in her way, and Willie could do with more hospitality like hers. Well, there was no saying what might happen if she were free and Macgregor attached to another girl...

"What are ye gaun to dae the nicht, Macgreegor?" he repeated, rousing himself as well as his friend.

"Dear knows," came the dreary answer. "I think I'll awa' back to the camp." Yet if he did not greatly desire Willie's company, he desired his own less.

"Cheer up for ony favour," said Willie. "If I could afford it, I wud stan' ye a feed."

The hint was not taken, and they strolled on, aimlessly so far as Macgregor was concerned.

About six o'clock, and while they were passing a large drapery warehouse, Willie gave his friend a violent nudge and hoarsely whispered:

"Gor! See thon!"

"What?"

"Thon girl!" – pointing to a damsel in a dark skirt and pink blouse, who had just emerged from the warehouse.

"What aboot her?" said Macgregor impatiently.

"It's her – the fat yin – the girl I burst the twa bob on!"

"She's no that fat," Macgregor remarked without interest. Then suddenly – "Here! What are ye efter?"

"Her! She's fat when ye're close to her. Come on! I'll introjuice ye."

"Thenk ye! I'm no takin' ony."

"Jist for fun. I want to see her face when she sees me again."

"Weel, I'll no prevent ye. So long."

At that moment the girl was held up at a busy crossing.

"Hullo, Maggie!" said Willie pertly.

"I'm off," said Macgregor – but his arm was gripped.

The girl turned. "Hullo," she said coolly; "still livin'?" Catching sight of Macgregor, she giggled. It was not an unpleasing giggle. Lean girls cannot produce it.

"This is Private Macgreegor Robi'son," said Willie, unabashed.

She smiled and held out her hand. After a moment she said to Willie: "Are ye no gaun to tell him ma name, stupid?"

"I forget it except the Maggie."

"Aweel," she said good-humouredly, "Private Robi'son'll jist ha'e to content hissel' wi' that, though it's a terrible common name." She did the giggle again.

The chance of crossing came, and they all moved over; on the crowded pavement it was impossible to proceed three abreast.

"Never mind me." said Willie humorously.

"Wha's mindin' you?" she retorted.

"Gettin' hame?" said Macgregor with an effort at politeness, while fuming inwardly.

"Jist that. Awfu' warm weather, is't no? It was fair meltin' in the warehoose the day. I'm fair dished up." She heaved a sigh, which was no more unpleasing than her giggle. "It's killin' weather for you sojer lads," she added kindly.

Macgregor experienced a wavelet of sympathy. "Wud ye like a slider?" he asked abruptly.

"Ye're awfu' kind. I could dae wi' it fine."

Presently the three were seated in an ice-cream saloon. The conversation was supplied mainly by the girl and Willie, and took the form of a wordy sparring match. Every time she scored a point the girl glanced at Macgregor. He became mildly amused by her repartee, and at last took a cautious look at her.

She was certainly stout, but not with a clumsy stoutness; in fact, her figure was rather attractive. She had dark brown hair, long lashed, soft, dark eyes, a provocative, mobile mouth, and a nice pinky-tan colouring. At the same time, she was too frankly forward and consistently impudent for Macgregor's taste; and he noticed that her hands were not pretty like Christina's.

She caught his eye, and he smiled back, but absently. He was wondering what Christina was doing and how she would take his letter in the morning... He consulted his watch. A long, empty evening lay before him. How on earth was he to fill it? He wanted distraction, and already his companions' chaff was getting tiresome.

On the spur of the moment – "What aboot a pictur hoose?" he said.

"That's the cheese!" cried Willie.

But Maggie shook her head and sighed, and explained that her mother was expecting her home for tea, and sighed again.

"Ha'e yer tea wi' us," said the hospitable Macgregor.

She glanced at him under lowered lashes, her colour rising. "My! ye're awfu' kind," she said softly. "I wish to goodness I could."

"Scoot hame an' tell yer mither, an' we'll wait for ye here," said stage-manager William.

"I wudna trust *you* ... but I think I could trust *him*."

"Oh, we'll wait sure enough," Macgregor said indifferently.

"I'll risk it!" she cried, and straightway departed.

Willie grinned at his friend. "What dae ye think o' fat Maggie?" he said.

"Naething," answered Mac, and refused to be drawn into further conversation.

Within half an hour she was back, flushed and bright of eye. She had on a pink print, crisp and fresh, a flowery hat, gloves carefully mended, neat shoes and transparent stockings.

"By Jings, ye're dressed to kill at a thoosan' yairds!" Willie observed.

Ignoring him, she looked anxiously for the other's approval.

"D'ye like hot pies?" he inquired, rising and stretching himself.

An hour later, in the picture house a heartrending, soul thrilling melodrama was at its last gasp. The long suffering heroine was in the arms of the long misjudged, misfortune-ridden, but ever faithful hero.

"Oh, lovely!" murmured Maggie.

Macgregor said nothing, but his eyes were moist. He may, or may not, have been conscious of a plump, warm, thinly-clad shoulder close against his arm.

Hero and heroine vanished. The lights went up. Macgregor blew his nose, then looked past the fat girl to make a scoffing remark to Willie.

But Willie's seat was vacant.

Maggie laid her ungloved hand on the adjoining seat. "It's warm," she informed Macgregor. "He canna be lang awa'."

"Did he no say he was comin' back?" Macgregor asked rather irritably.

"He never said a word to me. I didna notice him gang: I was that ta'en up wi' the picturs. But never heed," she went on cheerfully; "it's a guid riddance o' bad rubbish. I wonder what's next on the prog –"

"But this'll no dae! He – he's your frien'."

"Him! Excuse me for seemin' to smile I can tell ye I was surprised to see a dacent-like chap like you sae chummy wi' sic a bad character as him."

"Aw, Wullie Thomsons's no near as bad as his character. A' the same, he had nae business to slope wi'oot lettin' us ken. But he'll likely be comin' back. We'll wait for five meenutes an' see."

Maggie drew herself up. "I prefer no to wait where I'm no welcome," she said in a deeply offended tone, and made to rise.

He caught her plump arm. "Wha said ye wasna welcome? Eat yer sweeties an' dinna talk nonsense. If ye want to see the rest o' the picturs, I'm on. I've naething else to dae the nicht."

After a slight pause. "Dae ye want me to bide – Macgreegor?"

"I'm asking ye."

She sighed. "Ye're a queer lad. What's yer age?"

"Nineteen."

"Same as mines!" She was twenty-two. "When's yer birthday?"

"Third o' Mairch."

"Same again!" She had been born on the 14th of December. "My! that's a strange dooble coincidence! We ought to be guid frien's you an' me."

"What for no?" said Macgregor carelessly. Once more the house was darkened. A comic film was unrolled. Now and then Macgregor chuckled with moderate heartiness.

"Enjoyin' yersel'?" she said in a chocolate whisper, close to his ear.

"So, so."

"Ye're like me. I prefer the serious picturs. Real life an' true love for me! Ha'e a sweetie? Oh, ye're smokin'. As I was sayin', ye're a queer lad, Macgreegor." She leaned against his arm. "What made ye stan' me a slider, an' a champion tea, an' they nice sweeties, an' a best sate in a pictur hoose – when ye wasna extra keen on ma comp'ny?"

"Dear knows."

She drew away from him so smartly that he turned his face towards her. "Oh, crool!" she murmured, and put her handkerchief to her eyes.

"Dinna dae that!" he whispered, alarmed. "What's up?"

"Ye – ye insulted me."

"Insulted ye! Guid kens I didna mean it. What did I say?"

"Oh, dear, I'll never get ower it."

"Havers! I'll apologize if ye tell me what I said. Dinna greet, for ony favour. Ye'll ha'e the folk lookin' at us. Listen, Mary – that's yer name, is't no?"

"It's Maggie, ye impiddent thing!"

"Weel, Maggie, I apologize for whatever I said, whether I said it or no. I'm no ma usual the nicht, so ye maun try for to excuse me. I certainly never meant for to hurt yer feelin's."

She dropped the handkerchief. "Ha'e ye got a sair heid?"

"Ay – something like that. So let me doon easy."

She slid her hand under his which was overhanging the division between the seats."I'm sorry I was silly, but I'm that tender-hearted, I was feart ye was takin' yer fun aff me. I'm awfu' vexed ye've got a sair heid. I suppose it's the heat.

Ony objection to me callin' ye Macgreegor?"

"That's a' richt," he replied kindly but uneasily.

Her fingers were round his, and seemingly she forgot they were there, even when the lights went up. And he hadn't the courage – shall we say? – to withdraw them.

The succeeding film depicted a throbbing love story.

"This is mair in oor line," she remarked confidentially.

Every time the sentiment rose to a high temperature, which was pretty often, Macgregor felt a warm pressure on his fingers. He had never before had a similar experience, not even in the half-forgotten days of Jessie Mary; for Jessie Mary had not become the pursuer until he had betrayed anxiety to escape from her toils. And he had been only seventeen then.

The warm pressure made him uncomfortable, but not physically so – and, apart from conscience, perhaps not altogether spiritually so. For, after all, it's a very sore young manly heart, indeed, that can refuse the solace, or distraction, offered in the close proximity of young womanhood of the Maggie sort and shape. In other words, Macgregor may have been conscientiously afraid, but he had no disposition to run away.

About nine-thirty they came out. While he looked a little dazed and defiant, she appeared entirely happy and self-possessed, with her hand in his arm as though he had belonged to her for quite a long time. But at the gorgeous portals she stopped short with a cry of dismay. It was raining heavily.

"I've nae umburella," she said, piteously regarding her fine feathers. "Ma things'll be ruined."

"I'll get ye a cab," he said after some hesitation induced less by consideration of the expense than by the sheer novelty of the proceeding. Ere she could respond he was gone. Not without trouble and a thorough drenching he discovered a decrepit four-wheeler.

Maggie had never been so proud as at the moment when he handed her in, awkwardly enough, but with a certain shy respectfulness which she found entirely delicious.

He gave the man the address, learned the fare, then came back to the door and handed the girl the necessary money.

"Na!" she cried in a panic, "I'll no gang unless ye come wi' me. I – I wud be feart to sit ma lane in the cab. Come, lad; ye've plenty time."

He had no more than enough, but he got in after telling the man to drive as quickly as possible.

"Sit here," she said, patting the cushion at her side.

He obeyed, and then followed a long pause while the cab rattled over the granite. She unpinned and removed her hat and leaned against him heavily yet softly.

"Ye're no sayin' a great deal," she remarked at last. "What girl are ye thinkin' aboot?"

"Ach, I'm dashed wearit," he said. "I didna sleep a wink last nicht."

"Puir sojer laddie!" Her smooth, hot cheek touched his. "Pit yer heid on ma shouther… I like ye because ye're shy… but ye needna be ower shy."

Suddenly he gave a foolish laugh and thrust his arm round her waist. She heaved a sigh of content.

By making all haste Macgregor managed to get back to the camp in advance of Willie. He was in bed, his eyes hard shut, when his friend appeared in the billet.

Willie, who was unusually flushed, bent over him and, sniggering, asked questions. Getting no response, he retired grinning and winking at no one in particular.

Macgregor did not sleep well. If you could have listened to his secret thoughts you would have heard, among other dreary things –

"But I didna kiss her; I didna kiss her"

Conscience And A Cocoa-nut

WITH one thing and another Christina, during her first evening in Aberdeen, had no opportunity of sending her betrothed more than a postcard announcing her safe arrival; but she went to bed with every intention of sending him on the morrow the longest and sweetest letter she had ever written. The receipt of Macgregor's letter, with all its implied reproaches, however, not only hurt her feelings, but set her pride up in arms. "He had nae business to write as if I was a selfish thing; as if I had nae right to decide for masel'!" As a matter of fact, her sole reason for accepting Mrs. Purdie's invitation had been a fear of offending Macgregor's important relatives by a refusal. Heaven knew she had not wanted to put 150 miles between her lad and herself at such a time.

Still, as Macgregor might have known by now, it was always a mistake to try to hustle Christina in any way. Her reply condescended neither to explanations nor defence. Written in her superior, and rather high-flown English, which she was well aware he detested, it practically ignored his epistle and took the form of an essay on the delights of travel, the charm of residence in the Northern City, the kindliness and generosity of host and hostess. She was not without compunction, especially when Uncle Purdie expressed the hope that she was sending the lad something to "keep up his pecker," but she let the letter go, telling herself that it would be "good for him."

The postcard was received by Macgregor after an uneasy night and a shameful awakening. The meagre message made him more miserable than angry. In the circumstances it was, he felt bound to admit, as much as he deserved. Mercifully, Willie had such a "rotten head" that he was unable to plague his unhappy friend, and the day turned out to be a particularly busy one for the battalion. Next morning brought the letter. Macgregor was furious, until Conscience asked him what he had to complain about.

Willie, his mischievous self again, got in a nasty one by inquiring how much he had paid for the cab the night before last.

"Ye dirty spy!" cried Macgregor. "What for did ye hook it in the pictur' hoose an' leave her wi' me? She was *your* affair."

"I never asked her to spend the evenin'," Willie retorted, truthfully enough. "Twa's comp'ny."

Macgregor felt his face growing hot. With an effort he said coldly: "If ye had stopped wi' us ye wudna ha'e been back at the beer an' broke yer pledge."

"Wha tell't ye I was at the beer?"

"Yer breath, ye eediot!"

"Ho! so ye was pretendin' ye was sleepin' when I spoke to ye! Cooard to smell a man's breath wi' yer eyes shut!"

Macgregor turned wearily away. "It's nae odds to me what ye drink," he said.

"Ye should think shame to say a thing like that to a chap that hasna tasted but wance for near a year – at least, for several months," said Willie, following. "But I'll forgive ye like a Christian... For peety's sake len' us a tanner. I ha'ena had a fag since yesterday. I'll no split on ye." He winked and nudged Macgregor. "Maggie's a whale for the cuddlin' – eh?"

It was too much. Macgregor turned and struck, and Willie went down. Then Macgregor, feeling sick of himself and the whole world, assisted the fallen one to his feet, shoved a shilling into his hand, and departed hastily.

He wrote a long, pleading letter to Christina and posted it – in the cook's fire. Next day he tried again, avoiding personal matters. The result was a long rambling dissertation on musketry and the effect of the wind, etcetera, on one's shots, all of which, with his best love, he forwarded to Aberdeen. In previous letters he had scarcely ever referred to his training, and then with the utmost brevity.

The letter, quite apart from its technicalities, puzzled Christina; and to puzzle Christina was to annoy her. To her mind it seemed to have been written for the sake of covering so much paper. Of course she wanted Macgregor to be interested in his work, but not to the exclusion of herself. She allowed the thing to rankle for three days. Then, as there was no further word from him, she became a little alarmed. But it was not in her to write all she felt, and so she sought to break the tension with something in the way of a joke.

Thus it came about that on the fifth morning, Macgregor received a postcard depicting a light-house on a rocky coast and bearing a few written words, also an oddly shaped parcel. The written words were: –

"Delighted to hear you are doing so well at the shooting. Sending prize by same post."

This was better! – more like Christina herself. All was not lost! Eagerly he tore off the numerous wrappings and disclosed a – cocoa-nut! In his present state of mind he would have preferred an infernal machine. A cocoa-nut! She was just laughing at him! He was about to conceal the nut when Willie appeared.

"My! ye're the lucky deevil, Macgreegor! Frae yer uncle, I suppose. I'll help ye to crack it. I'll toss ye for the milk – if there's ony."

"I'm no gaun to crack it the noo, Wullie," Macgregor said, restraining himself.

"At nicht – eh?"

"I'll see."

By evening, however, Willie was not thinking of cocoanuts or, indeed, of anything in the nature of eatables. His first experience in firing a rifle had taken place that afternoon and had left him with an aching jaw and a highly swollen face. On the morrow he was not much better.

"I'll no be able to use ma late pass the nicht," he said bitterly.

"I'm no carin' whether I use mines or no," Macgregor remarked from the depths of his dejection.

Willie gave him a grostesque wink, and observed: "I believe ye're feart to gang into Glesca noo. Oh, they weemen!"

"If ye hadna a face for pies already, I wud gi'e ye yin!"

"Ah, but ye daurna strike a man that's been wounded in his country's service. Aw, gor, I wisht I had never enlisted! What country's worth a mug like this? ... Which girl are ye maist feart for, Macgreegor?"

Macgregor fled from the tormentor. He had not intended to use his late pass, but Willie's taunt had altered everything. Afraid? He would soon show Willie! Also he would show Maggie! Likewise he would show – Well, Christina had no business to behave as if she were the only girl in the world, as if he were a fool. He had a right to enjoy himself, too. He had suffered enough, and the cocoa-nut was the limit! ...

"Are ye for Glesca?" Willie persisted when Macgregor was giving himself a "tosh up" in the billet.

"Ay, am I!" he snapped at last.

"Hurray for the hero! Weel, gi'e Maggie yin on the squeaker frae me, an' tell her no to greet for me, because I'm no worthy o' her pure unselfish love, etceetera. I doobt the weather's gaun to be ower fine for cabs the nicht, but dinna despair; it's gettin' dark fairly early noo. Enjoy yersel' while ye're young."

"That's enough," said Macgregor. "Ye needna think ye're the only chap that kens a thing or twa!" And he left William gaping as widely as his painful jaw would permit.

On the way to town he decided to leave the whole affair to chance; that is to say, he would not arrive at the warehouse where the fat girl was employed until *after* the usual closing hour of six. If she had gone, no matter; if she was still there, well, he couldn't help it.

He arrived at 6.3, and she was there – in her fine feathers, too. She could not have expected him, he knew, but evidently she had hoped. He felt flattered and soothed, being unaware that she had had another swain in reserve in case he should fail her.

"Fancy meetin' you!" she exclaimed, with a start of surprise. "Where's the bad character?"

"Gumbile," answered Macgregor, who would not for worlds have betrayed his friend's lack of skill with the rifle.

"Lang may it bile!" she remarked unfeeling. "Wha are ye chasin' the nicht, Macgreegor?"

"You!" he replied more boldly than brightly.

"My! ye're gettin' quite forward-like," she said, with that pleasant giggle of hers.

"High time!" said he, recklessly.

After tea they went west and sat in the park. It was a lovely, hazy evening.

"Wud ye rayther be in a pictur' hoose, Maggie?"

"What's a pictur' hoose to be compared wi' this? If Heaven's like this, I'm prepared to dee." With three rose-flavoured jujubes in her mouth, she sighed and nestled against him.

In silence his arm went round her waist.

While waiting for the car back to camp he wrote on a picture postcard – "Cocoa-nut received with thanks. I wish I was dead," – and dropped it into a pillar box.

About the same hour, in the billet, Willie was disposing of the cocoa-nut by raffle, tickets one penny each.

"A queer-like present to get frae yer aunt," said some one.

"Ay; but she's a queer-like aunt," said Willie, pocketing the useful sum of tenpence.

“Fondest Love From Maggie”

MORNING brought no letter from Christina, but at breakfast time Macgregor received the astounding intimation that he was granted three days’ leave, the same to commence with the very next hour.

“What’s the guid o’ leave wi’ a jaw like this?” wailed the lop-sided William who, with several other members of the billet, had been included in the dispensation.

“I’ll tell ye what it means, onyway,” said Lance-corporal Jake; “it means that we’ll be gettin’ a move on afore we’re mony days aulder.”

Macgregor did not enter into any of the discussions which followed. Having hurriedly made himself as smart as possible, he took car for Glasgow, and there caught the ten o’clock train for Aberdeen. He spent the ensuing four hours in wondering – not so much what he should say to Christina as what she would say to him. For himself, he was determined to make a clean breast of it; at the same time, he was not going to absolve Christina of all responsibility. He had behaved like a fool, he admitted, but he still had a just grievance. Yet it was with no very stout heart that he alighted in the big station, where everything was strange except the colour of khaki, and found his way to the quiet hotel where his friends had rooms.

And there on the steps was Uncle Purdie sunning himself and smoking a richly-banded cigar – by order of his spouse.

“Preserve us!” exclaimed Uncle Purdie in sheer astonishment at the sight of his nephew. “Preserve us!” he repeated in quite another tone – that of concern. “But I’m rael glad to see ye, lad,” he went on somewhat uneasily, “an’ yer aunt’ll be unco pleased. Come awa’ in, come awa’ in! Ye’ve gotten a bit leave, I preshume. An’ ye’ll be needin’ yer denner – eh? But we’ll sune see to that. ’Mphm! Ay! Jist so! Eh – I suppose ye hadna time to write or wire – but what’s the odds? Ye’re welcome, Macgreegor, rael welcome.”

“Jist got leave this mornin’ – three days,” Macgregor

explained, not a little relieved to have found his uncle alone to begin with. "So I catched the first train I could."

"Jist that, exactly so," said Mr. Purdie with a heavy sigh that seemed irrelevant. "Weel, ma lad," he resumed hurriedly, "if ye tak' a sate here, I'll awa' up the stair an' get yer aunt. She generally has a bit snooze aboot this time – efter her meal, ye ken – but – "

"Dinna fash her aboot me, Uncle Purdie."

"Oh, but it – it's necessary to get her doon here. She'll maybe be able to break – I meant for to say – " Mr. Purdie stopped short and wiped perspiration from his face. "Jist a meenute," he said abruptly, and bolted upstairs.

Macgregor gazed after the retreating burly figure. Never before had he seen his uncle nervous. Was Aunt Purdie not so well? It was news to hear of her napping in the middle of the day. Then a likelier explanation dawned on Macgregor, and he smiled to himself. Uncle Purdie had been too shy to mention it, and now he had retired simply to allow of Christina's coming down by herself. So Macgregor prepared to meet his love.

And while he meditated, his aunt and uncle appeared together.

"Yer aunt'll explain," said Mr. Purdie, looking most unhappy. "I couldna dae it."

"How do you do, Macgregor?" said Aunt Purdie, shaking hands with stiff kindliness. "I am delighted to perceive you in Aberdeen. But what a deplorable catastrophe! – what a dire calamity! – what an ironical mishap! – "

"She means – " began Mr. Purdie, noting his nephew's puzzled distress.

"Hush, Robert! Allow me. I must break it gently to the boy. What a cruel fiascio! – what a vexatious disappintment! – "

"Whaur's Christina?" Macgregor demanded.

"Courage, boy!" said Aunt Purdie in lofty tones. "Remember you are a sojer – soldier – of the Queen – or rather, King!"

"But – "

"Christina left for Glasgow per the 1.10 p.m. train, one short hour before you arrived."

"Weel, I'm – "

"She decided very suddenly this morning. She did not hand me the letter, or p.c., for my perusual, but I understood her to observe that Miss Tod was not feeling so able and desired her presence. We were real sorry to let her go – "

"Ma impression," Mr. Purdie put in, "is that she was wearyin' for her lad. But for ill-luck this is the maist confounded, dampest – "

"Robert, behave yourself!"

"Weel, it's a fair sickener. But there's nae use talkin' aboot it. Come awa', lad, an' ha'e something to eat. Ye canna keep up yer heart on a toom kyte."

They were very kind to him and pressed him to remain overnight, but he was bent on leaving by the 3.40 express, which is due at Glasgow about 7.30. With good luck, he told himself, he might catch Christina at Miss Tod's. Meanwhile youth and health compelled him to enjoy his dinner, during which Aunt Purdie insisted on refunding the cost of his futile journey.

"Ye're ower guid to me," he said awkwardly.

"Not at all, not at all, Macgregor. It is quite unmentionable," she returned with a majestic wave. "Robert, give Macgregor some of your choice cigars."

In the train he smoked one of them, but finding it a trifle heady, preserved the rest for presentation to his sergeant, whom he greatly admired.

At 5.30 Christina was in Glasgow. Mrs. Purdie had commissioned her to deliver two small parcels – "presents from Aberdeen" – to Macgregor's sister and little brother, and she decided to fulfil the errand before going home. Perhaps the decision was not unconnected with a hope of obtaining some news of Macgregor. His postcard had worried her. She felt she had gone too far and wanted to tell him so. She would write to him the moment she got home, and let her heart speak out for once. Pride was in abeyance. She was all tenderness.

At the Robinson's house she received a warm welcome. Mrs. Robinson had almost got over her secret fear of her future daughter-in-law. Jeannie admired her intensely, and wee Jimsie frankly loved her. Aunt Purdie's were not the only gifts she delivered.

"Ye're hame suner nor ye intended," said Mrs. Robinson, during tea, which was partaken of without Mr. Robinson, who was "extra busy" over munitions. "Was Miss Tod wantin' ye?"

"Macgreeegor was wantin' her," piped Jimsie. "So was I."

"Whisht, Jimsie," Jeannie murmured, blushing more than Christina.

"We jist got hame frae Rothesay last nicht," said Mrs. Robinson, "so we ha'ena seen the laddie for a while."

"He hasna wrote this week," remarked Jeannie. "But of course *you'll* ha'e heard frae him, Christina" – this with respectful diffidence.

"He's been busy at the shootin'," Christina replied, wishing she had more news to give.

"I wisht I had a gun," observed Jimsie. "I wud shoot the whuskers aff auld Tirpy. Jings, I wud that!"

"Dinna boast," said his mother.

"What wud you shoot, Christina, if you had a gun?"

"I think I wud practise on a cocoa-nut, Jimsie," she said, with a small laugh.

After tea Mrs. Robinson took Christina into the parlour while Jeannie tidied up. Presently the door bell rang, and Jimsie rushed to meet the postman.

"It's for Macgreegor," he announced, returning and handing a parcel to his mother.

"I wonder wha's sendin' the laddie socks," she said, feeling it. "I best open it an' put his name on them. Maybe they're frae Mistress McOstrich." She removed the string and brown paper. "Vera nice socks – a wee thing to the lairge side – but vera nice socks, indeed. But wha – "

"Here's a letter!" cried Jimsie, extracting a half-sheet of white paper from the crumpled brown, and giving it to his dear Christina.

In bold, untidy writing she read –

"With fondest love from Maggie."

Pity the Poor Parents!

"IT'S a peety Macgreegor didna see his intended the nicht," Mr. Robinson observed when his son, after a couple of hours at the parental hearth, had gone to bed, "but we canna help trains bein' late."

Mrs. Robinson felt that it was perhaps just as well the two young people had not met that night, but refrained from saying so. "Hoo dae ye think Macgreegor's lookin', John?" she asked after a pause.

"I didna notice onything wrang wi' him. He hadna a great deal to say for hissel'; but that's naething new. Queer hoo a noisy, steerin' wean like he was, grows into a quiet, douce young man."

"He's maybe no as douce as ye think," said Lizzie under her breath.

"What's that?"

"Naething, John." She sighed heavily.

"What's wrang, wife?"

"I was wishin' we had a niece called Maggie... I suppose it's nae use askin' if ye ever heard o' Macgreegor ha'ein' an acquaintance o' that name."

"Maggie? Weel, it's no what ye would call a unique name. But what – "

"Listen, John. When Christina was here the day, a wee paircel cam' for Macgreegor, an' when I opened it, there was a pair o' socks wi' – wi' fondest love from Maggie."

"Hurray for Maggie!"

"But, John, Christina read the words!"

"Oho!" John guffawed. "She wudna like that – eh?"

"Man, what are ye laughin' at? Ye ken Christina's terrible prood."

"No ony prooder nor Macgreegor is o' her, Lizzie."

"That's no what I meant. Christina wud never put up wi' Macgreegor lookin' at anither lass."

"Weemen was born jealous; but it's guid for them."

"John Robi'son! ha'e ye the face to tell me ye wud approve

o' Macgreegor cairryin' on wi' anither lass when he's engaged to Christina?"

"Of course I wudna exac'ly approve o' it." Mr. Robinson scratched his head. "But surely ye're raisin' an awfu' excitement ower a pair o' socks."

"It wasna the socks, ye stupid: it was the fondest love!"

John laughed again, but less boisterously.

"Maggie's no blate, whaever she is. Did ye no speir at Macgreegor aboot her?"

"Oh, man! ha'e ye nae sense? I jist tied up the paircel again an' left it on his bed."

"Weel, that ends it," John said comfortably. "But" – with a wink – "let it be a lesson to ye never to tamper wi' yer son's correspondence. Ye're pretty sure to find mair nor ye expec'."

Mrs. Robinson clasped her hands. "Oh, dear! hoo can ye joke aboot it? What if Christina breaks her engagement."

"What?" he cried, suddenly alarmed. "Break her engagement! Surely ye dinna mean that! Did she say onything? Did she seem offended? Did she – "

"Never a word – but her look was different. But whatever stupid thing the laddie may ha'e done, his heart's set on Christina. It wud break his heart if – "

"This is bad," said John, all dismayed. "I didna think it wud be that serious. But I'll tell ye what I'll dae, Lizzie. I'll gang the morn and see Christina an' tell her – "

"What'll ye tell her?"

"Dear knows! What wud ye say yersel'?"

"Neither you nor me can say onything. Macgreegor'll ha'e to explain – if he can."

Mr. Robinson groaned, then brightened. "I yinst had a cousin called Maggie," he said; "unfortunately she's been deid for fifteen year. Still – "

"It's time ye was in yer bed, John. Ye canna dae onything, ma man, excep' hope for the best."

At dead of night –

"Lizzie!"

Silence.

"*Lizzie!*"

"Eh? – what is 't, John?"

"I was thinkin', wife; I was thinkin' it's no sae bad since her name's Maggie. Ye see, if it had been Henrietta, or Dorothea, or – "

"Mercy! Are ye talkin' in yer sleep?"

"I was gaun for to say that a Henrietta an' so forth wud be easier traced nor a Maggie, Maggies bein' as common as wulks at Dunoon, whereas – "

"D'ye imagine Christina – oh, dinna be silly, man!"

"But, Maggie – I mean Lizzie – "

"Oh, for ony favour gang to sleep an' rest yer brains."

When Macgregor, alone save for the slumbering Jimsie, had opened the parcel he muttered savagely: "Oh, dash it! I wish she had kep' her rotten socks to hersel'!" – and stuffed the gift behind the chest of drawers. The message he tore into a hundred fragments. Then he went to bed and slept better, perhaps, than he deserved. He expected there would be a letter in the morning, for Christina had left no message with his mother.

But there was no letter, so, after breakfast, he made a trip to the camp on the chance, and in the hope, that one might be lying there. Another blow! Managing to dodge Willie, he hurried home to meet the second morning delivery. Nothing again! ... His mother's anxious questions as to his health irritated him, and he so far lost his temper as to ask his sister why she was wearing a face like a fiddle. Poor Jeannie! For half the night she had been weeping for her hero and wishing the most awful things for the unknown Maggie.

"Ye'll be back for yer denner, laddie?" his mother called after him as he left the house.

"I dinna ken," he replied over his shoulder.

Mrs. Robinson felt that her worst forebodings were about to be realized.

"Never again!" she muttered in the presence of her daughter, who was helping her with the housework.

"What, mither?"

"Never again will I open a paircel that's no addressed to me."

"But it – it might ha'e been a – a fish," said Jeannie, who would have sought to comfort the most sinful penitent in the world. "Some girls," she went on, "dinna mean onything special by 'fondest love.' They dinna mean onything mair nor 'kind regairds.' "

Mrs. Robinson sighed. "I wud gi'e something if it had been a fish wi' kind regairds. I wonder what he did wi' the socks."

"I got them at the back o' the chest o' drawers. Weel, mither, that proves he doesna care for her."

"That's no the p'int, dearie." Mrs. Robinson paused in her work. "I'm beginnin' to think I should ha'e tell't him aboot the paircel bein' open when Christina was here. It's maybe no fair to let him gang to her –"

"I'll run efter him," said Jeannie promptly. "I'll maybe catch him afore he gets to Miss Tod's shop."

"Ay; run, Jeannie; run as quick's ye can!"

So Jeannie threw off her apron, tidied her hair with a couple of touches, and flew as though a life depended on her speed.

And, panting, she came in sight of Miss Tod's shop just in time – just in time to see the beloved kilted figure disappear into the doorway.

A Serious Reverse

THE fact that Christina had not written was a paralyzing blow to Macgregor's self-confidence and left him altogether uncertain of his ground. For the time being his sense of guilt as well as that of injury was almost swamped by the awful dread that she had simply grown tired of him. He entered the shop with foreboding – and received another blow.

A smartly dressed young man was lounging at the counter, apparently basking in Christina's smiles. As a matter of fact, the young man was merely choosing a note-book, and until the moment of Macgregor's entrance had been treated with the slightly haughty politeness which Christina made a point of administering to males under fifty. But with amazing abruptness she became so charming that the young man, a sensitive, susceptible creature, decided that an ordinary penny note-book would not do.

"Well," said Christina sweetly, "here are some at twopence, threepence and sixpence. The sixpenny ones are extremely reliable."

After some desultory conversation in low tones, during which Macgregor writhed with frequently averted gaze, the young man chose a sixpenny one and put down a florin, regretfully remarking that he had to catch a confounded train.

With a delicious smile Christina handed him his change, and with a graceful salute he fled without counting it. Immediately the door had closed Christina realized that she had given him one and ninepence. A small matter at such a time, yet it may have been the last straw. She had no word for Macgregor as he came to the counter, his uncertainty increased by that delicious smile given to another.

"Weel, ye've got back," was all he could utter, and her attitude stopped him in the first movement of offering his hand.

"Yesterday afternoon," she returned coldly.

"Ay, I ken. I wish ye had sent me word," he managed to say after a slight pause.

"It did not seem necessary. I suppose your mother told you."

"I heard it first frae Aunt Purdie. I missed ye by less nor an 'oor. It was gey hard lines."

Christina stared.

"I got leave yesterday mornin' an' catched the first train to Aberdeen – "

"Oh! ... What on earth took you to Aberdeen?"

"Christina," he exclaimed, "dinna speak like that! I gaed to Aberdeen because I couldna thole it ony mair."

"Thole what?"

"Oh, ye ken! ... Maybe I had nae business to be vexed at ye for gaun wi' Aunt Purdie, but oh, Christina dear, I wisht ye hadna gaed."

He dropped his gaze and continued: "I'm tellin' ye I gaed to Aberdeen because something seemed to ha'e come betwixt us, because I – " He stuck. Confession in the face of stern virtue is not so easy, after all.

"Pity you had the long journey," she said airily, "but you ought to have stopped for a day or two when you were there. Aberdeen is a delightful city." She turned and surveyed the shelves above her.

His look then would have melted the heart of any girl, except this one who loved him.

"Christina," he said piteously, "it wasna a' ma fau't."

Leisurely she faced him.

"May I ask what you are referring to?"

"Ye never said ye was sorry to leave me; yer letters wasna like ye, an' I didna ken what to think. An' then the cocoa-nut fairly put the lid on. I tell ye, a chap has to dae *something* when a girl treats him like that."

"Has he?"

He winced. "But I forgive ye – "

"Thanks!"

" – because I'm gaun to tell ye a' aboot it, Christina, an' ask ye kindly to forgive *me*. Ay, I'm gaun to tell ye everything

– everything! But I canna think," he blundered on, "I'm sayin', I canna think hoo I happened to get yer monkey up to begin wi' – "

"Excuse me!" she cried, indignant. "My monkey up, indeed!"

"Weel, maybe it wasna exac'ly yer monkey up; but I want to ken what way ye didna write a nicer letter afore ye gaed awa'. Nae doobt ye was in a hurry, but it jist seemed as if ye didna care a button for me. Maybe ma letter to you wasna the thing, either, but I was that hurt when I wrote it, an' ye might ha'e understood hoo I was feelin'. Christina, tell me what was wrang that ye gaed awa' like yon. Was ye – was ye fed up wi' me?"

Christina took up a pencil and began to spoil it with a patent sharpener. "Really, it is not worth while discussing," she said.

"What? No worth while? Oh, hoo can ye say a thing like that! ... But maybe I best tell ye ma ain story first."

"Many thanks. But I'm afraid I'm not deeply interested in any story of yours." She was almost sorry the next moment. It was just as if she had struck him.

Presently he recovered a little. "Christina," he said quietly, "that's no true."

"Hoo daur ye!" she cried, forgetting her "fine English" as well as her haughty pose.

"If it was true, it wud mean that ye've been judgin' me unfair, kennin' it was unfair, an' I'll never believe ye wud dae that... So, Christina dear, listen to me an' gi'e me a chance."

"Oh, what's the use," she sighed with sudden weariness, "what's the use o' pretendin', Macgreegor?"

"Wha's pretendin'?"

"You! What's the use o' pretendin' ye're hurt? Fine ye ken I'm no the – the only girl in the world."

"There's no anither like ye!"

"Weel," she said drily, "that means variety, does it no?" She drew a long breath and moved back from the counter. "I want to be as fair as I can, so perhaps I'd best ask ye a straight question."

"Ask it!" he said eagerly.

"Wha's Maggie?"

He was taken aback, but less so than she had expected, and possibly that increased her bitterness.

"She's a girl," he began.

"I could ha'e guessed that much. What sort o' girl?" she demanded, and wished she had held her tongue.

"She – she's kin' o' fat – "

"Fat!" Christina uttered the word with as much disgust as she would have evinced had she been handed a pound of streaky bacon without the paper. "How delightful! Anything else in the way of charms?"

"Christina, gi'e me a chance, an' I'll tell ye a' aboot it."

"Not another word! How long have you enjoyed the young lady's acquaintance?"

"Only a couple o' evenin's, but – "

"Case of love at first sight, I suppose!"

He flared up. "If ye hadna left me I wud never ha'e met her. If ye had wrote me a dacent letter – "

"Whisht, man!" she said in momentary pity. "Ye're talkin' like a wean."

"I canna help it. I'm that fond o' ye. An' it's no as if I had done a black crime. It was a pure accident – "

"Jist like a penny novel," she interrupted, merciless again. "Weel, I'm sure ye're welcome to ha'e as mony girls as ye like – only, ye'll ha'e to leave me oot. That's a'!" She took out her purse and from it something small which, stepping forward, she laid on the counter near him. Her engagement ring!

After a moment of strained silence – "Christina!" he gasped; "Christina! ye canna mean it serious!"

"Good-bye," she said stiffly, stepping back.

"But – but ye ha'ena heard ma story. It's no fair – "

"Oh," she cried harshly, "dinna keep on at that tune!"

All at once he drew himself up. "Noo I see what ye mean," he said in an almost even voice. "Ye had made up yer mind to be quit o' me. Still, it wud ha'e been honester to say ye was fed up to ma face. Weel, I'm no blamin' ye, an' I canna force ye to listen to ma story, no that it wud be worth ma while noo to shame masel' wi' the tellin'. I'll no even ask ye hoo ye cam' to hear aboot Maggie. Maggie's jist an or'nar' girl, an' I'm jist an or'nar' chap that done a stupid thing because he couldna think what else to dae. Weel, ye'll sune forget me, an' maybe I'll sune forget you – wi' the help o' a bullet – "

"Oh, dinna!" she whispered.

"An' as for this" – he picked up the ring and let it drop on the floor – "to hell wi' sich nonsense!" – and ground it under his heel. "So long!" he said, and went out quickly.

The Real Thing At Last

FOR an appreciable number of seconds after the door had closed Christina continued to gaze in its direction, her head well up, her face stern and rather pale. Then, quite suddenly, her bosom gave a quick heave, her lips parted, trembling, her eyes blinked, her whole attitude became lax. But she was not going to cry; certainly not! She was far too angry for tears; angry with herself no less than Macgregor. He had actually departed without being dismissed; worse still, he had had the last word! An observer – the thought struck her – would have assumed that she, weak wretch, had humbly allowed him to go and leave her in the wrong! Her maiden pride had somehow failed her, for she ought to have sent him forth crushed. And yet, surely, she had hurt, punished, humiliated him. Oh, no doubt of that! And for a moment her illogical heart wavered. She drew out her hanky, muttering "how I hate him!" – and blew her pretty nose. Then she clenched her hands and set her teeth. Then she went lax again. Then – oh, dear! he had even insulted her by leaving her to pick up the cast-off ring! – for, of course, she could not leave it there for Miss Tod or a customer to see.

Haughtily she moved round the counter and with scornful finger-tips took up the tiny wreckage of a great hope. The gold was twisted and bruised, the little pearls were loose in their places. All at once she felt a horrid pain in her throat...

Miss Tod appeared, fresh from the joys of strong tea.

"Oh, lassie, ha'e ye hurted yersel'?"

Christina choked, recovered herself and cried: "I've sold a blighter a sixpenny note-book for threepence, an' I'll never get over it as long as I live. B – but I hope that'll no be long!"

Just then Heaven sent a customer.

And perhaps Heaven sent the telegram that Macgregor found on his return home, rather late in the afternoon. The war has changed many things and people, but mothers most of all. Mrs. Robinson made no mention of the "extra special" dinner prepared so vainly in her son's honour. "Yer fayther missed ye," was her only reference to his absence from the meal.

The telegram was an order to return to duty. The mother and sister saw his eyes change, his shoulders stiffen.

"Maybe something's gaun to happen at last," he said; and almost in the same breath, though in a different voice – "Christina's finished wi' me. It was ma ain fau't. Ye needna speak aboot it. I – I'm no heedin' – greatly." He cleared his throat. "I'll awa' up to the works an' say guid-bye to father. Jimsie can come, if he likes. Ye needna tell him the noo – what I tell't ye."

Jimsie, summoned from play, was proud to go with his big brother. He was ill next day owing to a surfeit of good things consumed at high pressure, but not too ill to discuss what he would purchase with the half-crown that seemed to have stuck to his hot little paw.

Back from the works, Macgregor found tea awaiting him. His mother and sister were not a little relieved by his cheerfulness, though they were to doubt its sincerity later. But the boy had never made a greater effort for the sake of those who loved him than in that little piece of dissembling.

The parting was brief. An embrace, a kiss, a word or two that meant little yet all – and he was out of the home.

His laugh, slightly subdued, came up the well of the staircase – "Maybe it's anither false alarm!"

They looked over the rail, mute but trying to smile, and saw the last of him – a hurrying sturdy, boyish figure, kilt swinging and hand aloft in final farewell.

His route took him through the street of Miss Tod's shop. It was characteristic of Macgregor that he did not choose another and less direct course. He neither hesitated nor looked aside as he marched past the shop. The sense of injustice still upheld him. "She never gi'ed me a chance!" ... And so back to Duty.

Not more than five minutes later Private William Thomson came along in hot haste and banged into the shop.

"Macgreegor no here?" he demanded, and looked astounded.

"No," answered Christina, without laying down the book she had been trying to read.

"Jist left ye?"

"No."

"When did ye see him?"

"This morning."

"Gor! I could ha'e bet onything I wud ha'e catched him here. He had jist left the hoose when I – "

"Why are you so excited?" she coldly inquired.

"Me? I'm no excited. Jist been canoodlin' wi' ma aunt. She sprung five bob! Come oot an' I'll stan' ye a slider."

"I regret I cannot accept your kind invitation."

"Haw, haw! It's you for the language! But I say!" He leaned over the counter. "What way are ye no greetin'?"

She flushed hotly, wondering how much he knew or guessed, but replied coolly enough: "I have nothing to weep about. Have you?"

"Plenty, by Jings! I expected to see yer eyes an' nose rid, onyway, Christina."

"Indeed! Is that how it affects you?"

He looked hard at her. "My! ye're a game yin!" he said admiringly. "Weel, I maun slope," he went on, with a sigh that sounded absurd, coming from him. "I suppose ye've nae message for Macgreegor – something ye forgot to say at the last meenute? Eh?"

Christina was at a loss. Apparently he knew nothing, yet his manner was odd.

"No message, thank you," said she slowly.

"Then I'll bid ye guid-bye – an' I could bet ye a bob ye'll never see me again. So I'll tell ye something." His words came with a rush. "Ye're aboot the nicest girl I ever kent, Christina. Macgreegor's a luckier deevil nor he deserves. But I'll look efter him for ye in Flanders. Trust me for that. Noo that we're really boun' for the Front, in a day or so, things is different – at least I'm feelin' different. Dinna laugh! I – I dinna want to ha'e ony enemies but the Germans. I've just been an' kissed ma aunt – dammit! An' noo" – he caught her hand, pulled her to him – "I'm gaun to kiss *you*! There!" He turned and bolted.

Christina's hand went to her cheek, and fell back to her side. Her colour ebbed as swiftly as it had flowed. She began to shake. "Bound for the Front, in a day or so." ...

Later she went to the sitting-room where her employer was once more absorbing comfort from a cup. "Miss Tod," she said quietly, "I want to gang hame."

In the evening she posted a small package with this note enclosed –

"I am sending the ring Mrs. McOstrich said I was to give you when the time came for you to go. I hope it will bring you good luck. God bless you.

"CHRISTINA."

She lay awake most of the night, wondering if she might not have written more, wondering what answer he would send, wondering – wondering...

And as she fell asleep in the grey of morning, hours before the package would be delivered at the camp, a long train, at an outlying station, started on its way south, and six hundred eager lads shouted in the face of all things.

"We're awa' this time, by Goad!" yelled Willie in his friend's ear.

And Macgregor laughed wildly and wrung his friend's hand.

“Hullo, Glesca Hielanders!”

LIKE a trodden, forgotten thing Private Macgregor Robinson lay on the Flanders mud, under the murk and rain. A very long time it seemed since that short, grim struggle amid the blackness and intermittent brightness. The night was still rent with noise and light, but the storm of battle had passed from the place where he had fallen. He could not tell whether his fellows had taken the enemy’s trench or retired to their own. He had the vaguest ideas as to where he was. But he knew that there was pain in his left shoulder and right foot, that he was athirst, also that he had killed a man – a big stout man, old enough to have been his father. He tried not to think of the last, though he did not regret it: it had been a splendid moment.

He was not the only soldier lying there in the mud, but the others, friend or foe, were quite still. The sight of them in the flashes distressed him, yet always his gaze drifted back to them. His mind was a medley of thoughts, from the ugliest to the loveliest. At last, for he was greatly exhausted, his head drooped to his uninjured arm, his eyes closed. For a while he dozed. Then something disturbed him, and he raised himself and peered. In the flicker of a distant flare he saw a shape approaching him, crawling on hands and knees, very slowly, pausing for an instant at each still figure. It made Macgregor think of a big dog searching for it’s master – only it wore a helmet. Macgregor, setting his teeth, drew his rifle between his knees and unfixed the bayonet…

“Hist! Is that you, Macgreegor?”

“Wullie!”

“Whisht, ye – !”

“Oh, Wullie” – in a whisper – “I’m gled to see ye!”

“I believe ye!” gasped Willie, and flattened out at his friend’s side, breathing heavily. At the end of a minute or so – “Ha’e ye got it bad, Macgreegor?” he inquired.

“So, so. Arm an’ leg. I’m feelin’ rotten, but I’m no finished yet. Ha’e ye ony water? Ma bottle’s shot through.”

"Here ye are... Feelin' seeck-like?"

"I'm seeck at gettin' knocked oot at the vera beginnin."

"Never heed. Did ye kill yer man?"

"Ay."

"Same here... In the back... Ma Goad!"

"Ha'e we ta'en their trench?"

"Ay; but not enough o' us to haud it. We're back in the auld place. Better luck next time. No safe to strike a match here; could dae fine wi' a fag."

There was a silence between them, broken at last by Macgregor.

"Hoo did ye find me, Wullie? What way are ye no back in the trench?"

"Wasna gaun back wi'oot ye – I seen ye drap – even if ye had been a corp... Been snokin aroun' seekin' ye for Guid kens hoo lang. I'm fair hingin' wi' glaur."

"... I'm obleeged to ye, Wullie, but ye shouldna ha'e done it. Whauraboots are we?"

"I wisht I was sure. Lost ma bearin's. I doobt we're nearer the Germans nor oor ain lot. That's the reason I'm weerin' this dish-cover. But it's your turn to weer it. Ye've been wounded a'ready."

"Na, na, Wullie!"

"Dae what I tell ye, ye – !" Willie made the exchange of headgear... "I say, Macgreegor!"

"What?"

"This is Flanders. Ye mind oor bet? Weel, we're quits noo. I'm no owin' ye onything – eh?"

Macgregor grinned in spite of everything.

"Ay, we're quits noo, Wullie, sure enough."

"If ever we get oot o' this, will ye len' us dew francs?"

" 'Deed, ay... Wullie, ye're riskin' yer life for me."

"Awa' an chase yersel'! I wonder what that girl o' yours is thinkin'aboot the noo – if she's no sleepin'."

There was a pause till Macgregor said awkwardly: "Christina's finished wi' me."

"Eh?"

"I couldna tell ye afore; but she had got wind o' Maggie."

"Maggie! Oh, hell! But no frae me, Macgreegor, no frae me! Ye believe that?"

"Oh, ay."

Willie let off sundry curses. "But I suppose I'm to blame," he said bitterly.

"Naebody to blame but masel'."

"But did ye no explain to Christina? A' ye did was to canoodle wi' the wrang girl, pro tem. – a thing that happens daily. I couldna fancy a girl that naebody had ever wanted to cuddle; an' if I was a girl I couldna fancy a chap that – "

"Nae use talkin' aboot it, Wullie," Macgregor said sadly, wearily.

"Aw, but her an' you'll mak' it up afore ye're done. If ye dinna, I'll want to kill masel' an' Maggie forbye. A' the same, I wisht fat Maggie was here the noo. I could dae fine wi' a bit squeeze."

"My! ye're a fair treat!" said Macgregor, chuckling in his misery.

" '*Sh*! Keep still! Something comin'!"

The distant gun-fire had diminished. There were appreciable silences between the blasts. But during a flash Macgregor detected a helmeted crawling shape. Willie's hand stole out and grasped the bayonet.

"Number twa!" he muttered, with a stealthy movement. "I maun get him!"

But Macgregor's ears caught a faint sound that caused him to grip the other's wrist. "Wait," he whispered.

The helmeted shape came on, looking neither to right nor left, and as it came it sobbed. And it passed within a few yards of them, and into the deeper gloom, sobbing, sobbing.

"Oh, Christ!" sighed Willie, shuddering. "Put yer arm roun' me, Mac. I'm feart."

Five minutes later he affected to jeer at himself. "Weel, I'm rested noo," he continued, "an' it's time we was gettin' a move on. Mornin's comin', an' if we're spotted here, we're done for. Can ye creep?"

Macgregor tried and let out a little yelp.

"Na, ye canna. Ye'll jist ha'e to get on ma back."

"Wullie, gang yersel' – "

"Obey yer corporal!"

"Ye're no a corp – "

"If they dinna mak' me a corporal for this, I'll quit the service! Onyway, I'm no gaun wi'oot ye. Same time, I canna guarantee no to tak' ye to the German lines. But we maun risk that. Ye'll ha'e to leave yer rifle, but keep on the dish-cover till I gi'e ye the word… Noo then! Nae hurry. I'll ha'e to creep the first part o' the journey. Are ye ready? Weel, here's luck to the twa o' us!"

There is no authentic description of that horrible journey save Willie's, which is unprintable.

It was performed literally by inches. More than once Willie collapsed, groaning, under his burden. Macgregor, racked as he was, shed tears for his friend's sake. Time had no significance except as a measure of suspense and torture. But Willie held on, directed by some instinct, it seemed, over that awful shell-fragment-studded mire, round the verges of shell-formed craters, past dead and wounded waiting for succour – on, on, till the very guns seemed to have grown weary, and the rain ceased, and the air grew chillier as with dread of what the dawn should disclose, and the blackness was diluted to grey.

"Drap the – dish-cover," croaked Willie, and halted for a minute's rest.

Then on again. But at long last Willie muttered: "I think it's oor trench. If I'm wrang, fareweel to Argyle Street! I'll ha'e to risk gi'ein' them a hail in case some silly blighter lets fly in this rotten licht. Slip doon, Mac – nae hurry – nae use hurtin' yersel' for naething. I'll maybe ha'e to hurt ye in a meenute… Noo for it!" He lifted up his voice. "Hullo, Glesca Hielanders!"

It seemed an age until –

"Right oh!" came a cheerful response.

"Hurray!" yelled Willie, and rose stiffly to his feet.

Then with a final effort, he gave Macgregor the "fireman's lift," and staggered and stumbled, amid shots from the other side, into safety.

No Hero, Yet Happy

CHRISTINA was arranging the counter for the day's business when the postman brought her a letter in a green envelope with the imprint "On Active Service." Her heart leapt only to falter as her eyes took in the unfamiliar writing. Then under the "Certificate" on the left-hand side she perceived the signature – "W. Thomson." Something dreadful must have happened! She sat down and gazed at the envelope, fingering it stupidly. At last she pulled herself together and opened it. The letter was dirty, ill-written, badly spelt; but so are many of the finest-spirited letters of these days.

"If you are wanting a perfeck man, by yourself a statute from the muesum. Then you can treat him cold and he will not notice other girls when you leav him for to enjoy yourself. Mac was not for haveing anny when he first seen Maggie, but he was vext at you, and I eggged him on with telling him he was feared, and he took her in a cab becaus it was poring, and maybe he gave her a bit sqeese, I do not no for certin, but it is more like she began it, for Maggie would rather take a cuddel nor a good dinner anny day. Likewize there is times when a chap must sqeese something. It is no dash use for a girl to expeck her intended to keep looking at her when she is not there, unless she makes it worth his while with nice letters and so fourth. He gets soon fed up on cold nothings. Mac does not care a roten aple for Maggie, but you left him nothing better, and she is a nice girl and soft with a man, so God forgive you as I will not till I hear you are reddy to kiss him again. Mac is wounded in 2 places, but not mortle. He got wounded saveing my life. I am not wounded yet. He garded my back, which saved me. Probly you will see him soon, so prepare to behave yourself. Remmember you alowed me to kiss you??? Hopping you will take this good advice more kindly nor usual.

Yours resp.

W. THOMSON,

Lce. Corp. 9th H.L.I.

P.S. – If you was less proud and more cuddelsom, you would not loss much fun in this world. – W.T., Lce. Corp. 9th H.L.I.

Macgregor was in a small hospital not far from London. While not to be described as serious, his wounds were likely to keep him out of action for several months to come. He was comfortable, and the people were very kind. There English speech puzzled him almost as much as his Scotch amused them.

More tired than pained, he lay idly watching the play of light on his old-fashioned ring, the gift of Mrs. McOstrich. It had reached him just before he was borne from France, too late, he thought, to bring him luck. But the only luck he wanted now was Christina. He had her brief note by heart. There was kindness but no comfort in the words; forgiveness, maybe, but no promise of reconciliation. Truly he had made a horrid mess of it; nevertheless he rebelled against taking all the blame. Christina could not have cared much when she would listen to no explanations... Now he had a great longing for the touch of his mother and the smile of his father, the soft speech of Jeannie and the eager pipings of wee Jimsie. Also, he wondered, with a sort of ache, how Willie was faring.

A nurse appeared, sorted his pillow, chatted for a moment, then went and drew down the blinds against the afternoon sun. And presently Macgregor dropped into a doze.

He awoke to what seemed a dream. Of all people, Aunt Purdie was seated at his bedside.

In a hesitating way, quite unlike her, she put out her hand, laid it on his and patted gently.

"What's up?" he exclaimed in astonishment.

"How do you do, Macgregor?" she said formally yet timidly.

"Fine, thenk ye," he answered from sheer force of habit. Then – "Ye've come a lang road to see me," he said, gratitude asserting itself.

"It *is* a conseederable distance," she returned, with some

recovery of her old manner. "Your uncle said I must go the moment he heard where you were, and I quite homologated him. We was all copiously relieved to hear of the non-seriosity of your wounds. I have letters for you from your parents and sister, forbye your brother James. Your mother was anxious to come, too, but decided to wait for my report, your condeetion not being grave. All well at home and proud of you, but I was en rout before I heard the most gratifying news." She cleared her throat with an important cough, and Macgregor hoped none of the other chaps in the ward were listening. "I am exceedingly proud of you, Macgregor!"

"Me? What for?"

"Ah, do not distimulate, my boy; do not be too modest. You have saved a comrade's life! It was magneeficent!"

"Eh?"

"Oh, I know all about it – how you protected your friend William with your wounded body – "

Macgregor's hand went to his head. "I suppose I'm sober," he muttered. "Wha was stuffin' ye wi' a' this, Aunt Purdie?"

Aunt Purdie's manner was almost sprightly as she whispered –

"Your betrothed!"

"Ma what?"

"Christina, her own self, told me. So there you are, young man!"

Macgregor's head wagged feebly on the pillow. "There's a bonny mix-up somewhaur," he said; "it was Wullie who saved *ma* life." Then, with an effort – "When did ye see her?"

"Now understand, *Macgregor*, there must be no excitement. You must keep calm. I am doing my best to break it gently. H'm, h'm! As a matter of fac', I seen – saw – your fiancy about ten minutes ago. She is without!"

"Wi'oot what?"

"She is in an adjacent apartment."

"Here?"

"I am going to despatch her to you now," said Aunt

Purdie, enjoying herself thoroughly. "But mind! – no deleterious excitement!" She rose with a look on her gaunt face which he had never seen before.

"Aunt Purdie," he whispered, "did she *want* to come?"

"My dear nephew, without exaggeration I may say that she fairly jamp – jumped – at my invitation! Well, I'll see you subsequently."

"God bless ye," he murmured, and closed his eyes till he felt she had gone from the ward.

He knew when Christina came in, but did not look directly at her till she was beside him. By that time she had controlled the quiver at her mouth. And when he looked he realized that he had no defence whatsoever in the Maggie affair. Nothing was left him but love and regret.

She touched his hand and seated herself. "I couldna help comin'," she said, smiling. "Are ye feelin' better?"

"Oh, ay. But I maun tell ye the truth."

"No a word, Mac, noo or ever. I'll no listen."

"But it's a' nonsense aboot me savin' a comrade. Wullie Thomson saved me. I canna think hoo ye heard sic a story, but it's got to be stopped. An' though I'm terrible gled to see yer face again, I'm vexed ye cam' a' that lang road thinkin' I was a hero. Still, there's a chap in the next bed that's gaun to get a medal for – "

"We'll talk aboot it later," she interrupted gently. "But I'll jist tell ye that a' I took the journey for was to see a lad that was wounded. An' I think" – a faint laugh – "I've got a wound o' ma ain."

He sighed, his eyes on his ring. "Ye had aye a kind heart, Christina. I'm obleeged to ye for comin' … I wud like to tell ye something – no as an excuse, for it wud be nae excuse, but jist to get quit o' the thing – aboot the time when ye was in Aberdeen – "

"Oh, never!"

"Jist that. Weel, I'll no bother ye," he said, with hopeless resignation. Next moment he was ashamed of himself. He must change the subject. He actually smiled. "Hoo did ye leave Miss Tod? Still drinkin'?"

Christina may not have heard him. She was surveying the ward. Macgregor's only near neighbour was apparently sound asleep, and the only patient sitting up was intent on a game of draughts with a nurse. But had all been awake and watching, she would still have found a way.

She passed her handkerchief lightly across her eyes and put it in her sleeve. Then with the least possible movement she knelt down by the bedside.

"Christina!" he exclaimed under his breath, for her face was near to his.

Her fingers went to the neck of her white blouse and drew out a narrow black ribbon. From it hung, shining, the tiny wreckage of her engagement ring.

"Mac, dear," she whispered, "can – can we no ha'e it mended?"